Logan was transfixed by her.

As inconvenient as Jessica and the shop might be for the agency's expansion, he'd hate it if she wasn't there. It was a feeling he didn't want to examine too closely.

"What you're thinking isn't true," he said quietly. "In fact, the shop is why I wanted to talk. I've told my friends, or business partners, about your idea and we're all interested in seeing if it's feasible. But before a decision can be made, I have to do research on renovation costs, etc."

The glow from the lowering sun slanted across Jessica's face and turned her eyes an even more intense blue. He'd been impressed by her strong leadership during the meeting, but now she looked enchanted.

Would one kiss spoil everything?

There was only one way to find out.

Dear Reader,

It's a lot of fun to be a writer and have the power to create characters, explore lives and even establish towns that don't exist. That was the case with Regen Valley. While a talent agency was necessarily in a metropolitan area, I wanted a small town for Jessica and Lindsey's home. *Regen* comes from a German word referring to rain, which seemed eminently appropriate for the Seattle region.

Jessica's affection for Regen Valley is unsurprising, since she spent many happy summers as a child visiting her grandparents there. She finds it difficult, however, to believe Logan will stay. He's always lived in cities and worked on an international scale. As I wrote their story, I loved exploring whether, after all his travels, he just might find home and joy in a place and people he'd never heard of before.

I love hearing from readers and can be contacted through my Facebook page at Facebook.com/callie.endicott.author.

Best wishes,

Callie

HEARTWARMING

Finally, A Family

—

Callie Endicott

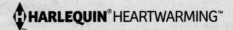

PLEASE RECYCLE · THIS PRODUCT IS RECYCLABLE

Recycling programs
for this product may
not exist in your area.

ISBN-13: 978-1-335-51068-6

Finally, A Family

Copyright © 2019 by Callie Endicott

All rights reserved. Except for use in any review, the reproduction or utilization of this work in whole or in part in any form by any electronic, mechanical or other means, now known or hereafter invented, including xerography, photocopying and recording, or in any information storage or retrieval system, is forbidden without the written permission of the publisher, Harlequin Enterprises Limited, 22 Adelaide St. West, 40th Floor, Toronto, Ontario M5H 4E3, Canada.

This is a work of fiction. Names, characters, places and incidents are either the product of the author's imagination or are used fictitiously, and any resemblance to actual persons, living or dead, business establishments, events or locales is entirely coincidental.

This edition published by arrangement with Harlequin Books S.A.

For questions and comments about the quality of this book, please contact us at CustomerService@Harlequin.com.

® and TM are trademarks of Harlequin Enterprises Limited or its corporate affiliates. Trademarks indicated with ® are registered in the United States Patent and Trademark Office, the Canadian Intellectual Property Office and in other countries.

Printed in U.S.A.

HARLEQUIN®
™ www.Harlequin.com

As a kid, **Callie Endicott** had her nose stuck in a book so often it frequently got her in trouble. The trouble hasn't stopped—she keeps having to buy new bookshelves. Luckily ebooks don't take up much space. Writing has been another help, since she's usually on the computer creating stories instead of buying them. Callie loves bringing characters to life and never knows what will prompt an idea. So she still travels, hikes, explores and pursues her other passions, knowing a novel may be just around the corner.

Books by Callie Endicott

Harlequin Superromance

Emerald City Stories

Family by Design
A Father for the Twins
Moonlight Over Seattle

Montana Skies

The Rancher's Prospect
At Wild Rose Cottage
Kayla's Cowboy

That Summer at the Shore
Until She Met Daniel

Visit the Author Profile page
at Harlequin.com for more titles.

To Missy, with love

PROLOGUE

TIME SEEMED TO stand still as Logan Kensington focused his camera on a magnificent buck, outlined by the first rays of sunlight. Mount Rainier rose beyond, white and majestic in the stillness. It was a fitting background to the deer, who surveyed his world with lordly arrogance.

The faint whirring sound from the camera caught the buck's attention and it looked at the undergrowth where Logan was hidden. He kept his finger on the shutter release button to take a continuous burst of pictures.

Earlier in the year, Logan had spotted the game trail and small stream on a hike. Suspecting it would be a good place for photos, he'd returned and spent last night under cover, alert to the faintest movement and sound. Deer, a fox, raccoons, a pair of skunks, rabbits, even a snuffling bear—each of their images captured by his sensitive equipment. Now he was getting daylight shots.

A moment later the buck was gone, leaping effortlessly over the stream.

Aware that time was passing, Logan crawled from his photography blind and stretched. His clothes were damp from the rain that had come and gone over the hours he'd waited, and he needed to get back to Seattle for a meeting at the Moonlight Ventures Talent Agency. He was one of four partners who owned the agency, but so far his participation had mostly been long-distance. Once his last contract as a fashion photographer was fulfilled, he could remain in Seattle permanently instead of spending a week or two whenever he could manage. In the meantime, he'd gotten a studio apartment and an SUV to make his frequent trips to the Pacific Northwest easier.

He and his partners had bought Moonlight Ventures over a year before, and he would be the last to come on board. Nicole George was the first, followed by Adam Wilding and then Rachel Clarion, who had just gotten there. They were his closest friends, met while on photo shoots. In the early days, Adam, Rachel and Nicole had all been models, but

Rachel had become a makeup artist after being injured in an accident.

Logan hiked out to where he'd left the SUV and drove back to Seattle, pleased with his night's efforts. Despite being late for the meeting with his partners, he hurried into the Crystal Connection for a cup of coffee. The shop was located in the large building owned by Moonlight Ventures and sold a mixed bag of merchandise, from petrified wood bookends to fanciful kites. Yet Logan suspected coffee sales were their mainstay; they had a reputation for making the best around.

"Hi, Penny," he greeted the woman behind the counter.

"Morning, Logan." Penny Parrish had an amazing memory and had remembered his name from the beginning of their acquaintance, though he wasn't a regular customer yet.

He studied the brews listed on the whiteboard. Some were the usual offerings, but he often got the flavor of the day. "I'll try the Southwest Twist," he told Penny.

"That's one of my favorites. There's a touch of roasted piñon nuts in the mix. It's so popular I'm planning to make it a regular item."

"Sounds great."

Logan took the cup she handed him and tasted the steaming brew. He gave Penny a thumbs-up. The rich scent filled his senses and he restrained the temptation to gulp the coffee down. Even though his hiding spot on the edge of the clearing had been upwind of the game trail, he'd refrained from eating or drinking to avoid attracting attention.

Penny's face was warm and friendly. While her eyes held the twinkle he'd enjoyed since getting to know her, he realized it couldn't be easy keeping a positive attitude—her husband had died just a month earlier. Logan hadn't been in Seattle at the time, though he'd sent flowers. On his visits before Eric's death, Logan had recognized how much the couple loved each other. Their commitment had been rare, but at least they'd had fifty-plus years together. They were among the lucky few, though he couldn't say that to Nicole or Adam, who'd both gotten engaged since moving to Seattle. Still, maybe they'd be lucky, as well.

Cup in one hand and swatting at his messy jeans with the other, Logan hurried into Moon-light Ventures. He waved at the office manager, Chelsea Masters.

"They're waiting for you," she called after him.

"I know, I'm late."

They were meeting in Nicole's office, which was the only one large enough for four people. Space was at a premium for the agency. Kevin McClaskey, the previous owner, had been a one-man show. He hadn't expected to expand, so he'd sectioned off most of the building and given long-term leases to people like Penny and Eric Parrish. Still, Kevin's overall office area was larger than he'd needed and it hadn't seemed an issue when they purchased the talent agency and building. They'd remodeled the office space extensively and had been fairly happy with it, but as each partner arrived, they were feeling increasingly cramped. Not to mention wanting more rooms for training purposes and other needs. His own office wasn't much bigger than a closet.

"I see you didn't have time to change your clothes again." Nicole tossed him the beach towel she had waiting. More than once on his trips to Seattle he'd arrived at a meeting wet or covered in mud from a photography outing, so she'd learned to be prepared.

"Nope." Logan's jeans had dried on the drive to the city, but despite his efforts to brush them off, they were stained with dirt and forest debris. He set his cup on a low table and covered a chair with the towel. "But I got some amazing shots."

Adam chuckled. "You always do."

"Here, take a look." Logan went over and inserted a memory card into the computer, bringing the images up to display on a wall-mounted television. One of the big remodeling expenses had been getting the best wiring and electronics into their offices.

"They're wonderful," Nicole said after seeing a number of the photos.

Adam nodded in agreement. "Absolutely. Are they for a magazine?"

"Actually, I'm doing a calendar, and a publisher has approached me about doing a book on the Pacific Northwest."

"I'll buy the first copy," Rachel promised. "But I wonder, are you going to be torn between full-time photography and the agency?"

The not-so-delicate question was probably something they were all wondering about.

"I've thought about it," Logan admitted. "But while I love the challenge of getting a great picture, I also want to work at the agency."

The discussion shifted and they compared notes on several prospective clients.

None of Logan's friends seemed concerned by his answer. They'd put contingencies into the partnership agreement in case any of them decided to go another direction at some point, but he didn't expect to change his mind about Moonlight Ventures. Being a talent agent would require him to find a balance between his competing interests.

Those interests didn't include a family, even though his parents had begun fervently lobbying for grandchildren. His father was a retired diplomat and his mother a former protocol expert. Now they wanted to dive into being grandparents with the same intensity they'd brought to embassy duties and official dinners. In fact, they acted as if marriage and kids were items on a list that everybody needed to check off.

Logan had firmly told them not to start buying baby booties; he intended to stay a bachelor. His decision partly stemmed from the fact that he'd seen too many bad relationships to have any faith in marriage. The statistics on divorce weren't encouraging. But the biggest reason was his own questions about whether he had what it took. He doubted he had the personality and commitment to make a marriage successful. After all, he'd have to change his personal life far more than a move to Seattle would require, and he couldn't see that happening.

Ultimately, it would be best to be an honorary uncle to his friends' children and leave the uncertainty of marriage and parenting to them.

CHAPTER ONE

Seven months later...

LOGAN SAT IN his car, gazing through the early spring rain at the Crystal Connection. It rained a lot in Washington in every season, which must be why it was called the Evergreen State.

Even in the dark weather, the crystals in the windows moved and winked with every breath of air inside the store. Small spotlights had been focused on them so they were sure to capture attention. He didn't understand why some people were so crazy about crystals and the New Age mysticism surrounding them, but that was their business. The problem was that he and his partners needed to expand and the crystals were directly in the way.

There was a knock on the window and he jerked; he'd been so deep in thought that he hadn't noticed Rachel Clarion approaching. Rachel *Kessler*, he reminded himself, since she'd joined the ranks of the recently married. Not only that, she was pregnant.

"What's up?" he asked, getting out of the car.

"Nothing much. Where is your sports car?"

"Traded it in over the weekend. I enjoyed it, but I decided to get this smaller hybrid since I want a place outside the city. I'm keeping the SUV for my photo ventures into the mountains."

"Simon has talked about getting a hybrid ever since Livvie learned about fossil fuels in school." Her face glowed at the mention of her new husband and his daughter. "He's a sucker when it comes to Livvie."

"So are you."

"True." Rachel laughed.

She adored her stepdaughter and was happy in a way Logan had never seen his friend before. He'd worried about her after the accident that had ended both her modeling career and first marriage. But everything had changed after she moved to Seattle and met Simon Kessler. Now, except for a few bouts of morning sickness, she seemed truly at peace. Logan just hoped it would last.

"I saw you brooding over here," Rachel added. "Is there a problem?"

"Just gathering my thoughts about the situation with the Crystal Connection. Today is my first official day as a regular agent and I need to evaluate how to approach this particular issue."

She made a face. "Being a landlord is my least favorite part of owning Moonlight Ventures."

He nodded.

The rapid growth of the agency had surprised him and the others. It was partly from name recognition since they were all known in the modeling world, but now they were victims of their own success. Even with Logan starting to work full-time they needed to hire junior associates, but they just didn't have space to accommodate anyone else.

As partners they shared administrative tasks and it was his turn to take the lead. Actually, it was well *past* his turn. So he was evaluating options for expansion…which mostly meant seeing if there was any way to move the Crystal Connection to another location in the building.

"It's a challenge since the new owner is Penny's granddaughter. She has a young daughter close to Livvie's age," Rachel told him. "I've been tempted to try setting up playdates between them, but it's tricky. I suspect we won't be popular once we've broached the subject of the shop moving."

"That makes me feel a whole lot better."

"Sorry. On the positive side, it's possible Jessica will like the idea of having a larger space for the same rent. We can't know until we ask. In any case, I'll leave you to beard the lioness in her den," Rachel said with a sympathetic smile.

"I probably won't do it today. First I'm going to check commercial real estate listings of rental spaces so I have other options to offer." They'd agreed they should pay the costs of a move, along with advertising to announce a new location—even if it was just around the corner of the building—but Logan wanted to start the discussion with real estate listings in hand. For all they knew, Ms. Parrish would love the opportunity to break her long-term lease and relocate somewhere else entirely.

"Sure you aren't being cowardly?" she teased gently. "Jessica isn't *that* fierce, except maybe when it comes to her daughter."

He gave Rachel a wry look. "I've faced grizzly bears, Bengal tigers, Mount Everest and prima donna models of both sexes. I'm not saying it'll be a piece of cake, but I can handle the situation."

Rachel said goodbye and walked toward the agency.

Logan glanced back at the Crystal Connection's storefront. Dealing with the issue would be part of the learning curve as he shifted from fashion photographer to businessman, but he wasn't required to enjoy every single aspect of it.

Maybe they should have anticipated a change in ownership over the eight months since Eric Parrish's death. Penny and her husband had started the store together, so it may have been too painful for her to continue running it alone.

Logan had spent the last month in Italy, which was why he still hadn't met the new owner. His partners had mentioned she'd been there for a couple of weeks, working alongside her grandmother, but they'd assumed she was just helping. Then, last Friday, Penny had sent a note, asking them to change the name on the lease to her granddaughter, Jessica Parrish, saying the shop now belonged to her. The lease specifically stated it wasn't transferable, but that was a technicality. While they weren't legally required to honor a change to the rental agreement, it seemed wrong to refuse under the circumstances.

They knew Penny, but Jessica Parrish was a lesser known quantity. Maybe he should call Kevin McClaskey—the previous owner of the agency might be able to tell him about Jessica. Kevin knew most of his former tenants the way he knew his own family.

Logan sighed. Getting more information was definitely wise before discussing business with Ms. Parrish. In the meantime, he may as well go in and get a cup of coffee.

The thought made him pause.

The Crystal Connection was known for its great coffee, but what would it be like with a new owner? Well, even if it was awful, diplomacy demanded he continue getting his coffee there for a while. In the interim, he might learn something useful.

As he came closer, he looked to see if there were any visible changes, not that Jessica Parrish would have had much time for alterations. Everything mostly looked the same except for the small spotlights in the windows.

"Hello?" Logan called as he walked inside. There was no one in sight.

"Welcome to our store," said a small voice. "Can I help you?"

He saw a little girl sitting on the floor next to the sales counter, a sketch pad resting on her up drawn knees. From what Rachel had said, he figured she was Jessica Parrish's daughter, which meant she was around seven or eight years old.

"Uh, hi," he said. "Is this your place now?"

"Kind of. It used to be Grandma and Grandpa's, but Momma has it now."

"I see."

"Hello. Can I help you?" another voice inquired.

He turned and saw a young woman standing behind him, holding a large box in her arms. Her striking blue eyes held a friendly glint.

"Yes, I'd like a cup of coffee. I've been here before. I'm one of the partners in Moonlight Ventures."

Her smile flashed. "Are you the large Southwest Twist, the low-fat mocha latte—"

Logan shrugged. "I don't have a usual."

"Oh, yes, you must be the one that Grams calls Magellan."

"I beg your pardon?"

"Because you try different things and don't

like routine. But maybe you'd prefer a different nickname."

"If anything, I've thought of myself as a Stanley. You know, of Stanley and Livingstone," Logan said, surprised that Jessica's grandmother had read him so well. He'd be bored to death following a routine every single day.

"Ah, another explorer." Jessica put the box she was carrying on the counter. "What can I get you?"

"I'm in a plain coffee mood this morning, so a large organic medium roast. By the way, I'm Logan Kensington."

"It's nice to meet you. I'm Jessica Parrish. This is my daughter, Cyndi." Jessica gestured to the child sitting nearby. "She's helping me out because her school isn't in session this week."

Cyndi smiled and wiggled her fingers in a wave.

Logan smiled in return and then looked back at Cyndi's mother. "We didn't know the shop was changing ownership until we got Mrs. Parrish's note."

"There was a delay in getting everything settled. Something or other with the will.

Grams prefers having her ducks in a row before making announcements."

Jessica went into the coffee bar in a corner of the shop and he evaluated her the way he'd evaluate a model he needed to photograph. Great skin. A steady gaze and firm jawline that suggested stubborn resolve. The unusual shade of her blue eyes complemented her hair, which was brown with a coppery tone. And while she didn't have a particularly bold figure, he preferred her slim curves.

He glanced at her ring finger and was annoyed with himself. It would be dishonest to deny he found her appealing, but he couldn't let it be an issue. Whether she was married or single, his interest was entirely on behalf of the agency.

"Do you have your own cup?" Jessica asked.

"I forgot to bring it," he said.

Many of the Crystal Connection customers were ecologically conscious and brought their own cups, getting a discount in return. She was probably continuing the policy.

"That's okay." She filled a tall paper cup and handed it to him. He added cream and fastened a lid on the top, noticing it was different than the ones Penny and Eric had stocked. He appreciated that it was biodegradable, instead of regular plastic.

Jessica went to the cash register and punched in some information. "I see we have your credit card number on file. Do you want me to continue charging your account once a month?"

"That would be great."

"I just remembered—an advance copy of your calendar arrived a few days ago." Jessica took out a large envelope from under the counter. "I'm sure you've already seen it."

"Yeah, but I didn't know advance copies had been distributed."

On the calendar's thick, glossy cover was a photo of two magnificent stags, charging each other in a battle for supremacy, their breath steaming in the cold air. Logan's signature was printed at the bottom right in bold silver ink. He hadn't wanted his name to be so prominent, but the publisher had insisted his reputation was one of the selling points. Logan wasn't convinced. He wasn't an Ansel Adams or a Pulitzer Prize–winning photographer; he was best known in fashion circles.

"The photographs are stunning," Jessica said, flipping through the pages. "I've shown it around and already have a waiting list for copies."

"I loooove your pictures," Cyndi chimed in. "My favorite is the one of the baby mountain lions. It's splendiferous."

The photo had taken patience, dumb luck and a huge dash of imprudence since mountain lions were notoriously protective mothers. Logan didn't want to confess how close he'd actually gotten to the small family; he was letting everybody assume he'd used a very powerful telephoto lens.

"Thanks, Cyndi," he said to the child. "That's one of my favorites, too. I didn't know the Crystal Connection was going to carry my calendars."

Jessica chuckled. "Grams sent an order as soon as Uncle Kevin told her you had one coming out for next year."

"*Uncle* Kevin? I hadn't heard you were related." Logan frowned. Discussions about moving the Crystal Connection would be even more sensitive if Jessica was Kevin McClaskey's niece.

"We aren't, but I've known him all my life. Grams and Kevin's wife were childhood friends. He's an honorary grandfather, but it was easier to call him 'uncle.'"

The explanation wasn't much comfort. Kevin's anxious concern for the people he cared about could get irritating, but he was also a tireless advocate for the people in his sphere—he knew what was happening in their lives and actively promoted their interests. Retiring had made no difference in how he behaved. Though Logan still wanted to talk to Kevin about Jessica, he'd have to be careful.

With a wink at Cyndi, Logan took his coffee and headed for the agency next door. When he settled at his desk, he checked for messages before taking a sip. The coffee was as good, or better, than what he'd gotten in the past. So at least the brew hadn't changed, though he still didn't know what other impact there might be from the switch in ownership.

He picked up the phone, hoping to make an appointment to meet Kevin for lunch. There was only one way he could deal with a problem, and that was straight through.

JESSICA ASSEMBLED A new display cabinet, humming along with the music playing over the speaker system. She'd been planning things to do at the shop ever since Grams had explained that when the estate was settled, Jessica would get the Crystal Connection. Technically Granddad had owned the store, but they'd both wanted her to have it when he was gone.

It meant she wouldn't have to work a regular job anywhere else, or keep paying someone for childcare. Either Cyndi would be with her great-grandmother after school, or Jessica would bring her to the store where there was a place in the stockroom to study and play. This week would have been especially hard since the school had closed unexpectedly because of a virulent virus making the rounds. So Cyndi simply came to work with her.

As deeply as Jessica missed her grandfather, she was grateful for the generous bequest. Not that it meant things would suddenly be easy. Her grandparents had made a living from the Crystal Connection and been able to save for retirement, but it was mostly because they'd lived simply…something their son had hated. Jessica's father was devoted to making the money needed to support an extravagant lifestyle, a choice her mother appreciated, as well.

It was fine for them, but Jessica didn't have fond memories of her childhood. Mostly she'd been lonely except for the summer-long visits with her grandparents, who'd lavished her with love instead of belongings. It hadn't been unusual for Granddad to burst out in song or to sweep his wife and granddaughter into a dance with the sheer joy of living. He'd had a slight limp, but hadn't let that stop him.

The memory was so happy that Jessica danced across the store to fetch a box of Austrian crystals to unpack, feeling as if Granddad was dancing right along with her.

Cyndi giggled. "I like when you're silly, Momma. But I don't like this." She frowned and held up the picture she'd been drawing. Clearly it was supposed to be Logan Kensington's mountain lion cubs. Cyndi's interest in art had started at a young age and she'd taken as many special classes as Jessica could afford.

Jessica walked over and studied the drawing. "Your perspective is a little off, but who says artists always need the same perspective?"

"I s'pose. Do you think taking pictures is the same as regular art?"

"It's just another type of art, the way sculpting isn't the same as painting."

"Yeah. Mr. Kensington's pictures are cool."

Jessica grinned. She loved when her daughter got enthusiastic about something, even if it meant she wanted to take a class that meant another expense.

At the display case Jessica experimented with the best way to arrange the new stock, tensing a moment when Cyndi coughed. It was hard not to listen for the wheezing that came with an asthma attack. But nothing followed the cough and Cyndi relaxed into happy activity.

The shop was fun, carrying a hodgepodge of items from around the world. Though the Crystal Connection's coffee was popular, they were best known for their crystals, both manufactured and natural stones. Jessica especially loved the intense greenish-blue apatite crystals, but each kind had its own special appeal.

Some customers shopped there because they simply enjoyed the beauty of the rocks and crystals. Other folks had mystical beliefs about their powers. Meeting new people and discussing their ideas was one of the things she loved about the shop.

It was sad that her brothers had preferred visits with their grandparents to be brief. Maybe it was because they had other interests, but they'd never really gotten to know

Granddad, and would never have the chance now. She was grateful for the move she'd made to Seattle the previous year. She'd been offered a good job at a department store during a visit and then her grandparents had insisted she move into the other side of the duplex they owned in the small community of Regen Valley. It meant she and Cyndi had spent more time with Granddad before he was gone.

There was an encouraging stream of customers in the first part of the morning, though some just came for coffee. Eventually she'd learn the names of the regulars and what they liked.

Shortly before noon, her grandmother bustled through the door. "Hello, dear," she said. "How is everything going?"

Penelope Parrish was a lively, beautiful woman of seventy-two. She had a keen intelligence and a generous heart. A few people thought she was flaky, but Jessica figured it was from her involvement with the store and extensive knowledge about the beliefs and legends surrounding rocks and gemstones. Her grandfather had shared the same reputation, even though he had been a published anthropologist before opening the Crystal Connection.

"Pretty good so far," Jessica replied.

"Have you had a lot of customers?"

"About what you said there'd be."

Jessica didn't care if she got rich, but she hoped to expand the shop's customer base. Her grandparents hadn't used social media to promote the business, and they'd never considered selling over the internet. By adding online sales she could save more for her daughter's future and have a cushion to tide them through slow times.

Doing well was important to her, just not at the expense of being a good mom. Her own parents had been so intent on making money there'd been little energy left for their children; she didn't intend to make the same mistake.

"Remember what I told you," Penny said. "Whenever you need me to cover for you, just say the word. I plan to stay active so when I get old, I won't feel it so much. In the meantime, I'll take my great-granddaughter home so we can have a serious bout with a new jigsaw puzzle."

"That's a terrific idea." Jigsaw puzzles had been a constant presence during Jessica's childhood visits with her grandparents. Working on a puzzle together was a great time to talk, or just be in silent accord. She was glad her daughter would have the same experience. Though they'd lived next door since early last summer, she'd rarely accepted her grandmother's offer of babysitting. It had been clear that Granddad was failing and she'd wanted her grandparents to have as much time together as possible.

In the early afternoon there was another flurry of customers for coffee. Several were from Moonlight Ventures and she hated feeling intimidated in their presence. For the most part they were startlingly good-looking. Who would have guessed she would someday serve coffee to Nicole George—now Nicole George Masters—or Adam Wilding, two of the hottest models in the past fifteen years? They weren't just average attractive, they were bigger than life.

Logan Kensington came back at 2:00 p.m. Of all her customers from that morning, he stood out the most. Maybe it was because she'd taken a better look at his gorgeous calendar; there was a biography on the back, along with a thoroughly intriguing picture of him, the image of a bold adventurer. He was ruggedly handsome and had an unusual background, having grown up not just in the United States but in various countries as a diplomat's son. It explained the faint hint of an accent in his voice. With a degree from Oxford and a post-grad stint at Harvard, he was as far removed from her realm of experience as a man could be.

She'd also noticed he was described as "committed to bachelorhood." The remark must have come from him and she had rolled her eyes upon reading it. Some men felt the need to advertise their lack of interest in settling down.

"Where's Cyndi?" Logan asked as she started a fresh batch of the organic medium roast coffee he wanted.

"With Grams. She's helping me with childcare."

"That's nice. The coffee this morning was superb," he said as he waited. "I admit to being skeptical when I realized someone else was making it for the shop."

"You aren't the only one who was concerned. With two major coffee companies having been founded here, Puget Sound residents are passionate about their brew."

"Did your grandmother show you how to make it?"

Jessica shook her head. "Actually, I'm the one who taught her and Granddad when they decided to put in the coffee corner. I'd been working as a barista, so I kind of knew the ropes."

"'Kind of' is an understatement."

"Thanks. It's been years since I had that job, so it's good to know I haven't lost my touch." She'd enjoyed being a barista, though there'd always been a few customers each day who thought they were too busy to wait their turn. The main reason she'd looked for another job was her need for a higher income.

"Did you grow up in the Seattle area?" Logan asked.

"I visited every summer as a kid, but until moving here last year, I mostly lived in the Washington, DC, region. I saw from your biography on the calendar that you aren't a Seattle native, either. What is it like, living outside your own country?"

Logan rested an elbow on the narrow coffee bar. She'd found it at a barn sale a couple of weeks earlier, along with four brass barstools. They'd come from an old bed-and-breakfast inn under renovation. The new setup didn't take much room, but it helped separate the coffee corner from the rest of the shop and gave customers a place to sit if they wanted.

"Living abroad can help broaden your view of the world and its people," Logan explained. "You realize it's ridiculous to assume that everyone does things the way we do at home."

"Conjuring a sense of humility?"

"In a way, I suppose. Still, it's easy to slide back into being egocentric. My folks might have been even more successful as diplomats if they'd fully embraced other customs and viewpoints."

Jessica was aware that her smile had become strained. "My parents have a similar problem. They know people make different choices than theirs, but usually believe those choices are foolish or wrong."

Logan gave her a sympathetic grin. "Including the ones you've made yourself?"

"They would have understood me becoming a high-powered lawyer or going into a corporation and climbing the ranks. Or even if I'd become an actress. But my lack of interest in wealth or fame is a mystery to them. Instead I prefer my grandparents' way of living. Simplicity, core values and not leaving too big of a footprint on the earth."

"An old-fashioned girl, huh?"

Girl? She cocked her head, wondering if Logan was showing his true colors.

"I wouldn't put it that way," she said casually. "People claim you're old-fashioned if you choose certain things an earlier generation valued. But there's nothing new in the world. People have adopted the hedonism of the Romans or the wild antics of the roaring twenties without being called old-fashioned. My parents have a huge amount in common with the robber barons of the nineteenth century, yet everyone calls it the 'modern' way."

"Good point," Logan acknowledged.

The coffee had finished brewing, so she refilled the paper cup he'd brought back from earlier that morning. "Anything else?"

"No—" He stopped. "That is, not at the moment."

Jessica frowned after he left. There had been something unusually intent about how Logan Kensington had watched her. He also seemed to be trying to make a connection. There wasn't anything creepy about it, but it was enough to make her wonder if he had a hidden agenda.

At the same time, she was reasonably certain he wasn't interested in her as a woman.

Why would he be?

Logan Kensington was a handsome man who'd photographed some of the most beautiful and sophisticated women in the world. She was a single mom who'd often shopped at yard sales to help make ends meet…just not for Cyndi's school clothes. Kids could be cruel about that kind of thing and she was fortunate that she could spare her daughter having to deal with it at such a young age. Logan couldn't possibly understand something like that. If he ever had kids, they'd probably go to private schools and shop at trendy clothing stores.

Yet it really didn't matter that he was out of her realm of experience. She'd already made too many mistakes with relationships and wanted to focus on making the shop an even bigger success while raising her daughter. Those were the things that counted.

CHAPTER TWO

LOGAN RETURNED TO his office, wondering if he should have initiated the conversation about moving the Crystal Connection. He'd been considering possible openings the entire time he was talking to Jessica. But maybe it was just as well he hadn't said anything because he still thought searching real estate listings beforehand was a good idea. Also talking with Kevin.

Oddly, Logan hadn't been able to reach him after several calls and two voice mail messages suggesting they get together. Being out of contact was unusual for the agency's former owner.

The next day an email arrived from Kevin, apologizing that he hadn't called back and explaining he was away for a few weeks. His daughter had given birth and he was in Chicago to see the baby and help out, possibly the only thing that could have pulled him from anxiously hovering over his friends and former clients. Kevin McClaskey was a classic overachieving nurturer who wanted to help everyone he met.

Logan sorted through the rental listings he'd compiled. Several were in excellent retail locations, but they had higher rental fees than what Jessica was currently being charged. Surely that would convince her that moving to the rear of the Moonlight Ventures building would be best. That way she'd stay their tenant, expand her retail space, and they could ensure it was well worth her while.

His gut instinct said he should talk with Kevin in person, but Logan wasn't in the mood to wait. So that afternoon he tucked the listings in his pocket and headed for the Crystal Connection, hoping to find Jessica alone. Instead, two customers were there, picking up merchandise and examining it carefully, then moving on to something else.

"Coffee?" Jessica asked.

"In a while. I'm going to look around."

He began peering into various display cases so it wouldn't be obvious that he was just waiting for the others to leave. The customers spent an inordinate length of time deciding which crystals spoke to them. Jessica was friendly as she dealt with their questions, while impatience welled inside of him.

"Do you have to endure that very often?" he asked once the couple had departed with their purchases.

"Excuse me?"

"I'm talking about that sort of customer. You know, looking at everything and all the discussion about healing properties and whether a crystal is speaking to them. I wouldn't have the patience to put up with it very often."

Her smile grew stiff. "I'm not putting up with anything. That couple has been coming to this shop since I was a kid. They're good customers, are awfully nice and attended my grandfather's funeral because they cared about him and my grandmother. But even if this had been their first time through the door, they were fine. I've heard people say a certain photograph or painting speaks to them. Why not a rock?"

Logan could have kicked himself. Despite having grown up with diplomats, sometimes he had a talent for saying the wrong thing. "Sorry, I shouldn't have said anything. I'm sure all businesses have aspects that seem odd from the outside."

"No doubt."

Her manner was polite, but it lacked the easy friendliness she'd shown on his earlier visits.

"Honestly, I'm sorry. I have a big mouth," he said, hoping to regain lost ground. "It's one of the many reasons I didn't follow in my parents' footsteps."

"Not diplomatic enough?" Her tone suggested she was sure of the answer.

"The State Department prefers people who think before they talk so you don't inadvertently start a war. They also prefer people who don't have a talent for sticking their foot in their mouths."

"I see. What kind of coffee do you want today?" she asked.

"A Southwest Twist, please." He handed her the travel mug he'd brought from his studio condo. Hopefully he wouldn't be living there for long—though he was accustomed to hotel rooms after being on location most of the year, he was quickly starting to want more space, preferably out of the city.

As Jessica filled the cup, he wondered if he should wait another day or two to talk with her. She hadn't said anything outright, but he was fairly sure her opinion of him wasn't at a high point right now. On the other hand, she didn't seem the type to turn something minor into a major incident.

As he was putting cream into his brew, the door opened. Great. More customers. Then he saw it was Jessica's daughter, along with Penelope Parrish, which was worse. They might be planning to spend the rest of the day.

"Hi, Penny," he called. "Hey, Cyndi."

"Good afternoon, Logan," Penny said, smiling. "I want to compliment you. The calendar is lovely."

Cyndi eagerly bobbed her head. "Does it take forever to get pictures like that, Mr. Kensington?"

"Call me Logan. Some photographs take quite a while since the animals can be difficult to find. Then you have to wait and take as many as possible, hoping to get the right one."

"Is it hard to do?"

"Yes and no. Mostly you have to be very, *very* patient."

Penny's eyes twinkled. "You have a wholehearted admirer, Logan. My great-granddaughter has been talking about photography ever since she saw that calendar and met you. She even pulled out our old family albums and asked questions I didn't know how to answer."

"I like old pictures, too," he said. "But the technology is different now, with digital cameras instead of using film. With digital, you can get an idea of what you've captured right away without having to wait for it to develop."

"I have a digital camera," Cyndi exclaimed. "Momma gave it to me for Christmas."

"Good, so you can take plenty of pictures and get the hang of how you want them to look. You can also get books at the library about composition and how to frame a shot."

In the back of his mind he was hoping the conversation would be a distraction from his less-than-tactful remark about Jessica's customers. He admired her respect for others and wished he'd voiced the same respect.

Since he wanted to conduct his business with Jessica in private, he went back to his office and spent the next hour evaluating the photos he'd taken of clients that morning down by the lake. Now that he was in the Seattle area full-time, Moonlight Ventures wanted to improve their clients' portfolios. There was a distinct difference between a standard head shot and a more creative approach that might excite a prospective advertiser.

It was late afternoon when he headed over to the Crystal Connection, the copies of the real estate listings still in his pocket.

Jessica looked up from where she was unpacking a large box. "I'm sorry. We stop making coffee at three thirty and there aren't any leftovers."

"I understand." He glanced around and was glad to see she was alone. "But there's something I've been wanting to discuss with you. It's about the space you're leasing from Moonlight Ventures."

Her eyebrow lifted. "Is there a problem? Grams told me she'd paid the rent for three months ahead."

"No, that isn't it. It's just, well, you may not have realized that the lease isn't transferable."

Her soft complexion went pale and Logan instantly felt like a villain in an old melodrama, threatening the beautiful heroine with eviction.

JESSICA STRAIGHTENED HER shoulders and injected steel in her spine. She'd survived setbacks before and would again. Besides, there was an option.

"If the lease isn't transferable," she said, "I'm sure my grandmother will be happy to continue renting the property. I'll work it out with her."

"Please understand, we aren't trying to throw you out," Logan said hurriedly. "It's just that we need to expand the agency."

"The lease is for another three years."

And Kevin McClaskey promised we could stay as long as we liked, Jessica wanted to tell him. She was quite certain that Uncle Kevin wouldn't have had a problem with transferring the lease to a family member. He'd be horrified to learn the new landlords had even mentioned the matter.

"I know what's in the lease," Logan said, "but no matter whose name is on it, we'd hoped to discuss an accommodation that might work for all of us. This issue would have been raised, whether or not the ownership had changed. After remodeling we thought our space was adequate, but we've realized it isn't. We planned to bring the matter up before, but given what happened with your grandfather...it seemed best to wait."

Jessica fought a renewed stab of panic and reminded herself that Grams's name could remain on the paperwork. She'd known the lease agreement wasn't permanent, but in the past it had always been renewed automatically. Granted, she'd questioned whether the situation would change now that Uncle Kevin was no longer the landlord, but she'd figured she had three years to talk with the new owners and sort things out. Now, no matter what Logan claimed, it sounded as if he and his partners wanted the Crystal Connection gone much more quickly.

He *said* it was because they wanted to expand the agency's space. But she had to wonder. His earlier comments had given her the impression that he had a low opinion of the shop and its customers. Perhaps he felt it wasn't as highbrow as his talent agency and didn't want her next door.

Some people thought it was ludicrous to be passionate about crystals, particularly when metaphysical beliefs were part of the attraction. But she knew folks who thought *modeling* was a skewed and ridiculous business.

"What do you mean by accommodation?" she asked warily.

"For one thing, this is a very large building. It covers the better part of a city block. There's space down around the end, off the smaller road. The Crystal Connection could move into one of the available rentals for the same rent, with over twice the square footage."

"Except we have easy parking here. More importantly, the street out front is a busy thoroughfare. Our visibility nets a huge amount of drop-in business."

The expression on Logan's face didn't flicker. "It isn't a big deal for someone to park and walk around the back of the building. And there are ways to minimize the impact of moving. Signs, advertising, that sort of thing. You must have a contact list for your regular customers."

Jessica seriously doubted advertising was the solution. She'd already heard new customers saying it was the large display windows that had enticed them into visiting. The back of the building bordered on a one-way street so narrow it almost functioned as an alley. The store would come off like a hole in the wall, hiding from the world. She shook herself and remembered that Logan was waiting for an answer.

"We don't have a contact list. Not yet. My

grandparents didn't do mailings or promote on the internet. I put out a sign-up sheet last week, but it's just a start."

"The move wouldn't have to be done immediately. If you're interested, I found rental listings for other locations, too."

Jessica wasn't interested; she was insulted. So he'd found a few available rentals. How very patronizing of him. Not to mention presumptuous. It was as if he expected to snap his fingers and have the whole situation resolved to his satisfaction. Moreover, with either solution, the Crystal Connection would be neatly tucked out of his tender sight. He might not even lose sleep if she went out of business altogether.

She gave him a tight smile. "It's early to be looking at other rentals, and if needed, I can certainly find them on my own."

His cool brown eyes were unreadable. "Yes, naturally."

"As for a contact list," she continued, "while I think it's a good idea, it has no relationship to walk-in traffic. Location is everything." Still annoyed, Jessica felt another wave of anxiety. She had three years before she *had* to do what Logan and Moonlight Ventures wanted, but they could make life miserable for her in the interim.

Her gaze fell to the counter by the cash register. The wood was warmly burnished from years of use and polishing, and there were various dents and grooves. Decorators would likely call it "distressed." It was a part of her childhood. As a little girl she'd perched on it and watched her grandparents unpacking merchandise. Sitting on a stool, she'd leaned over its wooden surface and drawn pictures or strung crystal necklaces with her grandmother.

On one of her summer-long visits with her grandparents, she'd written numerous letters to her parents on that counter. Back at home, she'd found them with the junk mail, never opened. Her folks hadn't meant to be uncaring—from their perspective, they'd been working for their family's security, providing a large home, putting money away for college and building a diversified financial portfolio. Though hurt, she'd gathered up the letters and put them in her memory box.

A group of customers came in and Logan moved aside, appearing to study a display of books on crystals, geology and rock collecting. His expression suggested poorly concealed scorn at their enthusiasm, though she tried not to read too much into it. When it got right down to it, he might feel that way about everything. But as far as she was concerned, true sophistication included an open appreciation of the world.

Once the shoppers were busy looking at merchandise, Logan returned to the counter. "What do you say?" he asked in a low voice. "Is it all right if we discuss this further?"

She couldn't refuse and risk antagonizing one of the building's owners. "I suppose, provided you know I haven't agreed to anything. I don't want to make a decision too quickly."

"Naturally." He gave her a crooked grin. "My friends and I talked and planned for years before changing our careers. Of course, we hope to resolve the situation faster with you."

"I understand," she said in a neutral tone.

"Could I take you to dinner Thursday night? That way we can have some uninterrupted time. If you have plans for Thursday, what about the evening after?"

She didn't have any "plans" to coordinate around, no appointments and certainly no dates. Being a single mother made socializing tricky. Now that she lived next door to her grandmother, childcare wouldn't be a problem, but she wasn't eager to explore love again. And she hadn't been in the Seattle area long enough to have much else on her social calendar except for her committee work to get an urgent care medical clinic started in Regen Valley.

"Thursday should be fine," she said, "provided Grams is available to watch Cyndi."

"I'd suggest bringing your daughter along, but it would be better to talk business with just the two of us."

"Right."

Privately she wondered what Logan's attitude might be toward single mothers. She'd met more than one guy who had personal rules about not dating a woman with "encumbrances." That was fine with her. Even if she'd been interested in finding someone, she wouldn't get involved with a man who saw children that way.

"By the way," he said, "to keep things simple, I'll be the only one at Moonlight Ventures discussing this with you. We thought it was best to have a single contact point, also to limit mix-ups in communication."

"That makes sense." It was the best solution and Jessica wouldn't have to dread the subject coming up whenever one of the other Moonlight Ventures partners came into the shop. She didn't want this to impact how she felt about them…which was decidedly negative at the moment, so maybe the most she could hope for was cordiality.

A customer approached the counter with a basket of items and Jessica went to ring up her purchases.

"I'll check with you when I come for coffee tomorrow," Logan said after the woman had left. "Is that all right?"

"Sure."

Jessica breathed easier when she was alone again, but only a little. Logan Kensington had unloaded a potential nightmare for her. With so much to consider, she suspected she wouldn't get much sleep that night.

"I'VE BROACHED THE subject with Ms. Parrish. We're supposed to have another discussion on Thursday," Logan explained to his partners at a meeting an hour after his chat with Jessica.

"Is she open to what we're proposing?" Rachel asked.

He shrugged. "I wouldn't call it open. Although it upset her, she didn't completely reject the idea. Presumably the store operates on a narrow margin, so she has a good deal to consider."

Adam grimaced. "We don't want to hurt her business."

"Her grandparents have leased that location for over thirty years," Rachel added. "This must be the last thing she expected."

Logan nodded. Even though Moonlight Ventures needed more space, they wanted to be responsible and decent. He'd actually found it reassuring when Jessica shot back the assertion that her grandmother could continue the lease. It was preferable to deal with someone who was able to stand up for herself.

"I know I've said it before, but our new career has issues I never thought about," Nicole said. "Especially the part about being a landlord."

They were in equal accord that owning such a large property and dealing with rentals was a challenge they hadn't fully anticipated.

"But it's been good, too," Rachel asserted. "After all, working with Matt Tupper has helped both of our companies."

Matt Tupper owned a recording studio in the back section of the building where they hoped the Crystal Connection would be willing to move. He hired their voice clients for various jobs and they helped find volunteers for his work recording books for the blind. One of those volunteers, Gemma Paulsen, had rapidly become a popular voice-over artist in commercials and other projects…and was now engaged to Matt. The couple expected to get married in a few months.

Logan almost squirmed at the thought.

It felt as if everyone around him was either recently married or getting married. Even their office manager, Chelsea Masters, had a wedding coming up. And his friends seemed to think he'd do the same, joking that falling in love had a domino effect—one fell and the rest began toppling. Hardly. He was glad they'd found people they cared about, but he refused to be swept into the nuptial frenzy.

"I wonder why Kevin originally leased space to the Crystal Connection," Adam mused, breaking into Logan's thoughts. "It's quirky compared to the other businesses here."

"I can answer that," Rachel volunteered. Years ago she'd been a client of Moonlight Ventures and knew the history better than any of them. "When the Parrishes wanted to open a store, Kevin offered them a deal. Of course,

I think the street was still run-down back then, so after he renovated the building, he probably needed tenants. He's been loyal to the ones who took a chance on renting from him."

"It isn't run-down any longer," Logan pointed out. The popularity of converting industrial structures to apartments and businesses had revitalized the area. The building they owned had become a desirable commercial location, yet several of their tenants were paying rent that was significantly under market value. He and his partners didn't plan to increase rents dramatically, but gradual raises seemed appropriate.

As for the Crystal Connection?

Even if it didn't fit with the other businesses in the building, the shop and its coffee were popular. Logan had noticed rocks and crystals on office desks and hanging from the rearview mirrors of various renters. Whether it was due to Kevin's enthusiasm in supporting the shop, or people's natural liking for those things, it was hard to tell.

"What do you think, Logan?" Adam asked.

"What's that? My mind was wandering."

Adam chuckled. "Are you in love?"

"No." Logan gave him a dark look. "And no

more pushing, okay? I'm leaving romance to the rest of you."

Smiles swept across their faces. Being the only unattached member of the group made him the odd man out. He was reluctant to explain that he questioned his ability to fall in love and that he didn't think it was fair to a woman to make a half-hearted commitment. Who knew? Maybe his emotional detachment came from looking at life through a camera lens. Or maybe it was the other way around. Maybe he'd chosen photography because the camera was a mask, hiding his true feelings.

He tried to clear his head. "What was the question, Adam?"

"I was referring to the Jessica Project." They'd taken to calling their expansion plan the Jessica Project since she was the key to getting what they wanted. "Do you think offering six months or a year of free rent might convince her?"

"I can't say," Logan replied. "She's worried about moving to a space that isn't visible from the main street. I'm sure signs and advertising could resolve the issue, but she seems doubtful."

Nicole leaned forward. "Basically, we won't

know how to make this work until you've spoken with her again."

"Right. I wanted to get information about Jessica from Kevin, but he's in Chicago with his new granddaughter, so I decided to just go ahead. It probably would have been a bad idea, anyway. The friendship is so close Jessica even calls him 'Uncle Kevin.'"

"I didn't know the baby had come," Rachel said. "His daughter wasn't due for another couple of weeks. What did they name her?"

"And how big is she?" Nicole asked before he could reply.

If Logan had needed proof he wasn't father material, this was it. He'd felt frustrated, rather than interested, when reading Kevin's email. He hadn't replied, either, because it hadn't occurred to him that there might be details he should ask about.

"Sorry," he apologized. "I was focused on the issue with the Crystal Connection. I'll forward the email to everyone."

His chagrin must have shown on his face because Adam laughed. "Don't feel bad. Blame it on being a bachelor. It's only since Cassie and I started talking about having more kids that I pick up on that kind of stuff. You'll see."

Logan tried to conceal his instinctive re-action. Adam's wife was raising her teenage niece and nephew, so by marrying Cassie, Adam had gotten a ready-made family. It was admirable, but Logan was surprised they wanted *more* children.

As for the "you'll see" remark? Once again it was an assumption that someday he'd join their married-with-children ranks. How many times did he have to tell them it wasn't hap-pening?

"Don't worry about it," Rachel said gently. "I'll send flowers and a gift from the agency."

The assurance reminded Logan of his mother and father. Ever the diplomats, they'd faithfully sent an appropriate gift, card, invi-tation or whatever was required—his father called it "playing the political game." But in Rachel's case, she genuinely cared about Kevin.

"That would be nice," he muttered.

It *was* nice; he just wished he'd thought of doing it himself.

CHAPTER THREE

THE NEXT MORNING Logan wondered whether getting coffee would be awkward, but Jessica simply gave him an impersonal smile and went over to the coffee corner.

"What brew does Mr. Magellan Einstein Stanley want to explore today?" she asked.

Logan liked the modified nickname, though Einstein hadn't been an explorer. "How about a latte? I missed breakfast this morning and at least it has milk." He glanced at a glass case that hadn't been there the day before. "I see you've expanded to an assortment of fresh food items."

"Grams told me that customers have been asking for food besides candy, granola bars or potato chips. This is from a local bakery in the town where I live. They'll package a selection for me and I'll pick up the order on my way to the store every day. We've talked about me carrying a few of their sandwiches, but this morning I told them the idea is on hold."

Ouch.

At a guess, Jessica had put the idea on hold because Moonlight Ventures wanted the Crystal Connection to move.

Feeling like slime, he took a bran muffin from the display case. "This looks tasty."

"It's supposed to be high in protein and fiber, but mostly it's delicious. I've sampled everything I'll be carrying. I didn't want to stock anything I haven't tried myself. My favorite is their cottage bread with jalapeño and cheddar, mostly because it's savory instead of sweet." She frowned at one of her insulated pots and ran her fingers over a brown stain on the bar towel beneath.

"I take it you don't have a sweet tooth."

Jessica lifted the pot and set it in the sink. "Not in the morning. After lunch I have to use all my resistance so I won't turn into a basketball."

Without thinking, he cast a swift glance down her well-formed figure. She wore a dress of soft fabric that flowed around her curves.

Logan reminded himself that their contacts were business-related and nothing else. Even if Jessica was available and interested, dating one of their tenants seemed a bad idea. Besides, call it old-fashioned, he'd pegged her as a forever type of woman. He might not be a properly warm and sensitive guy of the twenty-first century, but he knew better than to get involved with a woman who needed more than he was able to offer.

Once his coffee was shot with hot milk, she poured it into his cup and handed it to him. "Can I get you anything besides coffee and a muffin?"

"This is all. Have you checked with Penny to see if tomorrow evening will work for you?"

Her face tensed. "It's fine. My grandmother is already planning a taco-and-jigsaw-puzzle evening."

"She must enjoy having a young great-grandchild so close."

Jessica nodded. "She's thrilled. And it's a relief for me since it gives my daughter a second adult to count on. When we lived back east my parents were too busy to spend time with her, so it's mostly been just the two of us until I moved to Seattle last year."

It sounded as if Cyndi's father wasn't in the picture and Logan wondered why. Jessica was intelligent, attractive and appeared to have a pleasant personality, though those qualities didn't guarantee a successful relationship.

"That's great," he said. "I'll be here at closing time, if that sounds good."

"If you don't mind, I could use a few minutes after closing. Sometimes I have late customers and then I need to deal with the daily receipts."

"Then how about six?"

"That's fine." Her eyes had turned even more wary, a reminder that it would be a very sensitive discussion.

Moonlight Ventures didn't want her business to be adversely affected, but they needed space. There must be a compromise that would work for them both.

Logan left and Jessica resisted sticking out her tongue at him. It was childish and wouldn't change anything, but he annoyed her. How could he look so alert and well rested when she'd barely slept a wink?

Her cell phone rang and she saw it was one of the Flash Committee members. Regen Valley was a terrific town, outside the metropolitan area, yet within commuting distance.

Jessica had always loved her summer visits there and made a lot of friends over the years, but now that she lived in the small town, she was acutely aware it lacked an urgent care facility. Having a daughter with severe childhood asthma changed everything, so she'd started the Flash Committee to raise money for a clinic. With land for it recently donated, they were making great progress.

"Hi, Chris," she answered.

"I just wanted to let you know that I'll be at the next meeting, after all. Also, you'll be happy to hear we've already sold over a hundred and fifty tickets for the breakfast."

"Wonderful."

The Flash Committee's next fund-raiser was a pancake breakfast at the community center. The ingredients and paper goods were being donated by local businesses, so 100 percent of the proceeds would go into the urgent care clinic fund.

After Chris said goodbye, she shoved the phone into her pocket, annoyed that she couldn't relax and be happy at how well ticket sales were going. People were enthusiastically supporting the committee's efforts, but her worry over the shop was competing for emotional dominance.

She hadn't confided in her grandmother about Moonlight Ventures' request, or the need to keep "Penelope Parrish" on the lease. The night before she'd simply explained that she had a business meeting with one of the owners. Grams's eyes had gleamed when she learned the meeting was with Logan Kensington. She was obviously hopeful something more than business was involved. Jessica had nearly told her the truth, only to stop, reluctant to share upsetting news before she had additional information. But she would have to do it soon, or risk Grams finding out another way.

Jessica pressed a hand to her midriff to quell the flutters. She and Cyndi would be fine. She'd started over more than once, including the time she was pregnant and her brief marriage had collapsed. If necessary, she'd do it again.

Maybe she was borrowing trouble, but while the lease issue could be handled by keeping Grams's name on the paperwork, there were plenty of ways that Moonlight Ventures could make it difficult for her to stay in business. For one, several of the shop's best customers were connected to the talent agency, either as tenants or clients. Would they feel comfortable patronizing the Crystal Connection if Logan and his partners were unhappy with her?

It would be hard to stop thinking about the problem since Logan and his partners came in for coffee several times a day. They were going to be constant reminders that the shop was no longer welcome in the building, in this part of it, at any rate. As if in response to her thoughts, Adam Wilding showed up a few minutes later.

"Good morning, Jessica."

Her stomach tensed again. "Hey, Adam. Southwest Twist?"

"Yup." He held out his mug and she took it to the coffee corner.

Behave naturally, she reminded herself. Logan Kensington had promised he would be the only one speaking to her about moving the store. She needed to pretend everything was normal when dealing with the others, no matter what her private feelings might be. She filled Adam's mug and put it on the narrow bar. Perhaps it was her imagination, but he didn't seem anxious to meet her gaze. Instead, he was peering into the new display case filled with baked goods.

"Thanks," he said. "I talked to Logan on the walk over and he mentioned you'd just started carrying bakery items. What do you recommend?"

"The blackberry coffee cake is the bakery's specialty."

"Sold." Adam opened the case and selected a square of the pastry. "See you later."

He left and Jessica sighed as she entered the sales information into his account. It would be nice if she could have enjoyed owning the Crystal Connection without added complications. At least for a while. Thinking of which… she went to examine the insulated pot she'd put in the sink. She didn't see how it could be leaking, so she checked and found it to be an issue with the spout and pump mechanism. A minor adjustment corrected the problem.

She put it back with the other pots, wishing all of her problems were so easily solved. It wasn't as if she didn't understand Moonlight Ventures' position. They wanted more space and she was in the way. But their timing was lousy. She'd quit a good management job to take over the store. If she'd known something big was in the offing, she might have waited and negotiated with the new owners of Moonlight Ventures until a resolution was reached.

Grams would have been happy to continue running the Crystal Connection in the interim.

The situation was seriously messing with Jessica's business plan *and* with the modest security her grandparents had hoped to give her.

GRAMS CAME BY at noon. "I thought I'd help out with the store until I go pick up Cyndi from her playdate."

"Don't tell me you're bored already with retirement," Jessica teased lightly.

"Not bored, but still getting used to it."

Jessica didn't need to be told her grandmother was also still getting used to being alone. It had only been eight months. And she and Granddad had spent all of their time together; they'd shared a sweet, beautiful love story.

"I've been thinking about Logan Kensington," Grams said during a lull between customers.

"Oh?" Jessica asked warily.

"He's a fine-looking man. You could do worse."

"I agree, except I'm not interested. We have a business connection, that's all." Jessica kept her voice calm.

"Presentable single men are never just business," Penny returned with a grin. "Besides, you can't deny he's hot."

Jessica snickered. "I refuse to discuss something like that with my grandmother."

"Poppycock. We're both women. It's too bad Logan is a little too young for me. If he was ten years older, I'd make a move on him myself."

"Grams!"

Penny grinned. "Your grandfather and I both promised that if either of us ended up alone, we'd keep living to the fullest."

Jessica's grandparents *had* lived their lives to the fullest. Until her dad was in his later teens, they'd roamed the world while Granddad researched various cultures. The anthropology books he'd written during their travels were respected, but they were hardly a financial success. He hadn't cared. Learning had been more important to him, along with the friendships they'd made—Grams still corresponded with dozens of people in other countries.

"I'm glad you aren't giving up on living," Jessica said. "But my meeting with Mr. Kensington is purely business."

Penny waved her hand dismissively. "Ridiculous. There's nothing extensive to deal with as our landlord, so he must have personal reasons for asking you out."

Oh, great.

Jessica decided she'd have to explain so Grams would stop building castles in romantic fantasyland. "The thing is," she said slowly, "he wants to discuss whether the store can move to another section of the building, or even out of the building altogether."

PENNY STARED AT her granddaughter in shock. "What section?"

"Around the back. It's okay, nothing has been decided. He just wants to discuss the possibility, so I said we could talk."

Penny tried to keep her chin from quivering. When Eric had died, she'd determinedly held herself together. It wasn't as if she hadn't known she would spend years alone; her husband had been almost eighteen years her senior. But now... She touched the sales counter Eric had made when they were opening the Crystal Connection.

She gulped down a knot in her throat. "We worked together for so long. Right here. I have countless memories in this place."

"I know." Jessica gave her a hug. "I think of

Granddad all the time when I'm here. But remember, the building doesn't belong to us. As it is, your name will need to stay on the lease because I've been told it isn't transferable. We can work out a sublease arrangement."

"That's fine, but Kevin always said we could stay as long as we wanted."

Jessica took a deep breath. "That was my first thought, too, except Uncle Kevin doesn't own the building any longer and the new owners have a right to consider their needs."

"What needs?"

"They want to expand and because we're next door, this is where Moonlight Ventures needs to go."

"I see."

Penny glanced around the shop. Despite the changes her granddaughter had made, it was still the place where she'd spent years with Eric. With every step it was as if she was crossing paths with her husband's spirit. Sometimes she could sense him next to her or hear his voice and laughter.

How could the Crystal Connection move?

They'd poured themselves into creating a place that reflected their travels. Most of their stock came directly from friends in South America, Africa, the South Seas and Asia. With the shop they'd helped open up markets and create cottage industries for people they cared about.

"Nothing has been decided, Grams."

Penny tried to slow her racing thoughts. This might be hard for her, but it was also tough on her granddaughter.

"Please don't make any promises or commitments until we've discussed everything," she urged. "That is, the Crystal Connection is yours now, but I hope you'll talk with me first."

"I will," Jessica promised. "But please don't worry about it. And remember that no matter where the store is, Grandpa's counter goes with us."

Penny let out a choked laugh. "Good. You know, we could probably get his DNA off that thing. Eric cut himself and skinned his knuckles more times than I could count when he was cutting and polishing the wood."

"So when you used to say there was blood, sweat and tears in this place, you weren't kidding, right?"

"Right. Now I'd better go pick up Cyndi."

JESSICA'S HEART ACHED as her grandmother left, seeming more lonely and lost than she'd ever seen her. For the first time Penny looked her age.

As a rule, no one would guess she was seventy-two years old. With few wrinkles and brown hair barely streaked with gray, she could pass for fifty or younger. Granddad had been more than a decade older than her, but he hadn't looked his age, either.

Grams's first thought had been about losing the place where she'd worked with her husband, and it bothered Jessica that she hadn't considered that before. Was she more consumed by business success than she'd believed?

Swell. Now she had something else to keep her awake at night.

AT HOME THAT EVENING, Jessica tried to conceal her churning thoughts as she tidied the house. Her side of the duplex was roomier than their apartment back east had been, and it even had a small backyard.

A healthy dish her daughter actually *liked* was pasta primavera, probably because of the noodles, so after vacuuming, she cut up chicken and vegetables.

"Momma, do you think Logan would show me how to take pictures?" Cyndi wanted to know as they ate at the dinner table.

Jessica's first instinct was to say no and to tell her daughter not to ask. But it was a selfish reaction and she didn't want to discourage Cyndi from being excited about new things.

"I suppose it's possible," she answered. "But he might not have time. He's very busy."

"I was hoping he could help me get a hobby badge. Photography can be a hobby, right?" Cyndi had just joined a girl rangers' troop and was determined to earn every single badge they offered.

"Uh, yes."

Jessica had a sweet vision of siccing the entire group of giggling girl rangers on Logan. It might partially even the score for his having ruined a night's sleep for her. On the other hand, a few of the older kids had already developed romantic natures and they might get a crush on the handsome photographer. Then she'd have to listen to a steady diet of lovelorn commentary about a man she'd rather forget ever meeting.

CHAPTER FOUR

IN THE SMALL restroom off the shop's stockroom, Jessica studied her reflection in the mirror. Logan would arrive soon for their dinner together and she wanted to look calm, professional and not at all as if she was trying to catch his attention. She just wished her grandmother hadn't pointed out the obvious...how gorgeous he was. She didn't need to be reminded.

Grams believed Logan was a nice man, and he probably was. Of course, Penelope Parrish usually assumed people were nice unless they did something that proved the opposite.

But no matter how attractive Logan might be, Jessica wasn't interested in getting involved with anyone, not after making such a huge mistake with Cyndi's father.

For her daughter's sake, she'd gone to counseling to better understand herself and the decisions she had made. It had helped her realize that the way she'd grown up had left her hungry for love and attention. The counselor had chuckled when Jessica threw out the cliché, "looking for love in the wrong places," but it was what she'd done.

Despite it all, she had never regretted having Cyndi.

The old hunger for love still burned inside; only now she understood how it could lead her into making another mistake.

With a snort of disgust, Jessica ran a quick brush through her hair and clipped it back. Even if she met the right guy, she'd probably mess it up by being too needy. Neediness was death to a healthy relationship.

The shop's doorbell buzzed and she went to find Logan waiting.

"Ready?" he asked when she opened the door.

"Except for setting the alarm." She went to the back, punched in the code and locked the shop while he waited.

"My car is over there," he said, pointing to the opposite side of the lot.

"Perhaps I should follow you," she suggested. "That way I can head home right after we're finished."

A pained look crossed Logan's face. "One

car is best. Parking is limited at the restaurant where I made the reservation."

"All right." Having her own vehicle would make her feel freer, but she had a sneaking suspicion that Logan preferred driving because it gave him the upper hand. But if she wanted to end the conversation or if things got awkward, she'd simply get a taxi.

Logan's car confused her. It was a small, two-door sedan, which made it a lousy family vehicle, but it also was a hybrid, so it wasn't a stereotypical bachelor's ride.

"You seem surprised by something," he commented.

"I just figured you'd drive something sportier."

He shrugged. "I traded my sports car for this one. A hybrid makes more sense in today's world—better for the environment and less time in line at the gas station, which is appealing. That said, I have an SUV to use when I'm doing photography."

Jessica settled into the passenger seat and buckled the seat belt. "Do you miss the sports car?"

"You bet," Logan said. "It was great for running around the city."

Even without a sleek, sporty vehicle, he maneuvered through traffic with the ease of a race driver and soon pulled into a parking area.

"I chose a restaurant that does a cross section of foods. Is that all right with you?" he asked.

"Sure," Jessica said, despite her doubts. She didn't care what sort of food the restaurant served, but this place was small and exclusive. While she had little experience with that kind of establishment, she knew her outfit was far too casual.

It was yet another reminder, as if she'd needed one, that her world was very different from that of her landlord's.

LOGAN GLANCED AT JESSICA. "You sound doubtful."

"I'm not dressed for this sort of restaurant. That's all."

"You look fine to me."

Actually, he hadn't considered whether casual clothes were unsuitable. The restaurant was quiet and the tables didn't bump up too close to one another, so he'd figured it would be a good place for a business discussion.

On the other hand, he sincerely thought Jessica looked nice. Her clothes weren't sophisticated or the latest fashion, but she wore them with grace. Besides, *he* wasn't dressed any fancier, himself.

The maître d' showed no hint of disdain about their appearance, conducting them to a table with a view of the water. "Do you wish for anything from the bar while you look at the menus?" he asked.

"Thanks, not for me," Jessica said.

"Just water, please," Logan added.

Once they were alone again, she looked up from the menu. "What do you recommend?"

"Everything I've sampled is excellent, especially the seafood. The oyster appetizers are popular."

"I'm not much on shellfish. Or any type of seafood, for that matter. I'll just take the fettuccine Alfredo entrée," she said, "with the house vinaigrette on my salad."

"Please get an appetizer," Logan urged. "I'd like one and don't want to eat in front of you. How about the mushroom sampler?"

Her eyes were hard to read, but she finally nodded. "All right."

The server brought elegant goblets with water and lime wedges and Logan gave him their order. When they were alone again he wondered if it was okay to launch immediately into business, yet that *was* the purpose of the evening.

"Have you given any thought to moving the Crystal Connection?" he asked finally.

"It's been hard to think about anything else," she replied in a dry tone.

He suddenly realized the dark smudges under her eyes might be from lack of sleep. Was that his fault? It was an uncomfortable reminder that the business world had rocky aspects. Fashion photography had complications, as well; everything did, but he'd been accustomed to those problems.

"We truly want to find a good solution. Something that works for both our businesses," he said cautiously, hoping it didn't just sound like a platitude.

"I'm not sure that's possible. Anyhow, it's more than just a business to me."

"Oh?"

"For one thing, my grandmother is upset that the store might be moving from where she and Grandpa worked together for so long. And please don't say it's just another part of the building and you don't understand why it should be a big deal for her."

Logan's brow creased. "I wasn't going to say that."

He and his partners hadn't discussed sentimentality as a potential issue and it hadn't occurred to him on his own. His parents had moved around the world so often he'd never developed emotional ties to places or objects. It was a good thing, too, since his career had required frequent travel.

"I know her feelings aren't your problem and I didn't even consider it myself until she mentioned it," Jessica said with a hint of self-recrimination in her voice.

"That seems to bother you," he ventured.

Earlier in the day he'd managed to have a phone conversation with Kevin, who'd been surprisingly cagey about his surrogate granddaughter. So Logan still wasn't sure how best to respond to Jessica. But it was clear that the decisions she'd be making were as much about family as straight business, and he needed to accept it as part of the situation. If providing a sounding board for her was helpful, then he was prepared to do it, even if his efforts proved clumsy.

Her shoulders lifted and dropped. "Yes, it bothers me. The only thing my folks are passionate about is financial success. I've prided myself on choosing a different path, but in this case, the first thing I thought about was whether the Crystal Connection could survive a move, not about the emotional impact on my grandmother." Her face abruptly reddened. "Sorry, that isn't your problem, either."

"Hey, I'm new to business," Logan reminded her. "We can make up our own rules about how to get this done. It's natural the impact on the shop is a primary concern because you have a child to consider. No one can blame you for that."

Her face relaxed. "Maybe." She looked as if there was more she wanted to say but had decided not to open up any further.

"What sort of work did you do before taking over the Crystal Connection?" he asked, thinking it might help if he knew more about Jessica.

"I was a shift supervisor in a department store."

"Has your retail experience been helpful at the shop?"

She smiled wryly. "In a way, but department stores are quite different from a small shop, where one person does everything from choosing stock to sweeping the floor."

"I guess I was lucky to be the last to arrive in Seattle," Logan murmured reflectively.

"How so?"

"As you know, there are four of us who bought Moonlight Ventures together. But when the sale was finalized, three of us were still tied up with other commitments. Initially, Nicole was the only one who was free to move here, so she took the lion's share of work in the beginning. She oversaw all the remodeling at the same time she was juggling the original client list and taking on new ones."

"You've mentioned the remodeling. How extensive was it?"

Logan thought about the endless blueprints and design options they'd had to choose from, plus decisions about wiring requirements for the high-tech equipment they wanted. They'd had long debates over the expense of moving plumbing versus changing the floor plans, ultimately agreeing the cost was worthwhile. Then had come the decision to pay the contractors a bonus to have the work completed faster. Nicole had spearheaded the process. In his opinion, she deserved a medal for patience, grit and sheer willpower.

His laugh held a rueful note. "The place was completely gutted. I got off lucky, aside from writing some very large checks. By the time my last photography contract was satisfied, I was able to enter a smoothly functioning agency. That's why it was only fair that I take the job of, uh, working out everything with you." Too late he realized his last comment might sound offensive.

Jessica's expression was hard to decipher. "So you drew the short straw?"

"That isn't quite what I meant, and I'm not suggesting that working with you is unpleasant," Logan said hastily.

"Only that it's something none of you wanted to do."

"Exactly," he agreed, latching onto her statement as a way out of the dilemma. Then he winced. "On second thought, let me rephrase that."

FOR THE SECOND time Jessica wished her grandmother hadn't said anything about Logan's more pleasing qualities. Right now he looked like a little boy caught with one hand clutching a frog and the other on the teacher's desk drawer. Chagrin was an appealing expression on him—she'd almost call it endearing, but she wasn't going there.

"Feel free to rephrase once again," she offered. "I'm eager to discover how deep a hole you can dig."

Logan's mouth twitched as if he wanted to laugh. "Uh, it's simply that being landlords is new territory for us. We don't want to do anything that upsets you or makes it hard for your business to continue being a success. Who'd want or look forward to that?"

Pointing out the truth wasn't a job Jessica wanted, either, but she didn't have the luxury of staying silent. "Your hole just got deeper. Basically, you're acknowledging Moonlight Ventures expects to do something that will negatively impact the Crystal Connection."

He closed his eyes for a brief moment. "Didn't I mention a chronic problem with sticking my foot in my mouth? Please try to hear the spirit of what I'm saying. We want to find a way where no one will be hurt."

She decided to relent, temporarily at least. "Fine, I'll concede the four of you aren't bad guys joining together to gleefully destroy my business."

"Thanks, I think. So you haven't assigned an evil persona to me?"

"I didn't say you were evil. You might even turn out to be a hero."

An ambiguous hero, she added silently, *but a hero.*

Logan lifted an eyebrow. "You don't sound confident."

"I barely know you, but I'm trying to be open-minded, even if so far you've mostly caused me headaches and two sleepless nights."

He looked contrite. "I'm sorry. Once again let me emphasize that we want this to be a win-win scenario. We have a number of things to offer that could make it beneficial for you."

Jessica was skeptical because anything too good to be true usually was.

The appetizers were delivered, offering a breathing space to regroup. The menu hadn't listed prices, something that filled her cautious mind with apprehension, and she wondered if the plate in front of her cost enough to pay for a trip to the grocery store. It was why she'd originally said no to the appetizer and chosen the fettuccine entrée, hoping it might be one of the less expensive items on the menu.

Pushing the thought away, she tried a stuffed mushroom. It was delicious, though the rare treat was difficult to enjoy under the circumstances.

"What are your biggest concerns about moving to another location?" Logan asked after he'd eaten one of his oysters.

Jessica sat straighter, trying to appear reasonable and professional. "For one, as I've already mentioned, drop-in business would suffer and I'm not convinced that advertising or signs would have the same draw with passersby as seeing my display windows. I've considered ways to increase the store's profile through a website and social media, but that takes time and would have little impact on drop-in trade."

"Did your grandparents do any mail-order business?"

"No, though I'm sure there's a market for it. Buying rocks based on a photo can be tricky, but folks who believe in the healing power of stones and minerals seem willing to purchase that way." She paused and her jaw was tight as she glanced at him. "From our prior contacts,

I gather you don't have sympathy for that sort of belief."

Once again Logan wore the contrite expression of a small boy caught in mischief and she wondered how he planned to defend himself.

Shifting uneasily, Logan realized it would have been better if one of his partners was dealing with Jessica. Technically he'd volunteered, at the same time pointing out his awkward habit of saying the wrong thing. They'd laughed and said he would manage, probably relieved they wouldn't be tackling the problem themselves.

Of course, none of them were the type who stuck to a safe and cautious road. They'd each gambled for high stakes through most of their careers. Even buying the agency had held risks, financially and professionally, so it wasn't a surprise that they were okay about him taking charge of the Jessica Project.

He leaned forward. "I was hoping you'd forgiven my ill-considered remarks about your customers."

"Forgiven, yes. Forgotten, no. It's a question of self-protection. You still think people are foolish to believe in stones and crystals, right?"

Looking at it from Jessica's point of view, Logan understood why she was skeptical of his motives. Strangely, he was reminded of the period when he'd been disdainful of fashion photography, seeing it merely as a stepping stone to his ultimate goal of photojournalism. It wasn't until he'd accepted it as an artistic challenge that his career had skyrocketed.

"I may not agree with some of your clientele's ideas, but that doesn't mean I'm opposed to the Crystal Connection," he said, choosing his words with care. "You have the right to make a living in whatever way you want."

Her faint smile showed she didn't really believe him, but she didn't say so, eating another bite of her appetizer instead. "This is delicious."

Logan nodded, uncertain whether the change in subject was good or bad. "The restaurant was originally recommended to me by Jordan Masters. You may have met him already—he's married to Nicole, one of my partners. I needed a good place to host a dinner party when my parents visited last year. My studio apartment is too small for gatherings."

"I thought you just moved here."

"Yes, but whenever possible, I've come to Seattle to help at the agency. Having an apartment made it easier. My mother and father visited during one of my longer stays—they claimed it was too hard catching up with me in Los Angeles." Logan tried to keep the frustration out of his voice. He loved his parents, but he'd been in Seattle for work, not socializing. Fortunately, it had just been the one time.

A curious expression flickered across Jessica's face. "Where are they based now?"

"My father's last posting was in France, but he and my mother retired eighteen months ago to Florida. Unfortunately, they have a yen for grandchildren and have started pressing their point whenever possible. I'm an only child, so the pressure falls on me."

"But you don't intend to comply with their wishes." It was a statement rather than a question.

Logan leaned forward. "What makes you say that?"

"The biography on the back of your calendar. It mentions you're committed to bachelorhood and are in love with freedom…or something of the sort. Are you saying that statement isn't accurate, or is it just to warn marriage-minded women away?"

He couldn't deny that he intended to stay single, though his reasons were more complicated than the blithe statements on the calendar. "The editor chose what to put in the biography, but it's accurate to say I'm leaving love and child-rearing to my friends. They'll be much better at it than me, and I can be an honorary member of the family, the way Kevin McClaskey is for you."

Jessica sipped from the water goblet the server had brought and Logan was struck by how graceful her hands were.

"Is France one of the countries where you lived as a child?" she asked.

"No, though I always hoped we'd be sent there. Imagine spending as much time as you want at the Louvre or exploring the streets of Paris—above ground and below."

"I'm sure it would be wonderful. I've read about museums such as the Louvre and Uffizi, but I've never gone abroad." Her expression seemed wistful.

"Would you like to travel?"

"Absolutely. My grandparents went everywhere after they got married. I wouldn't want to wander for years the way they did, but it's a big planet, with fascinating stuff to see."

He was surprised. "I hadn't realized that Penny and Eric traveled so much."

"Why should you? You're a landlord, not a buddy, and you only just started full-time at the agency."

"Perhaps, but Kevin didn't mention it. He, uh, knows a great deal about his old tenants."

A smile warmed Jessica's face. "The McClaskeys used to take us sailing on Lake Washington when I spent summers here as a kid. My mom's parents aren't the warm, fuzzy type, so I asked if Kevin and Allison would be my other grandpa and grandma. Allison cried and said yes. They didn't have any grandchildren then, so I was their 'first.' To keep things less confused, I called them Uncle Kevin and Aunt Allison."

Perhaps that was why Kevin had said so little about Jessica, because the intensely personal friendship differed from the connections with his other clients and tenants.

"Where do your maternal grandparents live?" Logan asked, hoping to keep the conversation going.

"New York. Mom and Dad met there when they were both trainee stock traders."

"That's what they do?" he asked in some surprise.

"Not any longer. Dad is a real estate broker in the Washington, DC, metro area, specializing in high-end properties. Mom works with him and…well, it keeps them pretty busy."

There was a story behind her hesitation, but he wasn't certain how in-depth the conversation should go. The more he learned about Jessica, the harder it might be to press the issue of the lease. But he couldn't back off and let his friends down.

Jessica finished her appetizer and stood. "Please excuse me for a moment."

He nodded and she crossed the room, moving in a gentle glide. She spoke to the maître d', who gestured to a stained glass room divider, then followed her with his gaze as she disappeared around it.

After a minute, Logan realized he was staring after Jessica, as well, and forced his attention to his remaining oysters. He needed to focus on getting the space the agency needed without destroying Jessica Parrish in the process. Because Moonlight Ventures was, unquestionably, threatening the livelihood of a single mother.

The guilt he felt was predictable. But finding her attractive was a complication he hadn't expected.

CHAPTER FIVE

PENNY GAZED FONDLY at her great-granddaughter, who was busily fitting two pieces of the puzzle together. She was bright and loving, just like her mother, and it was a gift from heaven to have them next door. Particularly with Eric gone.

A sigh welled from within.

It seemed selfish to be glad Jessica was the one dealing with the new owners of Moonlight Ventures, but Penny knew her own emotions would get too much in the way. Her granddaughter was better suited to sort things out. The Crystal Connection just *couldn't* move; relocating it would kill the store and that would break her heart.

The idea for the shop had grown from years of watching friends from around the globe struggle to find a fair trade market for their local crafts and resources. She would continue coordinating the distribution network she and

Eric had established with similar shops across the United States, but it would hurt desperately if the Crystal Connection no longer existed. She had so many memories there.

It was curious. Penny didn't regret marrying a man so much older, but it was dawning on her that she didn't have anyone who shared fond memories of their travels. Her son had begged to attend boarding school and they'd finally relented. Maybe they should have insisted he stay with them, but he'd deeply resented their constant moving. In contrast, he had loved the regimented life of his school and fervently embraced its stuffy attitudes.

"Are you okay, Grandma?" Cyndi asked and Penny tried to smile.

"I'm fine. This puzzle just reminds me of happy times. Would you be surprised to hear your great-grandmother used to go scuba diving in places like this?" she asked, tapping the picture from the puzzle box.

It was a brilliantly colored ocean scene, with waves splashing over a coral reef, a vivid reminder of the time she and Eric had spent near the Great Barrier Reef. That was when he'd taught her to scuba dive. Eric had loved diving. It had given him freedom of movement, without the pain from the leg he'd injured on an Alaskan fishing boat during a college break.

Cyndi regarded her for a solemn moment. "I think you can do anything," she finally pronounced. "Did you see dolphins?"

"Dozens, and there was a green sea turtle who used to get curious and come around to watch us. I have pictures in one of my albums."

"Cool."

Penny's memories kept stirring, memories of all the natural beauty she'd seen, the cultures she'd been privileged to be part of. That was what life with Eric had been like…experiencing things other people just dreamed about. She missed him terribly, but she was finally remembering the good days first, before the reminder of the loss.

Until now, prodded her ever-active brain.

Right, until now, when this issue about the shop moving had turned her upside down.

She'd liked Logan Kensington the times she'd met him. He seemed emotionally reserved, but he was talented, had an explorer's spirit and was willing to take risks to get what he wanted. And he was also single. If only he'd asked Jessica on a real date, everything would be fine. Instead it was this business about the lease and wanting to move the store.

Penny absently fingered a puzzle piece and wondered if she should call Kevin. He was a nice man. He'd married her best friend from childhood and she'd worried that they would drift apart when Allison died, and then later when she'd lost Eric. Instead he'd remained a friend.

Her granddaughter had rightly pointed out that Kevin couldn't do anything since he no longer owned the building, but it would still be nice to talk it over with someone who understood how she felt.

JESSICA WASHED HER hands and dried them carefully. Logan was too intense for comfort, so she'd excused herself, needing a few minutes of breathing space. A part of her was even tempted to call a taxi so she could slip out the rear door and leave him sitting at the table.

She laughed to herself. If running away was a viable solution to problems, the wimps of the world would have a lock on success.

Squaring her shoulders, Jessica marched back to the dining area and then slowed to look at Logan. What would his face reveal if he didn't know he was being observed? He was gazing out the window and his profile seemed filled with focused energy, yet he was half smiling in a way that made her think about kisses and laughter.

The thought was annoying.

It had been ages since she'd spent time with a man in an atmosphere more conducive to socializing than business. Why had he brought her here? She was a family restaurant kind of woman, which was the type of place she'd expected them to go.

On the other hand, Logan Kensington had lived and worked all over the world, associating with people who were rich and famous. No doubt he'd visited restaurants in Rome, London, Paris and Tokyo that made this place seem rustic by comparison. He operated on a level she'd never dreamed of approaching, so if there were any future business discussions outside the shop, she needed to make sure they did it in a setting where she felt comfortable.

Fastening a calm expression onto her face, she returned to the table and sat quickly, though he'd started to get up as if to help her with the chair.

"This looks good." She gestured to the din-

ner salads the server had delivered, deciding
to enjoy the food even if she couldn't relax.

Jessica savored each bite, though it was difficult not to dread Logan's next question about
the Crystal Connection.

"I know you've lived in the Seattle area for
the better part of a year, but have you had a
chance to see any of the sights with Cyndi?"
he asked instead of launching back into their
business discussion.

"We go whenever possible and my grandmother is always eager to get out and do something. I live in the other side of her duplex, so
the adventures start there."

"I imagine that's both convenient and awkward, since you can't have much privacy."

Jessica assumed he meant privacy for dating,
or perhaps he meant having her grandmother
observing her comings and goings. She shook
her head. "Privacy isn't a concern for me."

"You've mentioned having Penny nearby
gives Cyndi another adult to rely on."

"Yes. Grams is looking forward to summer
because she plans to take Cyndi all over the
region, including British Columbia. When I
visited as a kid, my grandparents always made
sure I got to see places like Mount St. Helens

and Vancouver Island, along with museums and other sights. I would have loved hiking Mount Rainier, but Granddad wasn't able to do something so strenuous."

"Kevin mentioned Eric was much older than Penny. He sure didn't look like a man in his late eighties."

"No." Jessica felt a deep pang—if Granddad had been younger, he might still be alive.

"He must have loved the work at the shop to keep at it so long past the usual retirement age."

She smiled. "Granddad didn't care what he was doing, as long as it was with Grams. They met when he was thirty-five and she was eighteen. It was as if a lightning bolt had hit them, but he resisted getting involved because of the age difference. He also limped from an old injury and thought it wasn't fair to her."

"What changed his mind?"

"Grams. She's a force of nature."

"I see."

Jessica ate a bite of French bread, thinking how badly she'd messed up trying to follow her grandmother's example. She'd believed she was in love with Aaron and had gone after him the way Grams had gone after Granddad. It wasn't her ex's fault that they'd crashed and burned. He hadn't been ready for a relationship, especially with someone who needed a whole lot more than he could give. She'd never make that mistake again.

When their entrées arrived, Logan's expression changed from casual to formal. "Tell me some of your other concerns about moving locations."

"One is that I have a large number of regulars for coffee," she said. "If they have to go all the way around to the back of the building, some might not bother."

"Surely that wouldn't make a difference. Your coffee is excellent."

"Look, I know you don't think parking is a big deal, but time is important to people in this busy age," she countered. "It's a huge building. Often someone would have to park at one end, then walk the full length of the block and around to the back. Busy people will choose a shop with a drive-through window rather than put up with too much inconvenience, no matter how good the coffee might be somewhere else. Besides, out of sight, out of mind."

"Signs will help," Logan insisted, though she was fairly sure he saw the logic of her argument. Moving would inevitably impact her business, and not for the better. Coffee sales were a reliable income when other sales were slow, and losing them would be a huge problem.

Jessica pushed her slight depression aside. She'd been promised rapid advancement in her old job, but refusing her grandfather's legacy would have been unthinkable. At any rate, she still thought it was better to be her own boss, which meant she had to find a way to stay in business.

They continued talking, Jessica listing the issues that had occurred to her from the time Logan had first mentioned moving. He listened respectfully, which was surprising. He'd more or less scoffed at her concerns the first time they'd talked.

Jessica's conscience chided her.

She didn't know anything substantive about Logan beyond his amazing talent. And didn't expect to *ever* learn anything. He was a business associate, that's all.

THE NEXT MORNING Penny's head ached from lack of sleep. She got out her cell phone and debated. Several days earlier Kevin had dropped by the house on the way to the airport, both to say goodbye and encourage her to call if she wanted to talk. It had been thoughtful and she enjoyed their conversations, but she didn't want to intrude. Jessica was like a grandchild to him, but this was his daughter's first baby.

Besides, what could he do? The building had been sold even though he still came around and visited his former tenants. She worried he was lonely and didn't know what to do with his retirement.

A tap on the back door made her jump and she turned to see Jessica lean in through the opening.

"Hi, Grams. Just wanted to remind you that I'm taking Cyndi to the store this morning."

"Thank you, dear." Penny wanted to know how the meeting with Logan had gone but was afraid to ask. She put the hand holding the cell phone to her chest.

Jessica frowned. "Is something wrong?"

"No. I was thinking about calling Kevin, but he's probably busy with the baby."

"Maybe he wants to talk to you, too," Jessica said gently. "It must be hard, knowing Aunt Allison isn't here to see her new granddaughter. Anyhow, I'll see you later."

When Penny was alone again she realized Jessica was right. Why hadn't she thought of that? Kevin could have flown into Chicago full of expectation, only to remember his wife would never hold their sweet grandbaby in her arms. His emails had plenty of news—explaining that his daughter was recovering well from her scheduled caesarean and that baby Allie was gorgeous. Nonetheless, emails weren't the same as talking to an old friend.

She selected Kevin's number from her phone's contacts list.

"Morning, Penny," he answered, sounding pleased. "I was just thinking about you."

"How is everything going?"

Kevin raved about his granddaughter for a while, who was apparently the prettiest and smartest child born since his own daughter had arrived thirty-six years earlier. "Naturally, Jessica and Cyndi are perfect, too," he immediately qualified.

Penny chuckled. "Naturally. Are you having to fight Jill and her husband for a chance to hold the baby?"

"We're all taking turns. Bryan is a fine man. Isn't it wonderful that his employer gives paternity leave to both mothers and fathers these days?"

"Yes, it is," Penny murmured, recalling how she'd flown back east to help when her twin grandsons were born and again when Jessica arrived. After all, her son wouldn't have taken paternity leave if his company had begged him, and her daughter-in-law had barely recovered from childbirth before returning to work.

"Have to keep that nose to the grindstone," James declared each time, his wife vigorously agreeing. "It's the only way to get ahead."

Having a career didn't mean you couldn't be good parents, but her son and his wife had left child-rearing to other people. It was hard to admit that James didn't share his parents' love for home and simplicity. He'd wanted more and more, better and better. Penny wrinkled her nose. Definitely, they should have said no to the boarding school. Recognizing James was honest and hard-working was a comfort, but she hated how his children had grown up so lonely. It had been roughest on Jessica, though, since the boys had relied on each other.

"Penny?" Kevin prompted over the phone. Oops, her mind had been wandering. She would have claimed age or the stress of the past year, but she'd always been that way.

"Sorry," she apologized.

"A visit with the leprechauns?" he teased. It was an old joke, one that always made her smile.

"You know me too well. Listen, there's something I want to discuss, though I shouldn't bother you while you're away."

"Nonsense. What's up?"

"It seems that the…the new owners want to expand Moonlight Ventures right away. They've asked Jessica to move the Crystal Connection around to the back of the building. To the side that faces on that little street with no traffic."

"What are they thinking? It's a terrible site for a retail store. This must be why Logan called and was asking about you and Jessica." Kevin sounded grim. "I'll talk with them. You've had that space for a long time—it was almost a second home for you and Eric."

She let out a breath. "I know, but the new owners want to expand. Jessica can refuse since there are three years left on the lease, but that just postpones the problem."

"I'll still talk with them. They're young.

They may not realize how things should be done."

Penny felt better, though she knew there was little that Kevin could do if the new owners were determined. "Thanks. It's great talking with you. I've missed our chats."

"Me, too. We'll make up for it when I get back."

They spoke a few minutes longer before the baby started crying in the background and Kevin said goodbye.

Penny turned off her phone, feeling selfish that she wished he was home instead of being in Chicago. For months he'd been dropping by the shop each afternoon during the slow period. They would drink a cup of coffee or tea, sometimes sitting in silence, other times talking about everything under the sun. Perhaps she should have discouraged him, but it was the time of day when being alone weighed on her the most.

When Eric had suspected his heart was giving out, it was in the afternoons that they'd spoken about the future most often. It hadn't been easy for her, but they'd grown even closer as they talked about life and death, sorrow and joy. She hadn't wanted to continue running the store alone, so they'd decided to sell a piece of property they owned in Seattle to provide a nest egg for her and a bequest for Jessica's twin brothers. But there was never a question that Jessica should have the Crystal Connection. Now Penny feared the security they'd hoped to provide their granddaughter and great-granddaughter was fading away.

All at once she shook herself.

This kind of worry and fretting wasn't like her. Everything would work out.

IT WAS DIFFICULT for Logan to concentrate on the stack of work he'd planned to do that morning.

Wading through portfolios of prospective clients—otherwise known as hopefuls—was his least favorite part of running the agency, a sentiment his partners echoed. But that wasn't what was bothering him—it was how to resolve the issues with Jessica Parrish.

The agency's client list was growing and they needed to hire new agents, but they had zero space for them. Even working at home wouldn't take care of the problem because a professional setting for meetings was essential. A desk stuck in the corner of the reception area wouldn't reassure clients or advertisers that the agency had its act together. The room they had for photography work with clients was already inadequate. But even if they turned it into an office while he and his partners doubled up as an interim measure, it wasn't what they wanted long term. Crowded conditions also wouldn't project the image of success they were fostering.

Perhaps more coffee would help him get focused. It would be a good excuse to see Jessica and gauge how troubled the waters might be after their discussion the previous evening. He'd gotten a cup that morning, but there had been too many customers in the shop to determine anything. Grabbing his travel mug, he strode down the hallway, waving at Chelsea, the office manager. She nodded, accustomed to the partners going out on quick coffee runs.

Jessica was dusting a display case as he walked into the store.

"Hi," he said. "Is there any Southwest Twist ready?"

"Just made a fresh batch." She took his cup and headed for the coffee corner.

Several customers looked up from their

shopping and smiled as Cyndi ran from the back room, carrying a camera. "Hi, Logan."

"Hey, kiddo. I bet you're enjoying the break from school."

Cyndi's head turned thoughtfully and he noted a strong resemblance to her mother. She had the same soft hair with coppery highlights, the same striking blue eyes and the same bright expression.

"I didn't like it before Momma had the store and I had to go to day care. *Boring*," she declared. "Now I go to Grandma's house or the shop, so it's nice. But school is nice, too."

"I'm glad you like both."

He would have called it a win-win situation, except repeating the phrase within earshot of Jessica didn't seem wise. He'd told her to take a few days to think about moving the store and that they could meet again the following week.

"Can you show me how you took pictures of the baby mountain lions?" Cyndi asked.

"I can show you a few things." Logan examined her camera and then explained the zoom feature and various settings. "You'll need to experiment and see what works best."

"Is the sports setting the one you used taking pictures of the baby lions?"

"My equipment is different, but that's the setting to use on your camera for action shots," he said.

"Grandma says a lot of people just take pictures with their phones, so they aren't using cameras as much."

Logan was aware of the trend. "That's probably because they usually have their smartphones with them."

"But can they take the same kind of pictures as a camera?"

"Probably not," he admitted. "I haven't done comparisons, but I doubt camera phones can do as much as my equipment."

Cyndi's lips turned down with disappointment. "I was hoping to take pictures just like you."

Logan was flattered by her enthusiasm and didn't want to discourage her by discussing the thousands of dollars he'd spent on his professional gear. "I understand, but remember what I said before—your camera is a good place to start. This way you can get a feel for how the world looks through a camera and how you want to portray it. Practice taking pictures of kittens and puppies and things like that."

"But can you bring your camera and show me how you do it? Sometime, I mean."

"Here's your coffee, Logan," Jessica interjected, perhaps to head off her daughter's request.

"Can you?" Cyndi begged, though her mother was shaking her head at her. "I'd really like to see."

"Uh, sure," he said, unable to resist the pleading expression in the little girl's eyes. He'd mostly photographed adult models, so his experience with kids was limited, but she was refreshingly unaffected and eager.

"Cyndi, you need to finish your homework," Jessica said. "Remember, you can't go to the science center tomorrow with Grams unless it's done."

With a flutter of her hand, Cyndi quickly disappeared into the storeroom.

"I have a study and play area for her back there," Jessica explained, handing him the travel mug.

"Is that where you studied when visiting Penny and Eric?"

"It wasn't needed. My parents sent me here during summer breaks and I wanted to be wherever Grams and Granddad were. But I wanted a quieter place for Cyndi to focus on her schoolwork."

"A busy store would have too many distractions," he agreed.

A young man brought his shopping basket to the counter, so Logan moved away.

A sparkling object caught his attention. It was a piece of rock carved into a large sphere, with a natural cavity that revealed stunning blue crystals inside.

In the background, he heard the guy at the counter exclaim, "You've got a great selection."

"Thanks. Is this your first time here?" Jessica asked.

"Yeah, but I'll be back. I'm Jason Winslow. Is that your husband you were just talking to?"

Curious to see Jessica's response, Logan glanced over and saw her shrug. "He's one of my landlords. I'm divorced."

"In that case, is there any chance I can take you to dinner this weekend?"

Logan strained his ears to hear Jessica's reply.

"That's nice of you, but I just inherited the Crystal Connection and I need to focus on learning the business. The rest of the time I'm pretty busy being a mom."

"Maybe later when things are quieter? Uh, if it works better for you we could all go to a family movie or something."

"Perhaps. Would you like to be on our new email list? I'm going to use it for sales, coupons and promotions, but I won't send out constant emails or share it with anyone else."

The guy laughed. "Good to know. I mark that kind of thing as spam so I won't have to wade through it to find the stuff that matters."

Logan shifted his feet as a clipboard exchanged hands. It was illogical to be restless; getting Jessica's customers on an email list was helpful to his cause.

Picking up the blue stone ball, Logan examined it more closely. But he remained distracted, thinking about Jessica's casual manner when her customer had asked if he was her husband. He felt a wry chagrin. After all, he *was* just one of her landlords and didn't want to be anything else.

"Nice, isn't it?" Jessica's voice seemed to come from a distance and Logan realized his mind hadn't been present for a while.

"Yes, it is." At least he could say that honestly. "Is the color artificial, and what healing property are the crystals supposed to have?"

"The color is natural. It was carved from a celestite geode from Madagascar and I believe it's good for the eyes."

"Why is that?" Logan tried to make the question sound simply curious.

"Because it's so well-crafted and beautiful."

"Really?" he said. Odd, Jessica's eyes had the same blue as some of the crystals inside the stone ball.

"Yes," she said in a confidential tone. "Haven't you heard? Art is good for the eyes *and* the soul."

Logan stared, marveling at how smoothly Jessica had pulled his leg. How had he missed it? Easy answer…he'd been thinking about kissing her.

CHAPTER SIX

JESSICA GRINNED AT LOGAN, pleased to see him nonplussed.

"Okay," he said, "I deserved that. And you're right about this being a piece of art. I'll take it."

Her humor faded. "You don't have to buy something out of guilt or pity. Besides, one purchase, no matter how large, won't solve anything."

He shook his head. "This is for me, because I want it. I'm interested in doing microphotography and this would be a good subject. Microphotography is when you do extreme close-ups. The results can be extraordinary. You see details that aren't visible to the naked eye."

"I've read about it. Ever since she met you, Cyndi has been searching the internet for information on photography and asks about anything she doesn't understand. Your calendar has inspired her to new heights of enthusiasm."

"I'm honored."

Jessica's gaze fell to Logan's strong fingers holding the celestite ball and she swallowed. Once upon a time she'd dreamed of walking through life, hands clasped with a guy she loved more than anything. She still felt hungry for that kind of relationship and was embarrassed that Logan Kensington reminded her of the dream.

"Tell you what," she said, "if you bring one of your super-duper cameras and show Cyndi what you're doing, you can take extreme close-ups of the celestite ball and my other stock for free. Just let me know what afternoon you're free to come, and I'll make sure Cyndi is here."

The offer was self-serving—if Logan spent real time at the store he might get an inkling of why it was special. It probably wouldn't make any difference, but she wanted him to understand the shop was more than just a place that sold decent coffee and pretty things.

The cautious side of her nature was sending numerous warnings about Logan, but she had to ignore them. She was fighting for her livelihood and her grandparents' legacy.

Logan nodded after a long moment. "I'll

do that, but I still want to buy the sphere, or geode, or whatever it's called."

"It's your choice. Keep in mind the color will fade if you display celestite in sunlight," she said as she boxed the carved ball with its acrylic display stand. "Amethysts are the same."

"Thanks."

He walked out with his shopping bag and coffee cup, leaving Jessica with mixed feelings. Normally she would be pleased to sell one of the bigger-ticket items, but would he appreciate such a fine piece? Still, Logan had an eye for beauty.

A short time later Nicole George Masters came into the shop for her afternoon latte. Jessica said hello, struggling to smile. She'd been doing her best to act normally with everyone from the agency.

"Logan just showed me a fantastic blue crystal piece he got from you," Nicole said. "I'm envious. I think I've been rushing in and out too fast without paying enough attention to the displays."

"Rocks and crystals aren't everyone's cup of tea."

"It isn't that, I just get in a rush." Coffee cup

in hand, Nicole wandered through the aisles, stopping occasionally to look more closely at a particular crystal.

From Jessica's contacts with her, she knew the other woman wasn't only beautiful, she was intelligent and gracious, too. It was important to remember that her landlords were nice people, if removed from day-to-day realities. They'd succeeded fabulously in their former careers and were turning their talent agency into an equally stellar success, but they had troubles like everyone else. No one would know it looking at her, but Rachel Clarion Kessler's face had been scarred in an accident. And apparently Nicole and her husband had gotten married at the courthouse because their parents didn't get along, making a formal wedding out of the question.

Still, while none of them were wealthy, it had been a long time since they'd worried about putting food on the table or keeping a roof over their heads.

Nicole waved and left and Jessica threw her shoulders back. She despised feeling sorry for herself. After all, she was more fortunate than many people.

"Momma, I'm finished with my homework,"

Cyndi said, coming out of the stockroom. "Can I take pictures of the rocks now?"

"Sure. Maybe we can use them on the website I'm designing," Jessica told her.

Cyndi's eyes lit up. "Okay."

Before long her daughter was absorbed in taking pictures—having a purpose made it even more fascinating for her.

Jessica focused on the website she was creating. It hadn't been a top priority since she spent most of her free time on the Flash Committee. But now that the shop was in danger, she needed an online presence to promote the store and establish internet sales. Some people made their living that way, although Jessica enjoyed interacting with customers, hearing their stories and getting a sense of the items they liked best. Beyond that, the shop was a link to Granddad for her and Grams.

Nonetheless, whether it was now or a few years from now, she was going to lose this space. If she wanted to stay her own boss, she had to do something.

PENNY STOPPED PULLING weeds and sat back on the five-gallon plastic paint bucket she used as a seat and rubbed her knees. Gardening used

to be easier. There was no use pretending—
her legs were seventy-two years old. Not that
she was using age as an excuse; she just had to
find ways around arthritis and creaky joints.

With a snort of disgust, she grabbed the
trowel and dug at the weeds again. What had
she been thinking to neglect the yard for months
on end? Sorrow sapped everything, including
energy. No matter how much she'd promised
to keep embracing life when Eric was gone,
it was easier said than done. She was lucky to
have Jessica next door and be able to spend
time with her great-granddaughter. Kevin's
friendship was another help.

Still, Eric's absence remained an aching
wound. Their life together had been so good,
with great adventures and passionate love.
Now she was faced with years alone…which
was why he'd refused to date her in the beginning.

Penny dropped a handful of weeds into a
second bucket. At eighteen she hadn't truly
understood Eric's concerns, but she was still
grateful he'd relented. If being alone in her
senior years was the price, she'd gladly pay
it in return for all they had shared. She just

wished her granddaughter could have something equally joyful.

Jessica blamed herself for her divorce, but Penny didn't have any use for a man who abandoned his family that way.

Her cell phone rang. "Yes," she answered with a snap.

"Hey, Penny." It was Kevin. "Is something wrong? You sound annoyed."

"Sorry, I was thinking about the skunk who ran out on Jessica. It put my dander up."

His chuckle traveled over the line. "Understandable."

"I can't say things like that to her. She claims it's her fault. Besides, I don't want Cyndi to hear my opinion."

"She's never met him, has she?"

Penny sighed. "No. But what kid wants to hear her father called names? Half her DNA comes from Aaron, so I keep my mouth closed. All the good stuff is from Jessica, though."

"She's a treasure," Kevin said warmly. "Listen, I talked with Logan again and he assures me that they'll do whatever is possible to keep Jessica and the store from being harmed. Plus, I'll be home in a few days and can help keep an eye on everything."

"She'll still have to move, won't she?"

"It's possible, but let's not cross that bridge until the shoe drops."

Penny's lips curved. She liked the way Kevin sometimes mixed up his sayings and metaphors. With her, at least. She didn't know if he did it with other people.

"How is everything in Chicago?" she asked.

"Terrific, but I'm anxious to get back to Seattle, even if I can watch the Cubs and the White Sox on local stations here."

"You don't have a favorite between them?"

Kevin snorted. "I wouldn't dare choose. My daughter loves the Cubs and my son-in-law is a die-hard White Sox fan. It makes for spirited conversations in this household."

"I'll bet."

"How are you, Penny?" His voice was serious.

"Okay. I'm in the garden. My knees don't appreciate the effort, but there's a serious accumulation of weeds."

"I'll lend a hand when I get home."

She looked at the wilderness she called a garden. Jessica had been working on the other side and her efforts had extended into her grandmother's half. It was what had prompted

Penny to go out herself to work. Her granddaughter had enough on her plate.

"You don't have to do that," she told Kevin.

There was a long pause. "The thing is, I don't feel useful any longer. I don't regret selling the agency—my clients deserved young, energetic representation—but now I have nothing to do."

"Don't be a ninny," Penny said bluntly, concerned by his attitude. "You've got plenty to accomplish, and if you need more, give me five minutes and I'll make a list."

"If it would make a difference, I'd move to Chicago, but the kids don't need an old man around all the time. My life doesn't have a purpose any longer."

A deeper worry hit Penny. She'd seen too many people retire, only to live a short time because they lacked the will to go on. Men seemed especially vulnerable.

"I never expected to hear such ridiculous nonsense from you," she scolded. "Good grief, a man becomes a grandfather and the next thing you know, he's complaining about being old. It's time to fly home and start your second career. Just don't plan on becoming a comedian."

A chuckle sounded through the phone.

"Thanks, Penny. How about going out to dinner sometime when I get back to Seattle?"

Now it was her turn to hesitate. Having dinner was a new way for them to spend time together, almost date-like. No matter what she'd told Jessica about embracing life, it was a silly speculation for a woman her age, especially with a younger man. Not that Kevin was that much younger, being in his mid-sixties, and he'd already been married to an older woman. Sighing, she shook her head. Life was complicated.

"It sounds wonderful," she said, "provided my knees hold up after this gardening stint."

"Leave plenty for me to do. I'll see you soon."

"Safe travels."

Penny disconnected and attacked the flower bed while her mind buzzed over the conversation. Maybe she should take Kevin with her the next time she volunteered at the animal refuge center. Working with animals was a worthwhile activity and he needed to remember how much difference he could still make in the world.

She *had* to keep him busy and interested in living. With Allison gone and now Eric… she couldn't stand the thought of losing such a good friend.

AT THE AIRPORT the following Wednesday Kevin kissed his daughter and shook his son-in-law's hand. Reluctantly he handed his granddaughter back to her parents, only to spot tears streaking down Jill's face.

"Hey, kiddo, what's wrong?"

"I don't want you to leave."

It was sweet, but he knew she was extra emotional from postpartum hormones. Jill, Bryan and Allie needed time together as a family, without a grandfather hanging around.

"I'll be back soon," Kevin said gently.

Jill sniffed. "You'd better be. Allie needs to grow up knowing her grandpa."

Bryan put a comforting arm around his wife. "We realize you're close to the folks in Seattle, but don't forget, you have family here, as well."

"Thanks, son."

Kevin had enjoyed a good relationship with Bryan from the beginning and he was glad his daughter had a husband who loved her so deeply. Some couples struggled to keep a relationship strong when they had trouble conceiving, but Jill and Bryan had gotten through it and now there was little Allie to enrich their lives.

He hurried through the security checkpoint,

choking up as he turned and saw them still watching and waving. Once in his seat on the plane, he felt torn. He wanted to be home, but he also wanted to be with his family. Still, it wasn't hard to fly from Seattle to Chicago; he needed to plan more regular trips.

Before they asked everyone to turn off their electronic devices, he saw a text message from Penny Parrish, offering to pick him up. He replied that he'd left his car at the airport in long-term parking.

That was nice of her. Rachel had also offered to meet him when she learned he was returning. He'd always liked the four young people who'd bought his agency. After deciding to sell Moonlight Ventures, he had thought of them immediately. Perhaps he should have realized that with their talent and energy, the agency would expand and space could become an issue. If he had, he would have put a protection clause for the Crystal Connection into the sales agreement.

Hindsight was 100 percent, he reflected as he closed his eyes, hoping to sleep during the flight. He couldn't go back in time and fix anything, but he could do his best to help Jessica now.

FOR SEVERAL DAYS after buying the large celestite ball, Logan found himself spending any spare minute gazing into its sparkling depths. The art piece deserved a better location than his desk, but his office was too limited in size for more than the essentials.

Despite the money they'd spent on remodeling, certain issues had been impossible to work around. In the middle of the renovation it had belatedly dawned on them that they needed a combination lounge and break room. Rather than spend even more money to undo completed work, their architect had turned one office into a small lounge and divided the remaining square footage. Logan and Rachel had volunteered to take the resulting smaller rooms since they'd be the last to arrive.

The one thing he hadn't expected was to feel hints of claustrophobia in the closet-like space. Ultimately he'd move into one of the new offices and one or more junior agents would get his.

Someday they might even put in stairs and create a rooftop garden that everyone in the building could enjoy.

Logan yawned.

Cabin fever was making him less productive, resulting in additional coffee sales next door, even though seeing Jessica was a reminder of the conundrum facing Moonlight Ventures.

"You seem lost in thought," Rachel said. She was standing at the door he usually left open. "Any great insights on the horizon?"

"Nothing impressive enough to be called an insight. I just wish we had a better option for expansion. But I've checked and we can't get permits for adding a second floor to the building. So it comes back to us needing Jessica to move."

Rachel made a face. "We sure are struggling with the landlord side of the business. Regardless, we can't force the Crystal Connection to move until the lease expires, even if we wanted to."

"Which we don't want."

Logan glanced at the celestite crystals inside the carved sphere. He didn't know what he'd expected when he asked Jessica about their healing properties, but he hadn't expected her to tease him about art and beauty.

He focused on Rachel again. "I'd rather do business our way than ride roughshod over people, even if that's how some corporations operate these days."

"Absolutely," she agreed. "Simon admits he was ruthless when he first started, but I'm glad he's changed."

As always, her eyes sparkled at the mention of her husband, and Logan wondered again why some people seemed suited for love, while others didn't. Not that he was unhappy, and there were plenty of folks who felt the same about staying single. For him, the tricky part about dating was figuring out who genuinely didn't want commitment, in contrast with the women who claimed it wasn't a goal, yet privately hoped for an ending with orange blossoms and white lace.

It was interesting that Jessica had suggested he was trying to warn marriage-minded women away with his calendar biography. She hadn't rolled her eyes, but her tone had suggested it was arrogant. He didn't know. Wasn't it better for everyone to be up-front about expectations?

"I'm worried there may not be a good resolution," Logan said slowly. "We need the space, but I've been listening to Jessica's concerns and I'm afraid moving will have a negative impact."

"How about permanently lowering her rent as incentive or compensation? Perhaps halve it?" Rachel suggested. "I'm sure Adam and Nicole would agree. We aren't getting much income on those empty spaces in the back as it is. Some would be better than none."

"We could try, but when I talked to Kevin, he mentioned that he'd offered the Parrishes a lower rent on the shop during one recession and they'd refused. I suspect Jessica has the same sort of pride."

In fact, Logan was sure of it, considering the way she'd reacted when he wanted to buy the celestite ball, calling it a pity or guilt purchase. It was possible she'd accept a year's rent to move—incentives were a common business practice—but she'd likely refuse anything that smacked of charity to her. On the other hand, a rent reduction was appropriate for a less desirable location.

"I don't think it's pride, exactly," Rachel countered. "In the end, a person needs self-respect. If their values don't allow them to accept something, then all you can do is honor their decision."

"I realize that," Logan acknowledged.

Rachel knew too much about pity. Magazines and scandal rags had oozed sympathy about her accident, when they'd mostly been interested in titillating their readers. But Rachel had never wailed "poor me" or allowed her friends to do it. Instead, she'd resolutely built another career.

"The Crystal Connection closes at five thirty," he said. "Maybe Jessica would be willing to tour the alternate locations this evening and see what she thinks about them."

"Good luck."

Logan went to the lounge to dump his remaining coffee in the sink and rinse the cup. It was procrastination, the same as his contemplation of the celestite ball. Where was his normal drive to action? A photographer couldn't hesitate. When a great photo opportunity presented itself, he had to respond instantly.

That's before you met Jessica and her daughter, chided his self-honesty. Swift action could hurt them. Having his emotions challenged by Jessica wasn't helping his decisiveness, either.

He stepped into the store and saw Jessica was on the phone.

"That's good news," she was saying, "a nice boost to our income."

Hope sparked. The better her shop was

doing, the better it was for him and his partners. After a minute she got off the call and nodded at him.

"Good afternoon, Logan." Her voice was friendly, though he saw stress in her features. Most people wouldn't have realized it was there, but it had been his job to ensure he captured the right mood in photographs. He'd learned to detect when models were distracted and find ways to focus them.

"Hi. I wasn't trying to eavesdrop, but it sounds as if you got good news about the shop."

After a moment of looking confused, she shook her head. "If you're talking about the phone call, it was about a project I'm spearheading in Regen Valley."

"As I recall, Regen Valley is a little community, southeast of the city. I'm glad your project is going well."

"You bet. It's important for the town."

"Logan," Cyndi cried as she dashed out of the storeroom. "Did you bring your camera?"

"Sorry, I came to talk with your mom about the shop. Maybe next week."

Cyndi's face fell. "I have a troop meeting on Saturday morning and wanted to tell them all about your camera and taking pictures. Could you come and show them? I might get an extra point that way."

"The extra point is when you bring another girl your age," Jessica said quickly.

"I think it's anyone. The troop leaders claim it's another girl, but that isn't what the handbook says."

Logan couldn't suppress a chuckle. Cyndi was a neat kid.

"Will you?" she persisted.

He wavered. It seemed devious to agree, knowing it might win points with Jessica. But he liked Cyndi and didn't mind doing something for her.

"Please?" she persisted. "My troop never had anyone as good as you."

He capitulated. "All right. How can I resist so much flattery?"

"What do you mean?" She looked puzzled.

Logan glanced at Jessica and saw the humor in her eyes.

"You said I'd be good," he told Cyndi, "so I—"

"Because you will be. Courtney Willis got her uncle to come the last time and he's a plumber. It was dumb. He talked to us like we were babies. 'Sides, I knew hair clogs the drain by the time I was *four*. He didn't have to bring the gunky stuff he digs out to show us. It was totally gross."

Logan drew a deep breath. "Thanks for the vote of confidence, Cyndi. I'll try to be better than the plumber."

"Thanks. I'm going to finish my homework."

Her departure was a relief. It had belatedly occurred to him that discussion about moving the shop shouldn't happen in front of the owner's daughter. He turned to look at Jessica, whose face was still alive with humor. Today she wore jeans and a T-shirt that made her look far too young to be Cyndi's mother.

He'd worked with many beautiful women through the years, but Jessica had something special that made her attractive to him. He might as well admit the truth to himself and deal with it honestly.

CHAPTER SEVEN

JESSICA SAW WARMTH in Logan's eyes, almost as if he was seeing her as a woman, not just a tenant standing in the way of his agency's expansion plan.

But she didn't trust it.

He worked with women who were much prettier and far more accomplished. She should know—a good number of Moonlight Ventures' clients came in for coffee and several had raved about him. There would be an increasing number now that he was at the agency full-time.

She went to the storeroom and closed the door to keep her daughter from overhearing anything.

"If you'd prefer, I can tell Cyndi you remembered a prior commitment," she said, returning to the sales counter.

Logan shook his head. "I'm happy to do it. I've done several classroom visits and this is similar. Trust me, I'm better at communicating with groups than individuals. Who knows?

There might be a future professional photographer in the crowd."

"And my daughter is determined to be one of them."

Lately, Jessica couldn't escape hearing Logan's name. Cyndi talked about him several times a day and Grams kept making wistful comments about him being single, even though she knew the real reason he was coming around.

"You seem unhappy," Logan said. "Does it bother you that Cyndi is interested in photography? My own parents didn't think it was a practical career, but she's still young. Don't kids change their career goals a hundred times while growing up?"

Jessica was glad he hadn't guessed what she was really feeling. "Yes. So far Cyndi has wanted to be a princess, trapeze artist, botanist and a fire captain. Not a regular firewoman, you understand. She thinks being in charge is best. Oh, and a kitten tamer."

Logan grinned. "Kitten tamer?"

"She loves cats, as you may have guessed from her fascination with your mountain lion photos. Honestly, I don't care what field she eventually chooses, provided it's something she cares about. Passion is important. If she hopes to be an award-winning photographer, that's great. If she wants to be something else, that's fine, too. I want her to dream as big as possible. Impossibly big. You never know what you can accomplish if you believe in yourself."

"Does that also apply to you?" he asked, looking surprised by his own question.

"What do you mean?"

"You left your other job to run this shop. I'm sure you would have been a great doctor or teacher or engineer. Whatever you wanted to do."

"That's nice of you. It's just…" She glanced toward the closed door and then back at Logan. "My goals changed when I became a single mom."

He nodded. "Do you have any regrets?"

"None," Jessica said emphatically.

"Cyndi seems well adjusted and secure," Logan commented. "So you must be doing a great job."

"Thanks. By the way, it's after three thirty, in case you were hoping for coffee," Jessica said, anxious to change the subject. "But I have a small amount of the organic dark roast left if you're interested. You must have a caffeine addiction—you drink twice as much as your coworkers."

He shook his head. "It isn't the caffeine. I get restless working in a small office. Going for coffee is an excuse to get away for a short time."

"I see." The new subject wasn't an improvement, though she couldn't be sure he was referring to Moonlight Ventures' expansion needs. "And you'd much rather have a more spacious location, somewhere near one of my display windows."

Logan instantly looked contrite. "Yes. *No.* I meant that it's a challenge going from a physically active career to deskwork. I was either outside or on my feet as a photographer. Being an agent is a huge change."

She smiled tightly. As he'd once suggested, it was a good thing he hadn't followed in his parents' diplomatic footsteps. His verbal clumsiness might be charming if the Crystal Connection wasn't on the line, because while his mouth frequently said the wrong thing, it was thoroughly appealing in plenty of other ways.

Unfortunately, noticing Logan as a man wasn't helpful. If Aaron had been a mistake, Logan would be a disaster.

"I'll give you the benefit of the doubt," she said.

In a way she felt selfish, wanting to keep

her shop where it was doing well. But Moonlight Ventures wouldn't go out of business if they stayed in their current location, they just wouldn't have space for everything they wanted to do. She wasn't sure the same could be said of the store if it moved.

"Are you willing to tour the potential units we're proposing?" Logan asked. "I thought tonight would be good, after you close."

There was no avoiding it. At the very least she had to appear willing to consider the options.

"My grandmother just brought Cyndi over from school, but I'll see if she can come back." Jessica pulled a cell phone from her pocket and called. "Hey, Grams. I hate to ask, but could you come back and get Cyndi? Something has come up."

"No problem. I'm at the grocery store, only a few minutes away. I'll finish shopping and be there soon. I hope you have an unexpected date...maybe with that customer you told me about? You said he was cute."

Jessica tried to keep her expression neutral. "Sorry to disappoint, it's just work."

"Oh, honey, I know that tone. Please don't cut romance out of your life."

The moment was surreal. Jessica had a hand-some, single-but-off-limits man watching her from five feet away…and her grandmother on the phone, pushing for romance. Penny Parrish was a wonderful, wise lady, who treasured every memory of her marriage. She might be alone now, but Grams's life with Granddad was what happily-ever-after should look like. Not everyone was that fortunate.

"I promise to think about it," Jessica said brightly. "Thanks for the help, you're a peach."

"I'll make enough dinner for all of us. Come home when you can. It's nice having someone else to cook for."

"Don't worry about me, I can pick some-thing up. I'll fix dinner for all of us tomor-row. See you soon." Jessica turned to Logan after disconnecting. "Grams isn't far away— she stopped at the grocery store."

"In that case, I'll see you later. Before I for-get, I need the address and time for Cyndi's meeting on Saturday."

"Everyone takes turns hosting it and this week we're at my house," she explained re-luctantly. She didn't want him in her home, but that ship had already sailed. "I'll email the details."

Jessica kept thinking about Logan after he left. She'd visited the Crystal Connection often since moving to the Seattle area, but they hadn't met until the previous week. Her mental image of him had been skewed by his picture on the calendar, but meeting him in person had sent the image flying. Okay, it was stereotypical to envision a fashion photographer as a pale, artistic type with eyes that had turned glassy after years of taking pictures under hot lights. The reality was a strong, confident guy with muscles, a tan and a warm smile.

Grams arrived fifteen minutes later. Cyndi was confused to be going home earlier than expected, but she quietly gathered her homework and left with Penny.

Luckily for Jessica, a flurry of customers came in, distracting her from thoughts of Logan.

KEVIN WOKE REFRESHED as his plane landed at SeaTac. He already missed his daughter and her family, but it was good to see the familiar sights of Seattle as he collected his car in the long-term parking lot and drove home.

In the beginning, the condominium had seemed a good idea for him and Allison as they got older. Though it had a small patio garden, most of the exterior maintenance was covered by the monthly fee. The clubhouse was nice and the residents had monthly potlucks that were well attended. But with Allison gone, he was less certain that he wanted to stay.

"Hello, Kevin," a neighbor exclaimed, rushing out from her front door, which was unfortunately close to his. Mary Gentry was one of the reasons he questioned keeping the condo.

"Good evening, Mary."

She eyed the luggage he carried. "I'm glad you're back. Will you come for dinner? You can't have any edible food in the fridge after being away so long."

"Thanks, but I have plans for the evening."

His plans included staying away from a gregarious widow who was doing her best to collect a third husband.

"Come over if you change your mind. You're always welcome. I can't seem to stop cooking for two, so there's plenty." She followed him to his condo, still chattering. Most of the time she didn't wait for an invitation and he practically had to close the door in her face.

Phew.

He blew out a frustrated lungful of air. Allison wouldn't have been bothered at the thought of him remarrying, but he doubted she'd approve of Mary Gentry and he certainly didn't care for her style.

Slumping into a chair, he turned on the television and flipped through the channels. Wasn't that what old men did, watch TV and listen to their arteries harden?

Suddenly it was as if he could hear Penny scolding him, so he picked up the phone and dialed her number.

BY SHEER FORCE of will, Logan made the remainder of the afternoon productive, including setting up four appointments with prospective clients. There was also a modeling job to coordinate, along with a couple of go-sees, which was a model's version of an audition. He was building his own client list and a share of Kevin McClaskey's original clients had been transferred to him, so there was plenty to do.

Kevin had been a stellar agent on many levels, but his intense involvement in clients' lives didn't necessarily match how the new partners saw an optimum working relationship. Thanks to Nicole's efforts, most of them had adopted an engaged but more independent approach, though a few missed Kevin and still called him for advice. When buying the agency, the four of them had agreed he could stay in contact, but it was proving to be tricky.

Then there was the lifelong friendship between the Parrishes and the McClaskeys. Logan hadn't anticipated Jessica being part of it. Instead, from childhood, she'd looked at the McClaskeys as honorary grandparents. He might have handled things differently with her if he'd known about their close ties ahead of time; it was his own fault for being impatient.

At five thirty he locked his office and headed for the Crystal Connection. Jessica was busy with late customers, so he wandered around the displays as they shopped.

"Do you have any black tourmalines?" one woman asked. "They're supposed to be good for protection. I'm driving across country next week with my daughter, so it was providence when I saw your shop."

Jessica directed her to a basket on a circular display stand.

Fifteen minutes later, Jessica locked the door behind the last customer. "Sorry," she said. "I'm considering being open once a month on Saturday for people who can't get here during the week."

"Not all Saturdays?"

"My grandparents never opened on the weekend, which probably wasn't the best financial decision. On the other hand, this isn't a major tourist area, so weekend hours aren't as critical. Um, let me take care of something before we go."

Jessica removed the contents of the cash register and he followed her to the storeroom area, where she crouched and put everything in a safe.

"How about hiring a part-time clerk for the weekend?" Logan asked as he waited.

"I've thought about it, but this has always been a family-run operation, so that's a big leap. I've also considered being open Tuesday through Saturday, but the coffee regulars would dislike it and I'd have less time with Cyndi."

"Obviously being a good mom is important to you."

Jessica straightened and stared at him. "Well, *yeah*. Kids aren't kids for long—I don't want to miss out."

Over the years Logan had heard various comments about parenting. His mother and father were pragmatic, saying it was a duty to protect the young and raise productive human beings. Other people had mentioned not wanting to miss their kid's childhood, but it was the expression on Jessica's face that struck him—she genuinely enjoyed being with Cyndi.

"Why is her father missing it?" he asked but then stopped abruptly. "Sorry, none of my business. My big mouth again."

Jessica didn't look offended. "It isn't a huge secret. We fell in love and I wanted to get married, so we got married. He wasn't ready, though, and the prospect of a baby was too much for him. He left and I haven't heard from him since. Aaron could be on the other side of the world for all I know."

A rush of outrage hit Logan. "That's terrible. A real man doesn't run away from his responsibilities."

She shook her head. "You've been talking to my grandmother. I'll tell you what I've told Grams—it wasn't Aaron's fault. He wanted to wait, I didn't."

"Penny and I haven't discussed it, but regardless, decent men don't abandon their children."

The corners of Jessica's mouth twitched.

"I'm the one who married the guy. Are you saying I lack good taste?"

Logan chuckled. "Not quite. You were just too young to know better."

Her expression sobered. "I was twenty, which is two years older than Grams when she met Granddad. Do you ever wonder why something works for some people and not for others?"

The question was eerily similar to the one Logan had been asking himself about relationships. Strangely, he didn't like hearing it come from Jessica.

"Penny lucked out," he said firmly. "And even if your ex wasn't ready to settle down, he didn't say no, either. On top of that, he's had years to grow up and make contact. If he knows anything about your family, you can't be difficult to locate."

"I suppose. As for Grams being lucky? I don't know if it was luck or inspiration. I just know I don't expect to get married again myself. The risk of repeating my mistakes is too great."

Logan sensed there was more to it. A whole lot more. Jessica was strong and independent. She'd be an equal partner in a relationship.

He saw it, even if she couldn't.

JESSICA DIDN'T KNOW what to make of the expression on Logan's face and decided not to try. It had been an unusual conversation, but nothing was usual these days.

"Shall we walk to the potential sites?" he asked. "It doesn't make sense to drive the length of the parking lot."

"That's fine," she said, though she suspected he hoped to prove the new space wasn't an impossible distance from her current location.

The walkway was wide and Logan strolled beside her with a comfortable ease. He was hard to figure out. It was odd that he'd tried to reassure her about the mistakes she'd made with Aaron. They'd already discussed his attitude toward marriage. If anything, she would have expected such a dedicated bachelor to take her ex's side.

They rounded the corner of the building. "This is the first available unit," Logan explained, opening the third door, "since Tupper Recording uses the first two. As you can see, a nice feature on this side is the band of grass, along with the protected green space across the street. I've noticed you put a bowl of water outside the shop for dogs, so the grass would be great for them."

"I've been down here. Cyndi and I often take a walk after I close the store. The recording studio is the only occupied rental on this end, right?"

"Er…yeah, for the moment. But the studio is completely soundproofed, so you wouldn't have a noise issue. The layouts of the units are similar, but you should check all of them. The paint and flooring are in poor condition, but that's a cosmetic fix we'd take care of before you moved," Logan said. "Each unit has a private restroom, which means routing water to a coffee bar wouldn't be a big deal. We'd handle that, as well. Take a look around."

Jessica wandered through the space, wrinkling her nose at the musty odor. Clearly it had been empty for a while, which should have been enough to tell Logan that it wasn't desirable commercial space. A booming economy and they had four large empty rentals while the rest of the building was filled to capacity? Hardly a promising sign.

So, why hadn't Moonlight Ventures considered moving to the rear of the building themselves? There was more than enough space and the nature of the agency didn't require a high-visibility location. She almost asked but then remembered Logan's remarks about the expensive remodeling they'd already done. It was unlikely they wanted to do it all over again.

He locked the door and they toured the next two spaces, then the last, which was the most appealing because it had more windows, except it was even further from potential customers. But nothing could change the fact that they all fronted on a quiet, narrow street, with no neighboring businesses except a recording studio.

"I wanted you to see what we could offer," Logan said as they walked back to the Crystal Connection. "Each unit is twice the size of what you've got now. Moving costs would be covered, along with the other incentives we've discussed."

Jessica smiled noncommittally, her nerves twisting tighter. Even the push-pull attraction she felt for Logan was swamped by worry. She believed the owners of Moonlight Ventures were ethical people who intended well, but good intentions weren't always enough. If she didn't agree to move to one of the empty spaces, when the lease ran out she'd probably have to find another location altogether. After all, they were offering incentives to move *now*, not in three years.

"Where would you like to go for dinner?" Logan asked.

She blinked. "Uh…what?"

"From what I heard when you were talking to Penny, you don't need to rush home and feed Cyndi. I figured we'd catch a bite."

"That isn't necessary."

"It will give us a good chance to talk. It's a challenge when the store is open and you have customers coming and going."

Tiredly, she considered what to do. Logan was right that discussing business at the shop was problematic, but she refused to eat at another expensive restaurant where she felt out of place.

"How about a pizza?" she suggested.

"Good idea. We can eat in the agency's break room."

Jessica would rather stay on her own turf, but the store didn't have a place to eat aside from the sales counter and the narrow coffee bar. Besides, if she had an idea of what the Moonlight Ventures offices looked like, she might get a better sense if it was feasible for *them* to move instead of her.

"Okay," she said. "I'll come over when I've closed out the register."

"Didn't you already do that?"

"No." She resisted rolling her eyes. Logan really didn't know anything about retail if he thought stashing cash and checks in a safe was the same thing as closing out a register.

"All right, no need to hurry. At this time of day, the pizza parlor will take an hour to deliver. Are there any toppings you don't like?"

"No anchovies. I'm not picky otherwise, but some veggies would be nice."

Glad for the brief reprieve, Jessica went inside the store and locked the door behind her. She tallied the day's receipts, filled out a bank deposit slip and then returned everything to the safe…which raised another question. Would Moonlight Ventures move the safe to a different location? The thing weighed a lot and was solidly installed so it couldn't be stolen by someone with a screwdriver and a strong back. Moving it wouldn't be easy.

There was plenty to discuss with Logan and she still wasn't sure if she should agree to the move. It was a huge risk, either way.

CHAPTER EIGHT

PENNY STIRRED HER spaghetti sauce on the stove and then checked the meatballs in the oven.

"I'm glad Mr. Kevin is coming for dinner," Cyndi said. She was peeling carrots at the kitchen island, her brow creased with concentration. "Can we play a game after we eat?"

"He might enjoy that. Let's ask."

"Good. He isn't like Grandpa Eric, but..." Cyndi's voice trailed away and she looked puzzled.

"Is something wrong, dear?"

"A kid at school told me I shouldn't talk about Grandpa Eric. *His* grandpa died and his mom gets mad if he says things about him 'cause it makes his grandma cry."

Penny kissed her great-granddaughter's forehead. "It's okay to talk about Grandpa Eric to me. I'm sad he isn't here, but it also makes me happy to know how much people loved him."

Cyndi's nose wrinkled. "You're happy and sad at the same time? That's weird."

"I know. You'll figure it out when you're older."

"That's what my teacher said when I asked why Doug Thornton was so mean. But I'm older now and I still don't know why. And he's still mean."

Penny laughed ruefully. She remembered being told she was too young to understand. She'd disliked it as much as her great-granddaughter.

"I'm afraid we can only learn some things through experience," she admitted. "But about Grandpa Eric, think of it as having different voices inside, telling you different things at the same time. Remember when you didn't want to go to a classmate's birthday party, then felt funny when you weren't invited?"

"Oh. So I guess it's okay to like Mr. Kevin. It doesn't mean I don't love Grandpa Eric any longer. I do, bunches and bunches."

Penny was beginning to understand what troubled Cyndi. Kevin was around a good deal, even more now that Eric was gone, and in her little-girl way she was wondering where he fit into her world.

"It's good to like lots of people," Penny said, not wanting to make too much of the matter.

"Okay."

Penny washed the carrots Cyndi had peeled and sliced them into the salad. It had seemed natural to invite Kevin to dinner when he called, the way she would have invited him and Allison if they'd just gotten home from a trip. True, the situation had changed, but was she supposed to behave differently now? They were old friends and had grieved together through the loss of their spouses.

A breathy gasp came from Cyndi, catching Penny's full attention. "Do you need your inhaler, hon?"

"I don't think so." Cyndi closed her eyes and mouthed numbers as she inhaled and exhaled slowly.

Penny thought about running for the inhaler, but the specialist had been teaching Cyndi relaxation techniques to help deal with her asthma attacks. In very mild cases, she was able to get by without medication.

Her doctor said she might grow out of the condition, but in the meantime, it was a serious worry. If only the urgent care clinic was up and running. Getting a facility was simply the first step. After that they'd need both medical staff and an administrator.

Within a few minutes Cyndi was smiling and feeling well enough to answer the door when the bell rang.

"Hi, Mr. Kevin," she said. "I love the postcard you sent me. Why do they call Chicago the Windy City? Aren't other cities windy?"

"Yes, but in Chicago they get wind off Lake Michigan and it sometimes blows pretty hard. Cities have nicknames for different reasons, but that's the one I like best."

"Oh."

Penny had stepped out of the kitchen, annoyed at feeling awkward. Kevin was a dear friend and it was her job as hostess to make him comfortable.

"Dinner is almost ready," she said. "It's great seeing you, but it must have been tough to leave your daughter and the baby."

"You have no idea. Little Allie is a bundle of heaven. It didn't help when I ran into Mary Gentry before I could escape inside my condo." He clutched his forehead in mock horror. "I'm sure she'll bring me an inedible casserole tomorrow. Her last husband probably kicked the bucket just to get away from her cooking."

Penny grinned. She'd never met Mary but had heard stories. "She's just lonely, Kevin. You can't blame her."

"I realize that." He dropped grumpily into a chair. "But I refuse to become number three. I have standards, you know."

"What does kicked the bucket mean?" Cyndi asked, looking puzzled.

Oops.

Kevin ruffled her hair. "Right now it means I wasn't being kind about someone who means well but gets on my nerves."

"There's a boy at school who gets on my nerves, too. He thinks he knows everything."

"Cyndi, will you get the salad dressing while I bring the hot dishes to the table?" Penny asked.

"Okay."

The meal was simple, but Kevin seemed to enjoy every bite, asking for seconds and complimenting them both when she explained that Cyndi had helped with the salad. After eating, Penny asked to see pictures of baby Allie and the three of them clustered together on the couch to look at the shots he'd taken with his smartphone.

"She's absolutely beautiful," Penny said. She wanted to say the baby took after her grandmother but was reluctant to remind Kevin that Allison had died before she could see her first grandchild. With a start, Penny recalled Cyndi's worry that she shouldn't talk about Grandpa Eric. She drew a deep breath. "And Allie looks just like her namesake."

Kevin beamed. "I think so. Jill is certain her mom was with her, every single step of the pregnancy and caesarean."

Cyndi's eyes grew large. "Is Mrs. Allison a ghost?"

"No, dear." Penny kissed her forehead. "But many of us believe the people we love can visit in spirit after they're gone. It's wonderful, isn't it, to think Grandpa Eric and Allison come back to see us, hoping we're happy?"

"I guess, but I miss Grandpa Eric's hugs."

I miss them, too, cried Penny's heart. She was certain she'd see Eric again, but it wasn't the same as hearing his voice and holding his hand.

"I'm not Grandpa Eric, but would one of my hugs help?" Kevin asked gruffly.

"Uh-huh." Cyndi scrambled to her knees and threw herself into his arms.

Penny's gaze met Kevin's and she wasn't surprised to see him blink moisture from his eyes. He was sentimental, the way Eric had been. She and Allison used to joke that they'd been forced to be practical so their husbands could remain corny romantics. It was only partly true—Penny and her friend had been corny and romantic, as well.

Cyndi dropped back on her heels. "Mr. Kevin, do you want to watch a movie or play a game tonight?"

"A game, but I'll be glad to watch a movie if you prefer."

Cyndi's tone had revealed which activity she preferred and Kevin was too fond of kids to choose anything different.

"Scrabble?" Cyndi asked hopefully.

"Careful," Penny warned. "This kid is scary good at word games."

Cyndi giggled.

"That's all right, I'll take my chances. Scrabble, it is."

His gaze met Penny's again and they both smiled. How could she have felt awkward before? With Allison and Eric gone, Kevin was the best friend she had in the world.

LOGAN PAID THE pizza delivery guy and brought the food to the break room. Jessica had arrived a few minutes earlier and he noticed she didn't seem comfortable.

"I hope the lounge doesn't give you claustrophobia," he said, setting everything on the table. "Without a window, I can feel trapped in here. Someday we hope to install skylights. The dome kind, so they'll work with a rooftop garden, which is another one of our dreams."

"I prefer rooms with windows, too. But this is fine."

He took plates and silverware from a cabinet.

Jessica's eyebrow rose. "Can't we eat pizza with our fingers?"

Logan gestured to a bag. "I also got their deluxe Greek salad. The tangy dressing is a great contrast to the pizza. I hope you like it—they use a variety of vegetables, along with olives, feta cheese and pickled peppers."

He'd seen Jessica's pleasure when she was eating her salad at the restaurant, so he'd ordered a dish he hoped she would enjoy just as much. It had nothing to do with sweetening their business negotiations, though he couldn't have proved his intentions.

"Sounds good."

"Have you seen anything of the agency?" he asked as they served themselves.

"Not much. I was here often as a kid, but it's quite different now."

"I'll give you a tour later. We're proud of the renovations. We moved walls and some of the plumbing, updated the decor, and made sure the wiring supports twenty-first century technology." Logan decided not to mention their design mistake, which had resulted in two of the offices being much too small. It made no difference, because ultimately they still needed additional space.

It wasn't a relaxing meal. Jessica asked perceptive questions about details he hadn't considered, including whether they'd move her safe and reinstall it in a new location. Since he was authorized to make the decision without consulting his partners, he reassured her that they'd cover any cost incurred to get the Crystal Connection up and running at full speed, with no downtime.

Curiously, he wasn't worried she'd start making unreasonable demands.

"By the way," Jessica said, "I phoned Grams before coming over and she says Uncle Kevin flew into Seattle this afternoon."

"Oh?" Logan had a feeling he'd be getting a visit from Kevin McClaskey in the near future. It promised to be another difficult conversation.

"Yes. I'm glad to have him home. She invited him to dinner and they were getting ready to play Scrabble. That's Cyndi's doing. She loves games, but most of them aren't as much fun with just the two of us. Did your family play board games when you were a kid?"

"My folks used to say politics and international relations are such high-stakes games that they didn't have energy for anything else."

"Wow." Once again Jessica's expression suggested she was holding something back.

"What are you thinking?"

"That you must have had an even more unusual upbringing than I'd realized."

Logan leaned back in his chair, gazing at a picture he'd taken of the Sydney Opera House.

"There were challenges," he admitted. "It might have been even stranger if Mom or Dad had been appointed as ambassadors, instead of being part of the diplomatic service. Even so, I was continually warned to mind my manners and never say anything about our host nation that might be construed as negative."

"So you didn't dare dis the country, even in jest."

He gave a mock shudder. "Absolutely not. I was routinely warned about the dangers of creating an international incident, especially when I got older and interested in girls."

"You're kidding, right?"

"If only that was true. My parents took their work very seriously and it put a major dent in my teen social life. That's probably why I got into photography. Nobody was going to be offended by a kid excited at taking pictures of their country."

Jessica cocked her head. "So the bio on your calendar is accurate—photography is a life-long passion."

"More or less. I usually think of how the world will look in a photograph before anything else." Logan barely remembered a time when he hadn't been framing a scene, either in his head or through a camera lens.

Jessica ate a slice of bell pepper that had fallen off the pizza. "Doesn't the camera put a barrier between you and the nitty-gritty of living? I mean, you're observing and documenting the world, instead of participating. Of course, it must be easier to deal with people that way. They're just superficial images, not real human beings with real problems and concerns. But it also means you're alone."

"I'm more than an observer," Logan insisted. But for some reason he looked again at the photo he'd taken of the Sydney Opera House. He'd gotten it at dusk while in Australia doing a fashion shoot for a hot new designer. But as visually stunning as the building might be, he'd never gone inside.

Jessica gathered their plates together and tidied the table. "I wasn't criticizing. We all experience the world in different ways. What's the first thing you'd do at the great Colosseum in Rome? Take pictures, right?"

Logan shrugged. "I've been there a few times. First I figured out the best angles and then got photographs. What would you do?"

"I'd listen for the ancient echoes of the crowd and the yell of gladiators. Granddad used to say human history is a river so powerful that it even flows through stones."

Prickles shivered up Logan's spine. He'd never see the Colosseum again in the same way. Whether that was good or bad he didn't know.

Jessica stood and smiled at him. "Sorry

about the flight of fancy. How about the tour
of the agency you promised to give me?"

"Sure." He got up, as well.

Although he'd accepted a measure of detachment was an innate aspect of his character,
it was unsettling to see himself through Jessica's eyes. He wanted to argue that he had an
involved, passionate personality, but he wasn't
sure he'd win the argument...either with her
or with himself.

JESSICA WAS INTERESTED in the changes to Moonlight Ventures, but reminding Logan about the
tour also prompted a less personal topic of discussion.

As a rule she tried to understand differing
points of view, but that meant she sympathized
with her landlords and their wish to expand.
Her dad would tell her it was a terrible way
to do business unless she could turn it to her
advantage by using the opponent's issues to
strengthen her own position. She didn't agree.
Using people was wrong.

However, she needed to be cautious in case
Logan tried to do the same thing—influence
her emotions by demonstrating their need for

more space. It didn't seem like him, or she hoped it wasn't, but she still had to be careful.

Two of the offices were relatively large. Nicole's was located where Uncle Kevin's had once been, though the dimensions were different and one end of the room was set up for meetings. They'd put serious money into sending a message of classy success. The lobby decor alone must have cost a fortune with its hardwood paneling and plush carpet. Jessica remembered it as a poky area where Aunt Allison had sat at a desk, doing paperwork and greeting clients.

Adam Wilding's office was down the hall from Nicole's and was a decent size, too, except it didn't have a meeting area. Rachel's was quite a bit smaller, and Logan's was the tiniest of all. It was hard to imagine an outdoorsy guy being comfortable in such a confined space.

Still, plenty of people worked in small offices or cubicles. Anyway, *they* were the ones who'd allocated so much square footage to the lobby and front two offices. It even made her wonder if the new owners had expected from the beginning to take over the Crystal Connection's space.

"What do you think?" Logan asked.

Jessica lifted her chin and smiled. "You have a nice setup. But I've been wondering about the empty rentals—it would be helpful to know what type of businesses have rented those units and why they aren't there any longer. I can ask Uncle Kevin, if it would be easier for you."

Logan's forehead creased. "The information must be in the files he left. Why is it important?"

"I'm curious. Grams mentioned several businesses had come and gone, with the units largely staying empty. There must be a reason."

"I'll check."

"Great." She was sure of what he'd find—few businesses could thrive without visibility—but seeing it for himself might impress on Logan the enormity of what he was asking.

They finished the tour in the lounge where they'd eaten.

"Thanks for dinner," she said, anxious to leave.

Logan held the pizza box out to her. "Please take the leftovers. They'd just sit in my fridge until I got around to tossing them."

"That's nice, but leave them for your co-workers."

He scowled. "You won't even take a few slices of pizza? Rest assured, it won't obligate you in any way."

Jessica rolled her eyes. "I'm aware of that. Do you always make such a big deal out of how leftovers are handled?"

LOGAN COUNTED TO TEN, fighting frustration. Jessica was right; what happened with the pizza wasn't important. She had her reasons for refusing and it was rude to have pushed so hard. For all he knew, Cyndi was allergic to some of the ingredients.

"I overreacted," he said. "Sorry."

Jessica's face revealed little emotion. "No problem. We aren't friends, just business associates."

"Can't we be friends, too? That's what I want with all our tenants," he added.

Skepticism creased her forehead. "Friends in what way?"

"I don't know. Nothing complicated. *Friends*," Logan said, regretting that he'd brought it up in the first place. He hadn't expected her to put him on the spot by asking for a definition.

He liked Jessica and knew being friends was possible with a woman without male-female issues coming into play—Rachel and Nicole were perfect examples. Problem was…they'd never made him feel the way Jessica made him feel. It was almost as if his soul had recognized her from another life, which was absurd. He didn't believe in such fanciful ideas.

Oblivious to his inner turmoil, Jessica took the pizza box he was holding and slid it in the break room refrigerator. "I think you're talking about breezy, surface cordiality, which is fine for business associates. But I wouldn't call it friendship."

"Then what's *your* definition?"

"Well, it's more than exchanging pleasantries. You care about someone because their welfare makes a difference to your own happiness. To be a real friend you have to be willing to give part of yourself, and other times be vulnerable enough to take the chance of getting hurt. Do you have anyone you feel that way about?"

"My partners," Logan said instantly. "I'd

trust them with my life. We know each other's best qualities, along with our quirks and weaknesses. We don't argue often, but when we do, it doesn't change a thing. I can rely on them, no matter what."

Jessica's lips curved. "That's nice. Maybe my grandparents were so happy because they were married and also the best of friends."

"You don't think your parents are happy?"

She shrugged. "In their own way they are. They have the same goals and work together. I guess that's important. Anyway, I'm hardly an expert on relationships." She tapped her left ring finger and he suspected she was thinking about her failed marriage again.

"So, what led you to move here?" he asked.

"Cyndi and I were visiting my grandparents and I heard about the department store job. Grams knew the manager of the human resource division and put a good word in for me. Moving across country was a big step, but now I wonder what took me so long. Washington has always felt like home." She gestured at the clock on the wall. "It's late. I'd better get going."

"I'll see you on Saturday, if not earlier when

I come for coffee. Thanks for sending the directions to your house."

He let her out the front door and watched as she headed for her car. Then he realized he was framing mental snapshots of Jessica in the parking lot. He'd tossed off comments about viewing the world through a camera lens, but Jessica was right; it was easier to deal with a photo than a real person with all their complexities.

CHAPTER NINE

JESSICA DROVE HOME, stressing even more than before, if possible.

She glanced at her reflection in the rearview mirror and made a face.

One of her counselor's frequent urgings had been to stop trying to control the uncontrollable, especially her childhood past, her husband's desertion and her parents' continued absorption in moneymaking. The important thing was to choose how she reacted to the events that had impacted her life. It was easier said than done, but she didn't have to pretend everything was okay when it wasn't. Being uptight was normal with so much at stake. The answer was applying her energy to find creative solutions.

So, what *could* she do?

There was the idea about the agency moving, instead of her.

It was true that Logan and his partners

had spent a truckload of money remodeling the original location, but if she moved, they wouldn't get that much more room. In contrast, taking over the empty units at the back of the building would nearly double their footprint.

Rather than continue worrying and losing sleep, she'd write out a list of pros and cons and propose the idea to Logan. Even if they'd considered moving already, she might come up with something that would swing the decision in her favor.

KEVIN THOROUGHLY ENJOYED the dinner and game with Penny and Cyndi, which they'd finished playing by the time Jessica arrived.

She gave him a hug. "Welcome home, Uncle Kevin. I've missed you."

"I missed you, too."

He looked at her closely, seeing shadows under her eyes that hadn't been there when he'd left for Chicago. When it came to Jessica he was biased and he felt a surge of anger at Logan.

"Show the baby pictures to Jessica," Penny ordered.

Grateful for the distraction, he took out his phone again and handed it to his honorary granddaughter. She went through the photos, oohing and aahing before giving it back.

"Newborns are so precious."

"Do you miss having a baby around?" he asked.

Jessica watched her daughter, asleep on the couch. "I'm sad to see Cyndi grow out of every stage of childhood, but it's inevitable. They grow and grow, no matter how often you tell them to stay little."

"You ought to have more kids. That way I'd have grandbabies on *this* side of the country."

Her smile wavered. "It's possible to have children without a partner, but that isn't the way for me."

"You're still young. You have time to meet someone."

"Hey, don't start matchmaking, I get enough of that from Grams." Jessica's voice was light but firm.

What was wrong with young men today? Kevin wondered. They ought to be beating her door down. He just hoped little Allie would grow up to be as fine a woman as Jessica.

"Do you want some dinner?" Penny asked. "I have spaghetti and meatballs."

"I'd love it, but the reason I had to stay late

was to meet with Logan. We shared a pizza. If I'd known your spaghetti was on the menu I would have told him to forget it."

Kevin frowned. "I'm sorry about what's happening, kiddo. I'd do anything to fix it."

"Don't worry. I'm sure everything will work out." Jessica went to the couch and bent to kiss her daughter's cheek. "Wake up, sweetie. Time to go home."

The little girl leaned against her mother groggily as they went out the door. It felt strangely natural when Penny stepped next to him as he watched to be sure the two got safely inside their half of the duplex.

He sighed.

It was hard to stand alone when you were used to having someone at your side.

ON SATURDAY MORNING Logan left his studio apartment by nine to be sure of getting to Jessica's place on time. Her instructions didn't accord with his GPS, but she'd indicated that the route missed the worst traffic, which proved to be true.

Ironically, Regen Valley was one of the areas he was considering in his house-hunting search. So far he'd looked at places in Enumclaw, Buckley and Issaquah. He'd also driven up to Black Diamond, only to decide that the community was a little *too* small.

Just outside of Regen Valley Logan spotted an interesting house for sale. The rear of the property looked out on an evergreen-crested hill rising above the town. He stopped and collected one of the real estate fliers. The description further intrigued him.

Knowing the house was in the same town where Jessica lived made him hesitate, but he finally shrugged. With so many Moonlight Ventures tenants and clients, the chances were good that he'd find one of them wherever he looked. Perhaps he'd contact the real estate agent and arrange a viewing once he was finished with Cyndi's meeting.

When he arrived at Jessica's home, he studied the duplex. She'd written that she lived on the right side of the midcentury home. The place was in good condition and bursts of colors filled the flower beds.

The door on the right flew open as he got out of the car. Cyndi came running down the walkway.

"Hi, Logan. You *came*."

"I promised to come, didn't I?"

"I know. See you in a minute. I'm helping Grandma in the kitchen. We're 'sposed to have healthy snacks." Cyndi leaned forward and dropped her voice to a conspiratorial whisper. "But there's a little bit of chocolate."

Jessica stepped onto the front porch as her daughter rushed back inside.

"Good morning," Logan said.

"I see you found us."

"Your directions were excellent. It was convenient coming out today because this is one of the towns I've considered in my search for houses. I'm going to look around after the meeting."

Her delicate eyebrows rose. "I would have pegged you as a city guy, all the way."

"I have been, but when I was moving to Seattle, I decided it was time for a change."

"This would be a big change. Regen Valley is nice, but we don't have embassies or art galleries. Instead we have community picnics, softball and amateur watercolors sold at our gift shop."

Her tone was skeptical and Logan was unaccountably annoyed. "You sound like a longtime native warning me away. I thought you just moved to Washington last year."

"Sorry, I don't mean to sound unwelcoming," Jessica apologized. "As a kid I spent my summers in Regen Valley—made good friends, learned to swim and drive…had my first real kiss. But my parents hate the place, so I know it isn't to everyone's taste."

"Your father never lived here?"

"Nope." She peered back at the duplex and then continued in a low tone. "Dad disliked roving the world and eventually talked my grandparents into sending him to boarding school. Grams still wishes they'd refused, but I think he would have turned out the same."

Logan thought about his childhood. At times he'd resented the constraints of diplomatic life, but he wouldn't have wanted to leave his parents. "I can't imagine boarding school."

"Me, neither. But on the question of moving to Regen Valley, will you be comfortable in a town where people are active in the community and expect their neighbors to be the same? It would be hard to stay behind a camera here."

Once again Jessica was holding up a mirror that reflected how other people saw him…and how he saw himself, deep down.

He was the guy with the camera, the watcher, the one who caught the perfect moment. And yet in many ways he was invisible. Who paid attention to the photographer at weddings or other events? But it was undeniable that he'd been restless. He had simply assumed it was about wanting to start the new part of his life at Moonlight Ventures. Now Jessica was making him wonder if it was more than that.

"Maybe I don't want to stay behind a camera. Not all the time."

She gave him a quizzical smile. "Really? Keep in mind, there's limited privacy in such a small community. I wouldn't call my neighbors nosy, but they have a friendly interest in what's going on."

Logan shifted the camera bag hanging on his shoulder. He'd enjoyed the frenetic world of fashion photography, but when the time had come to leave it behind, he hadn't been able to do it fast enough. Forays into the wilderness and living closer to nature were what appealed now.

"I'm willing to give it a try," he said.

"Then I wish you luck. Several nice houses are for sale."

"Uh, yeah. I picked up a flier for one of them on the way into town. Looks like an interesting place."

Jessica nodded. "That must be the Satterly House. A wealthy businessman built it years ago as a retreat. The property has been on the market for a while, so you might be able to pick it up for a good price."

On the market for a while? That could mean the house was a fixer-upper and Logan would prefer something move-in ready. Still, it wouldn't hurt to take a look.

With an inviting gesture, Jessica motioned him inside and he saw the living room was sparsely furnished.

"I'm buying a couch on layaway, but it won't be paid off for another couple of weeks. It was too expensive to move our stuff across country, so mostly I've been shopping at yard sales for what we need. Don't be alarmed, though, the girls sit on the floor." She grinned. "Grownups get the chairs. That's my rule."

Her tone was matter-of-fact and Logan realized being careful with her finances was such a normal part of her life she didn't think twice about buying secondhand.

"Is a yard sale where you found that vintage coffee bar for the Crystal Connection?" he asked. "It's a great piece."

Jessica's eyes sparkled. "An old inn was

being refurbished and they sold what they weren't keeping at rock-bottom prices. Their loss, my gain. I got these two chairs, too."

Intrigued, Logan went to look. For indoor shoots, he'd sometimes used classic furniture as a contrast to modern fashion. "These Morris chairs could be Stickleys."

He glanced up and saw Jessica typing into her phone. A moment later she shook her head. "According to what I see on the internet, Stickley chairs cost a bundle. There's no way I'd get two of them for forty bucks."

"Anything is possible. How do you think antique dealers stay in business? They buy valuable items that other people don't recognize."

She rolled her eyes. "You don't understand— I don't *want* them to be Stickleys. They're attractive, solid and comfortable. That's what counts. If they were valuable, I couldn't enjoy sitting in them any longer."

Hmm. Jessica had a curious point of view— most people would do handstands at getting an extraordinary bargain. But then, she probably wasn't interested in designer labels, either.

"Are you partial to antiques?" she asked.

"Not especially. If anything, I prefer Mission-style. Or Shaker and Arts and Crafts," Logan added, though he hadn't given it much thought. "My studio apartment came fully equipped, so most of my furniture is in storage. But I just had a small condo down south, so I'll need to start shopping when I buy a house."

Logan wasn't wealthy, but his work had provided him with a comfortable income. His success had come early, so he no longer knew what it was like to buy what he needed piece by piece, looking for bargains.

"The Satterly House would look good with any of those furniture styles," Jessica said.

"Then if I buy it, are you going to roll out Regen Valley's red carpet for me?"

She just gave him a measured smile and shrugged.

PENNY SUPERVISED CYNDI'S efforts in the kitchen and made sure she used the knife safely, but she didn't do the work for her. The directions were clear about how she earned ranger points. Regen Valley Girl Rangers was a local program, unaffiliated with a national organization. Jessica had longed to join as a kid, but at least she'd been able to participate as a guest during her summer visits.

"This part is done," Cyndi said. "Now I have to do the celery with peanut butter."

"Are any of the girls allergic to peanuts?" Kevin asked. After hearing Logan was coming to give a program on photography, he'd promptly volunteered to be one of the adult helpers. Penny hadn't objected. They were both anxious on Jessica's behalf and wanted to be supportive.

Cyndi shook her head. "I checked. Everyone can eat peanuts, but Ella can't have apples. She likes them, but they give her a rash. That's why I decided on oranges for my fruit. It wouldn't be nice to eat apples in front of her."

"Good thinking."

"Girl rangers are supposed to be considerate and re-spect-ful," she said, spreading peanut butter on celery sticks and poking raisins on the top. "I'm reading the handbook and Momma helps with the big words. The other girls have been girl rangers longer than me, so I have to catch up."

Penny smiled as Cyndi picked up a tray, carried it to the living room and then returned for the second container. She loved having Jessica and Cyndi next door. Her grandsons rarely visited, but Jessica was a loving, thoughtful woman who was teaching her child to behave the same way.

"Pretty proud of that youngster, aren't you?" Kevin asked in a low voice.

"Extremely. I just wish I could take some credit for how she's turning out."

"Of course you can take credit. You've seen Cyndi every day since they moved here and had a big influence on her mother. Jessica is a fine young woman."

"I agree, even though it's basically patting myself on the back."

They chuckled and followed Cyndi to the living room, where Logan and Jessica showed distinct signs of being on edge with each other. So much for the hope they'd become a couple. Not that their discomfort was necessarily a bar to romance. There were awkward moments *whenever* two people were getting acquainted. She and Eric had been champions at it, what with her chasing after him, while he tried to do the noble thing and avoid temptation.

Logan nodded at them. "Hi, Penny. *Kevin*. I didn't know you were going to be here this morning. How was your flight from Chicago?"

"Not bad. My new grandbaby was restless the night before I left, so I slept most of the way. Thought I'd come into the agency on Monday or Tuesday to talk. If you're free."

Logan's jaw hardened. "I'll check my schedule and let you know."

The tension in the room was now so thick that Penny opened a window, needing air. When she turned around, she saw a wicked smile on Jessica's face.

"Grams, Logan just told me he stopped and got a real estate flier for the Satterly place. Isn't that nice?"

Kevin looked skeptical. "Really? You don't seem like the small-town, take-care-of-your-neighbor kind of fellow."

Logan's jaw muscles were clenched so hard now his skin turned white. "That's my problem, isn't it?"

"My girls live here, so it's my problem, too."

Oh, dear. Kevin was a sweetheart, but Penny suspected a bit of testosterone-driven competition was coming into play. She decided to intervene.

"Logan, I'm sure you'd enjoy Regen Valley. And the old Satterly home is wonderful."

"Have you been inside?"

"Several times. When Eric and I moved back to the States, Virginia Satterly was still hosting garden club parties there. It was lovely. Her formal gardens are gone now, but I think the less structured setting suits the house."

Penny really hoped Logan would buy the Satterly home. It wasn't the type of place a man chose when he expected a wife and family in his immediate future, but it was a decent size and no one could tell what would happen. It might be ridiculous, but she'd often thought Logan must be lonely, especially now that his closest friends were all married. The excitement of working around the world in exotic locales couldn't replace sharing your life with the right person.

Besides, it was a shame for a beautiful house to stand empty.

"The Flash Committee toured the property when it came on the market last fall," Jessica said. "We were hoping it might work for an urgent care but decided it wasn't feasible."

"Is it in poor condition?" Logan asked.

"No, the site just wouldn't be good for a medical clinic. From what our volunteer architect says, the house mostly needs cosmetic fixes."

His eyes narrowed. "Cosmetic, huh?"

She smiled sweetly. "Yes. You've heard of them, right?"

The interplay was interesting, though Penny didn't know what it meant. She still felt the impulse to play matchmaker, but anything she said might do more harm than good.

JESSICA TRIED NOT to laugh at Logan's expression. He knew she was referring to the "cosmetic fixes" needed in the empty rentals. Poor guy. He'd come to talk about photography with a group of little girls, only to be surrounded by people who supported her side of things.

She didn't have long to think about it because the members of Cyndi's troop began arriving. A divorced mother who hadn't expected to stay for the meeting changed her mind, despite the limited seating. Jessica suspected Logan was the reason.

Amy Irvine soon came over to stand near her. "I don't see a wedding ring," she whispered. "Are you involved with him?"

"He's one of my landlords for the shop," Jessica explained in a neutral tone. "That's how Cyndi got acquainted with him. She's been camera-crazy ever since."

"Oh. I see."

The twinkle in Amy's eyes caught Jessica's attention. Should she warn the other woman away? Amy was welcome to make a move on Logan, but she might be disappointed. Would a man who dated supermodels and brushed elbows with movie stars and world leaders get involved with a divorced, small-town soccer mom?

The usual troop business didn't take long and then the meeting was turned over to Cyndi, who explained that Logan was her guest and since she was in charge of the program, she'd invited him to talk.

"He takes super, super, *super* cool pictures," she said. "See?" Proudly she displayed each page of the calendar. Excited cries of admiration came from her audience when they saw the photo of the baby mountain lions. "Okay, now he's going to show us his camera."

Logan got to his feet. "Thank you for inviting me, Cyndi."

As he spoke with the girls, Jessica grew increasingly impressed. He didn't talk down to them the way the plumber had done; instead he described how digital cameras worked in words they could understand. He'd claimed to be better with groups than individuals, but she'd assumed he was exaggerating. As part of his demo he took numerous pictures, including a group photo, then displayed them on his laptop.

"Grandma says she misses film," Kitty Carman said when he invited questions. "What's film?"

Logan explained what film was and how it was processed, throwing in some of the history of photography, as well.

Ellie Smithfield put up her hand. "My mom just takes pictures with her smartphone."

Logan smiled. "Phones are easy and quick, which is great when you're busy. Some models have advanced features, but they may not have the same capabilities as cameras, especially the ones with special lenses and the optical zoom I mentioned earlier. Everyone has to choose which gadget works best for them."

Jessica appreciated his attitude. She'd known experts who dismissed amateur efforts, but Logan seemed made of better stuff. Surely she could recognize his positive qualities without putting her heart at risk.

When he was finished, the girls chorused a thank-you in unison.

"Can you come back again?" Kerry Stevenson asked.

"I'd love to." He sounded sincere and even the married mothers attending the meeting seemed dazzled.

Jessica sighed.

"I made the snacks myself," Cyndi announced. "I scrubbed my hands the way Momma says, and I washed the oranges and celery over and over. There are orange slices, ants-on-a-log, organic grape juice and gorp cookies. They have lots of oatmeal and raisins and healthy stuff along with some chocolate because Mom says chocolate is good for mental health."

Her troop didn't crack a smile, but the adults in the room snickered.

A moment later, Logan came over to stand next to Jessica.

"Good for mental health, eh?"

"Absolutely, and I read once that..." She stopped, realizing she didn't want to explain that she'd read chocolate made a person feel the way it felt to be in love.

"Yes?" he prompted.

"Nothing. It isn't important."

He looked both skeptical and curious,

though he didn't press the subject further. "In that case, what are 'ants on a log'?"

"Oh." Jessica shook her head. Considering Logan's unusual childhood, it was doubtful he'd ever perused the kids' section of a cookbook. "They're peanut butter celery sticks with raisins stuck on top. Someone must have thought it made a cute name. You've never eaten them before?"

"Peanut butter isn't popular in most of the countries where we lived. Anyway, my mother isn't a fan."

"Oh." Jessica knew people who didn't care for peanut butter, but even her own parents hadn't objected to their kids eating peanut butter and jelly sandwiches.

Cyndi approached, carrying two paper plates.

"This is for you, Logan." She handed one of the plates to him.

"That's very thoughtful, thank you."

"I brought you some, too, Momma."

Jessica smiled at her daughter and accepted the treats. "Thanks, sweetie. You're doing a fine job."

Cyndi beamed before hurrying back to the serving table. Jessica considered going over to help, but Grams and Kevin seemed to be enjoying themselves as assistant leaders of the event. As for Amy, she kept sending longing glances in Logan's direction but apparently couldn't summon the resolve to introduce herself. It couldn't be easy to become socially active again after being part of a couple.

Jessica understood.

Though she'd grown accustomed to taking the blame for her divorce, Logan's contempt for Aaron was making her reevaluate. While she'd been too needy in the marriage, her husband hadn't been honest with her. That didn't negate her mistakes, but maybe she didn't have to accept every single scrap of responsibility.

"Your daughter's a good hostess," Logan murmured, breaking into Jessica's thoughts.

"It isn't about being a good hostess, per se, actually, it teaches courtesy and respect for others." Jessica ate a bite of cookie. "The troop leaders are very clear that those qualities aren't gender-specific and they apply to all parts of life, including work and business."

"I've met too many people who are ruthless in business." He glanced at her. "But that isn't my style."

Jessica didn't believe Logan was ruthless, but he still wielded a huge amount of power over the Crystal Connection, and by extension, her future.

He bit into a loaded celery stick and chewed thoughtfully. "I wonder who thought of combining peanut butter and celery. They don't seem like a natural combination."

"Who knows? I've always wondered who was brave enough to eat a raw oyster the first time. They don't look appetizing."

He laughed. "Probably somebody who was extremely hungry."

"Yeah. I bet they never imagined they'd become so expensive. Even if I loved oysters, the price would keep me from eating them." Jessica abruptly wished she hadn't mentioned cost as a factor. Logan had ordered oysters as his appetizer the night they'd gone out to dinner.

"So, what are the treats you dream about having?" Logan asked.

She thought for a moment. "Dark chocolate, root beer floats, nachos…that kind of stuff. How about you?"

"Barbecued hot dogs with lots of mustard."

"Seriously?"

"Absolutely. They weren't common in the countries where we lived, but one of the ambassadors threw a birthday party for his daughter and that's what she wanted. He had them flown in on dry ice. They're exotic when you've never eaten one before. To this day, I can't resist a street vendor selling hot dogs."

"Wow. I figured it would be something like caviar, champagne or truffles," Jessica said, thinking how different his life had been from that of everyone else she knew.

It was a reminder of how far apart perception and reality could be. She'd always recognized Logan worked hard, but she'd also seen him as a guy who preferred fancy foods and exclusive parties. Yet inside the sophisticated man was a little boy who craved ordinary treats. The image was more endearing than she would have expected.

CHAPTER TEN

Logan didn't see judgment in Jessica's eyes, merely curiosity. "I never drank champagne as a kid, but I ate my share of leftover caviar and truffles," he admitted. "They were on my mother's favorite menu for formal dinners and if something was in the refrigerator, I ate it."

"The way kids in the United States eat peanut butter."

He smiled. "Something of the sort. My folks didn't try to give me the normal childhood they'd known, so I didn't realize what I was missing until I was twelve or thirteen. I craved it after that."

"But you didn't choose to lead a nine-to-five kind of life as an adult."

"Ironic, right? My career got in the way."

"People can end up in circumstances beyond their control, but our choices usually reflect what we want or what makes us comfortable,"

Jessica said. "You chose to be a globe-trotting fashion photographer."

"Actually, it was supposed to be a stopgap until I could get work as a globe-trotting photojournalist."

"You never had an opportunity to change direction?"

It would be nice to offer a simple explanation about why he'd continued working in the fashion industry, but he couldn't. Little decisions had piled up until it wasn't just one reason but many. The money had been great. He'd earned a reputation and it was flattering to be in demand. The challenge of filming in the range of diverse locations chosen by designers and advertisers had appealed to him. And he'd made friends, the first real friends of his life.

"I discovered I was good at working with models in difficult settings," he said at length. "So I stayed."

"Then maybe you aren't as bad at working with people as you've claimed." Jessica made a face. "I must be the one who brings out the worst in you."

Instant denial leapt to Logan's lips. How could Jessica bring out the worst in anyone? She was kind, beautiful and a devoted mother.

It was his sense of guilt that made their interaction difficult. From their very first discussion about the Crystal Connection moving, he'd felt like a villain.

"It isn't you," he said. "I'm adjusting to my new career as an agent, that's all. Instead of bouncing around the world constantly, I hope to develop ties with this area and make new friends. I also want to build something to be proud of at Moonlight Ventures. That's why we're looking for a way to expand, without hurting your business."

Her eyelids flickered and then half closed as if she was concealing her thoughts. Logan mentally slapped himself. It was one thing for Jessica to refer to their conflict over the store, quite another for him. He was here on Cyndi's behalf, not as a landlord.

"So, tell me more about chocolate," he urged.

"Researchers say it's loaded with antioxidants. The darker, the better."

"I've heard that, as well. Anything else?"

A deeper pink crept into Jessica's cheeks. "I once saw a health insurance tip sheet that said chocolate mimics how it feels to be in love. Temporarily. It could be why chocolate is popular on Valentine's Day. Have you ever noticed getting that kind of reaction?"

"I've never been in love, so I wouldn't know. But I enjoy chocolate."

"Most people do. Perhaps you're more like the rest of us than you think."

"So, a longtime ambition fulfilled by a candy bar."

Just then parents started arriving to pick up their daughters, pulling Jessica away. Logan swiftly finished the contents of his plate, tucked the laptop he'd brought into a carrying case and went to say goodbye, as well. Cyndi astonished him by throwing her arms around his neck.

"Thank you, Logan. You were fantabulous."

"Better than the plumber?" he teased.

She giggled. "Bunches."

Her approval gave Logan a warm sensation in his chest, and it lingered as he went out to his car and called the real estate agent for the Satterly House.

"Ms. Foley? I'm Logan Kensington. I have your flier for the Satterly property. Is there any chance I could see it right away?"

"Of course! I can be there in twenty minutes. And call me Carol."

"I'll see you then."

Logan got there first and had a chance to look around the exterior. The building seemed to be in good condition and the yard was more casual than neglected. When Carol Foley arrived, they went inside.

"Only two bedrooms, I see," he said after going through the house. It was just as interesting inside as out, reminiscent of iconic Frank Lloyd Wright designs.

"The square footage is wonderful, but I can't deny the limited number of bedrooms has discouraged house hunters with families. More could easily be added, though," Carol continued gamely.

Logan shrugged. "I don't have a family, but I need both a studio and a home office."

The agent's face lit up. "A studio? This is a perfect retreat for an artist. Every window has an attractive view and the natural lighting is perfect. The property is quite large. You could build a stand-alone studio away from the main structure or add to the existing building. Whichever would work best for your needs."

"I'm a photographer, actually." Logan restrained a smile. He didn't blame her for being anxious to make a sale, especially if the house had been on the market for an extended period.

"You're still an artist. I think the original blueprints included a plan for additional rooms on the north side. They might still be available if you're interested."

She continued chattering about architects, city permits and local contractors. Logan nodded politely at appropriate moments, but he'd already made up his mind. The house felt right and the drive into the city was well within his acceptable commute time.

He was also eager to get the house hunting over and be free to spend his weekends as he pleased. The closer it got to summer, the higher in elevation he'd be able to trek. If his work at Moonlight Ventures permitted, he even hoped to spend a couple of weeks hiking in the back country, getting pictures for the book he wanted to do.

Logan focused on the agent when she stopped to draw a breath. "I want to make an offer."

She looked dazzled. "Wonderful."

"My lease will be up soon on my apartment, so if they accept, I'd like to move in as soon as possible."

"We can negotiate an interim rental agreement if necessary. I have the papers in my car. Wait here, I'll get them." Carol rushed out, probably afraid he'd change his mind if given too much time.

Logan could have assured her it wasn't going to happen, though he *did* wonder what Jessica would say about his swift decision... then wondered why it mattered.

BY SUNDAY AFTERNOON, Logan's offer on the Satterly House had been accepted. First thing Monday, Carol Foley called to say a home inspection had been scheduled for late that afternoon.

Did he want to be there for it?

He did, and was pleased when the inspector confirmed that the building was solid, with no major issues except for a problem with the circuit breaker panel. A small negotiation ensued, with the owner agreeing to make the repairs. Logan would have paid for an electrician himself, but he didn't want to be seen as a pushover in case a larger problem loomed.

He'd soon be a homeowner.

In the interim, he was going to rent the house for a remarkably low amount. He reminded himself that Regen Valley wasn't Los

Angeles or even downtown Seattle, so rents were bound to be more reasonable.

The cramped studio apartment—which had been such an improvement on hotel rooms during his visits to Seattle—would soon be a thing of the past.

Another benefit?

He wasn't impacting anyone else's life, unlike what the expansion of Moonlight Ventures might do to Jessica's livelihood.

On Tuesday morning Jessica paced around the Crystal Connection, rehearsing what she wanted to say to Logan. She'd arranged an appointment with him through Chelsea Masters, the agency's office manager, but he hadn't said anything about it when getting coffee.

"Slow down," Grams urged. She'd come into town to cover the shop in her granddaughter's absence. "You'll wear a hole in the floor and you're making me nervous."

"Sorry." Jessica tried to slow her racing heart and feet. She'd spent the past several days researching and creating a list of pros and cons for her idea to relocate Moonlight Ventures instead of her store. She hoped the suggestion was unbiased, but Logan might think she was being ridiculous.

At five to eleven, she went into the agency and smiled at Chelsea, who was a frequent shopper at the Crystal Connection. Lately she'd regaled Jessica with her stories about the ups and downs of wedding planning. "But mostly ups," Chelsea had said. It was going to be a garden wedding, hosted by her fiancé's parents. She seemed to adore her future in-laws, so it boded well for the future.

"Hi, Jessica," Chelsea said. "I meant to give this to you last week, but I'm getting scatterbrained, juggling all the details."

It was an envelope made of thick vellum paper holding a wedding invitation. Jessica didn't know what to say.

"Please come if you don't have other plans," Chelsea urged. "We want Cyndi to be there, too. See? It says children are welcome."

"The weekend before it is pretty hectic, but I don't think we have anything scheduled for this date. Let me check and let you know."

"Great." Chelsea picked up the phone. "I'll tell Logan you're here."

A moment later, Jessica was heading to Logan's office.

"Hi," he said, waving her inside his open door. "I didn't realize you had an appointment until I looked at my schedule this morning."

"Oh." She caught sight of the real estate flier on his desk. "Are you still considering the Satterly place?"

"More than just considering it. They've accepted my offer and I'll be renting the house until escrow closes."

"That was fast."

"I don't hesitate when I've decided to do something. Being part of a small town will be a new experience, so why wait to get started?"

Logan gestured to a chair and Jessica sat down, her brain moving furiously.

"In that case, do you want to get involved in a worthy project?" she asked before she could lose her nerve. "I'm leading a committee that's raising money for an urgent care clinic in Regen Valley. Participating would be a great way to get acquainted with people and become part of the community."

She didn't expect him to accept, but he was talented and his public profile could add a lot to their efforts. The clinic was too important to let her discomfort around him get in the way.

"You mentioned a committee on Saturday—the Flash Committee, right?"

"Yes." She shouldn't be surprised that he was so observant. "We have doctors in Regen Valley but no hospital, and the closest urgent care clinic is a half hour away. It won't be easy to change that, especially since we need support from the medical community. But doctors want us to guarantee we'll have a proper facility, with long-term funding, before they consider it a viable project."

Logan nodded. "You also have insurance, licensing and other issues to juggle."

Though he'd claimed to be new to business, he seemed to grasp the complex challenges facing the Flash Committee. A few members had even dropped out after recognizing the enormity of the task. The core group was dedicated, though. They wanted a clinic that operated seven days a week, right in town.

"It's a huge undertaking," Jessica acknowledged. "But we're making progress."

"I see."

Logan's expression was impossible to read, probably because he was thinking of ways to say no.

"Look, I don't know why I asked," she said.

"You're busy and from what you've told me, you don't have experience with community projects. Besides, this kind of thing can be intense, with all the people involved offering different opinions about what to do and how to get it done. You'd probably hate it."

She was giving him an easy out, but she only wanted people on the committee who were sincerely motivated. It would also be wise to avoid too much contact with a man who was both exciting and dangerous to her heart.

THE LAST THING Logan wanted was another responsibility.

He was starting a new career, he was interviewing prospective new clients daily and he'd bought a house that needed renovations. He wanted time and freedom to explore his new state. So his plate was full. But he understood why Jessica was passionate about her project. His travels had taken him from major cities to little-known corners of the world, and more than once he'd been grateful for a drop-in clinic, either for himself or for someone on his crew.

It was also annoying that she'd more or less withdrawn her invitation. He could be useful.

After all, he was a hardworking guy and he had contacts with big business. Moreover, you didn't have to be a born diplomat to contribute to a committee.

Oblivious to his inner turmoil, Jessica gestured to the file she'd brought. "The Flash Committee isn't why I made the appointment, so let's forget it and move on."

"You have an unusual recruitment strategy— ask someone to join and then tell them to forget it."

Her jaw dropped. "I was being polite. You aren't even living in Regen Valley yet, and you're new to the area."

"That doesn't mean I don't care. A clinic would improve life for everyone, wouldn't it?"

"Yes, though parents with kids at home are especially sensitive to the need."

Logan envisioned the happy girl rangers he'd met that Saturday. He'd been working on the photographs from the meetings, isolating the face of each youngster for printing and matting as portraits. He was planning it as a surprise for Cyndi to give her friends.

He didn't have to be a father to understand how important ready medical care was for those kids.

"I'd be happy to join your committee," he blurted out, almost as surprised by his words as Jessica appeared to be.

Her mouth opened, closed and then opened again. "Are you sure? I mean, you just moved, and now you're moving again. And I know you must be working long hours here at the agency. You can't have much spare time."

"Another excellent recruiting technique, telling people they're too busy to get involved."

A delicate pink crept up her neck. "I don't want to feel as if I strong-armed you."

"Don't worry, I'm perfectly capable of holding my own."

"Hmm…okay. Our next meeting is tomorrow, 7:00 p.m., at the Regen Valley Community Center. I try to end promptly at eight—busy people don't need endless meetings. But I understand if it's too short a notice. The next one will be—"

"No problem, I'll see you there." He leaned forward in his chair. "Now, what did you want to discuss?"

With a start, Jessica glanced at the folder she held and straightened her back as if she was steeling herself for something.

"It's an idea I've been working on since you

showed me the empty rentals and the agency offices. I don't know if you'll be interested or are willing to consider it. Or if it's already been considered…" She stopped, looking flustered.

Logan was genuinely curious. At the same time he was trying not to notice charming details of Jessica's appearance…such as the strands of hair that had escaped her loose French braid and were brushing her cheek.

"Yes?" he prompted.

"Let me start again. It doesn't seem as if Moonlight Ventures needs street visibility. People who want to become models or actors go looking for a talent agency, usually on the internet. Or else *you* go looking for them."

"That's right," Logan said, trying to sound encouraging. He didn't know what she was getting at, but with Jessica, the journey could be interesting.

"Well, you need more space, but if you think about it, my store's square footage wouldn't give you that much. You'd only get a meeting room and maybe two or three extra offices, depending on what size they are."

"That's true," he agreed slowly.

Jessica took a sheet of paper from her folder and slid it across the desk. "This is a copy of the building map that Uncle Kevin gave my grandparents several years ago. Originally he wanted all the units to open onto the atrium, but it was too expensive and the space was too large to make it feasible. That's why there are the large rentals in the back. He hoped there would still be businesses that wanted those spaces, even if they didn't have access to the common atrium area."

"But it didn't work out that way."

"No, except when Matt Tupper opened his recording studio. The combined square footage of the three empty units is over twice the size of your current location."

Logan studied the map and the figures Jessica had written along the edge. It was easy to see where she was going. Displacing the Crystal Connection wouldn't be a permanent solution. But moving to the back of the building would give Moonlight Ventures all the space they currently needed and room for future expansion, as well.

Jessica handed him a second sheet of paper with two columns, one titled "Pros" the other, "Cons."

"I'm just suggesting this as an alternative," she said, "and you may have already thought of the idea. Clearly you spent a bucket of money remodeling your current location, and this would mean doing it all over again."

Logan mentally groaned. Renovations to the back section of the building would make the additions he wanted on his new house look like child's play.

"Logan?" Jessica prompted.

"Yes, doing it again would be pricey and I can imagine what Nicole would say. We had a general contractor, but she was the one who was here, on-site, having to deal with everything."

"At least you wouldn't have to move until the remodeling was done, which means you wouldn't have any disruption to the business."

"True."

Jessica reached across the desk and tapped the sheet of paper she'd given him. "There are other advantages to consider. You mentioned the remodeling didn't quite turn out how you'd hoped, so this way you could start with a clean slate. Also, you wouldn't be losing much rental income back there since those spaces are usually empty. But you could turn around and lease your existing offices for a premium rate.

Units in the front of the building are rarely vacant, and never for long."

Logan was impressed. There were genuine advantages to Jessica's proposal, though, to her credit, she hadn't whitewashed the drawbacks, either. The considerable initial expense was his biggest concern. The agency was doing well, but they couldn't be careless with finances.

He studied the list.

It seemed comprehensive, except for one thing—she'd left the Crystal Connection out of the equation. If Moonlight Ventures moved instead, Jessica wouldn't need to consider a risky move herself, either in the near future or in three years when her lease ran out.

Logan wasn't sure if the omission was admirable or cagey.

His gut instincts told him she was too honest and straightforward to manipulate people.

Admirable, he decided.

JESSICA KEPT HER lips pressed together while Logan looked at the pros and cons list.

It had been a bizarre morning.

Much as she liked Chelsea, she hadn't expected to be invited to her upcoming wedding.

Uncle Kevin and Grams were going, but they'd known Chelsea a lot longer.

Then she'd gone and invited Logan to join the Flash Committee. Huge mistake, at least personally. He kept reminding her of old dreams she'd rather forget. Dreams of being loved, completely and wholly. But the problem with wanting something so badly was that you made bad choices trying to get it.

Jessica shook herself. She'd often wondered if the reason Aaron couldn't handle marriage and impending fatherhood was because her neediness had frightened him. He'd been lousy at expressing his feelings and she'd wanted far more reassurance than he'd been willing or able to give. A baby on top of that must have scared him witless.

And even if Aaron was partly responsible for the divorce, there were no guarantees she wouldn't slip into the same old pattern with another man.

The rustle of paper yanked her attention back to the present. Logan was studying the floor map again and she tried to be optimistic. At least he hadn't immediately rejected the idea of Moonlight Ventures moving. She was uncomfortable, having basically suggested they spend a lot of money so that she wouldn't have to move, but she honestly believed it could be better for everyone in the long run.

Logan looked up. "I wish you'd been around with this idea when we first got started. Of course, there was a renter next to Matt Tupper's studio when we bought the place, but they moved out a month later, after we were deep in plans for the renovations. That's probably why taking over those units in the back never occurred to us."

Her tension eased marginally. "Moonlight Ventures has always been located right here, so it's hard to imagine it being anywhere else, even another part of the building."

Jessica decided not to explain that she'd already discussed the idea with Uncle Kevin. She'd worried that he would have reservations about Moonlight Ventures moving, but instead he'd seemed pleased with the idea and had added items to her list of pros.

"No promises about the outcome, but I'll discuss this with my partners," Logan added. "Keep in mind, it could be a while before we make a decision."

"That's understandable. Now I need to get to the store, since I think Grams has plans."

It surprised her when he stood and put his hand out to shake. The formal gesture was businesslike, but the contact sent electric tingles up her arm.

Don't be a ninny.

Logan hadn't shown a shred of interest in her as a woman and she was too aware of the reasons she shouldn't get involved with any man, much less one with his commitment issues.

Grateful the meeting was concluded, she hurried back to the shop.

Penny looked at her anxiously. "How did it go?"

"Logan is willing to discuss it with his friends. I couldn't expect more than that."

"I suppose. They haven't been here for long, so it may be too large an investment for new business owners. You're awfully flushed. Was it difficult?"

"A little." Jessica didn't want to go into details. "Dad would tell me to keep emotion out of it, but he has more experience with business negotiations." She tried to sound as matter-of-fact as possible, since her grandmother didn't enjoy being reminded that her only child had chosen a lifestyle his parents had rejected.

Only one customer was in the store, a

woman deep in the crystals aisle. She approached with her basket and Jessica rang up the purchase.

"Would you like me to stay and help?" Grams asked when they were alone again. "I was going to have lunch with a few friends, but it isn't urgent. They'll understand if I don't come."

"I'm fine," Jessica assured her. "Go eat with your friends."

Grams hugged her. "I'm so proud of you. It took gumption to have that meeting with Logan. You've turned into such a lovely, accomplished woman."

"Gumption?" Jessica laughed. "I haven't heard *that* word in a while. Have you been reading some of Granddad's old Westerns again?"

Penny grinned. "Cheeky kid."

She left on a happy note and Jessica decided to focus on paperwork for the Flash Committee between customers. It made her think even more about Logan, but she might as well get used to it. He was a member of the committee now.

CHAPTER ELEVEN

LOGAN KNEW HE was strongly biased in favor of Jessica's proposal, but he also knew it was a good idea.

That afternoon he shot photos of the empty units and their current offices, then created an electronic presentation to show his partners. He also sketched out ideas for floor plans and took pictures of what the view would be— while they'd lose the vista on the other side of the building, the green space across the one-way street was appealing in its own right.

His friends were excited at their Wednesday morning meeting, particularly since it wouldn't disadvantage one of their renters. Still, the potential cost sobered them.

"We need general estimates on the renovation costs," Nicole said. "It could be much higher than when we did this space."

"I'll work on getting ballpark figures from general contractors," Logan told her. "We'll also need an architect to tell us what he or she thinks, and a structural engineer to take a look."

"Talk to real estate agents, too," Adam suggested. "See what rental possibilities are for our current space. I'd hate to have to renovate again just to make them commercially viable."

Rachel winced. "What an awful thought. But even though we designed the space for our needs, it might work for a law office or consulting firm."

"Shall I tell Jessica we're willing to consider it?" Logan asked.

"Absolutely," Adam affirmed and the others nodded agreement. "But we can't make any promises."

"She already knows that."

THAT EVENING LOGAN went directly to the Regen Valley Community Center from work, arriving early. He'd looked up the Flash Committee on the internet and found articles and editorials on the *Regen Valley Times* website. His real estate agent had been less informative about the project, though she'd claimed an urgent care facility might raise local property values.

"The town adores Jessica," Carol had gushed.

"We've wanted a clinic for years—we just didn't think we'd be able to get one. But Jessica says anything is possible when it's needed badly enough. Believe me, she got everything moving in a hurry."

A force of nature.

That was what Jessica had called Penny. Apparently Penny's granddaughter was a force to be reckoned with, as well.

The newspaper articles had mentioned a pledge for a grant that would match all money raised in a two-year cycle, up to a maximum amount. The town was providing meeting space and any other facilities needed for the committee's efforts. They'd considered renovating an existing building, but land had been donated recently in a great location. Perhaps Jessica's success was partly due to Penny and Eric's long ties with Regen Valley and her extended childhood visits, but it was still impressive.

Logan had also learned Cyndi had asthma. In an interview, Jessica had mentioned it was one of the reasons a clinic was so important to her. Being a single mom of a daughter with health problems couldn't be easy.

As he came up the walkway of the community center, Jessica was coming out.

"Hi, Logan. It's the first door on the right. Back in a minute, I've got another load in the car."

"I'll help." He followed her to a small compact in the parking lot. Without making a fuss out of it, she handed him a box and took another.

"I've been reading about the Flash Committee," he said as they returned. "Your financial plan is intriguing."

"Thanks. We've got a long way to go."

Several members of the committee were already waiting in the meeting room.

"Hi, all," Jessica said. "This is Logan Kensington. He's buying the Satterly House and wants to work with us on the clinic."

Warm smiles greeted him, along with handshakes and friendly cries of "Welcome to Regen Valley" and "I've always liked that place."

"My name's Perry Eastwood," one man introduced himself. "I'm one of the organizers of the pancake breakfast on Saturday. We've sold over three hundred tickets and expect more.

It's a drop in the bucket, but we won't let that stop us."

"Right," Jessica affirmed. "Enough drops and we'll get there."

"I'd be happy to help with the breakfast," Logan offered awkwardly. "Do you need any unskilled labor?"

"I could use another volunteer in the kitchen," Perry said. "It's at the Veterans Memorial Hall on Vancouver Street. We start serving at 7:00 a.m. Can you be there by six?"

"No problem."

Logan had planned to start packing for the move, but it would have to wait.

Jessica called the meeting to order and went through the agenda. Status reports were given and decisions made, but she kept everyone on track. As promised, they ended within the hour, with Jessica handing out stacks of brochures and fliers.

Logan couldn't add much to the discussion, though he offered to check if any of the agency's clients would donate time at the upcoming street fair. "Most aren't huge stars, but their presence might draw a few extra visitors," he explained.

He lingered to speak with Jessica and walked with her to the parking lot.

"You have a great group of folks," he said. "And they didn't seem to mind having me suddenly added to the ranks."

If anything, Logan had expected a hint of wariness about a newcomer horning in on their business, but the welcome had seemed genuine.

"Why should they mind?" Jessica asked. "They're terrific. No monster egos to be stroked or control freaks, and when somebody says they'll do something, you can count on them."

She was a natural leader and motivator, and totally committed to the project.

"Your talent seems wasted on a small shop like the Crystal Connection," Logan said without thinking.

Her eyes turned stormy. "You may have intended that as a compliment, but when will you figure out that I consider the store worthwhile? Honestly, I think you'd be happiest if I just closed the shop and disappeared."

Shocked, Logan stared at her. As inconvenient as Jessica and her store might be, he'd hate it if she wasn't there. It was a feeling he didn't want to examine too closely.

"That isn't true," he said quietly. "In fact, the store is why I wanted to talk. I've told my friends about your idea and we're all interested in seeing if it's feasible. But before a decision can be made, I have to do research on renovation costs."

The glow from the lowering sun slanted across Jessica's face and turned her eyes an even more intense blue. She almost looked enchanted.

Would one kiss spoil everything?

There was only one way to find out. He leaned forward and pressed his lips against hers.

JESSICA'S BREATHING STOPPED and she wondered if her heart had stopped along with it.

She couldn't remember the last time a man had kissed her that way and she wanted the soft caress to go on forever.

Distantly she heard an odd sound then realized it was Logan's stomach growling.

Stepping backward, she managed to smile at him. "Never mind kissing me, I think you'd better have dinner."

He looked chagrined. "I ordered a sandwich for lunch, but I was too busy to eat. Are there good restaurants in Regen Valley?"

"Several, but I especially like the Hong Kong over on Main Street."

"Would you join me?"

"Sorry, it's a school night. I have just enough time to get home, check Cyndi's homework and tuck her into bed."

With a casual wave, Jessica got in her car, but a few blocks down the street, she pulled over to wait while her trembling subsided. She wasn't sixteen any longer; an innocent kiss shouldn't affect her so much.

Logan had just been curious. That was all. Well, she'd been curious, too. It was perfectly reasonable. They were unattached adults and didn't have to be coy.

A knock on the car window made her jump—it was Logan. *Darn it.* Why had he followed her?

She rolled down her window. "How can you be lost? GPS works all over Regen Valley."

"I wasn't using it. When I saw you'd pulled over, I was concerned you had a flat or something."

"Nope. Just working out a problem in my

head." It was true—Logan Kensington was a big problem. "You aren't too far from the restaurant. Turn around, go three blocks, and then left. That will put you on Main Street in the downtown district. It's also where we're going to have the Flash Fair. The streets will be closed a block each direction from the city square."

"The town supports stuff like that?"

"Sure. They close downtown for all sorts of things, like the chili cook-off in July and the Christmas Gala in December. Only big-city types complain about having to take detours. No one else cares."

His forehead creased. "Come to think of it, cities close streets for parades and other special events."

"True." Jessica grinned. "When they close streets in DC, you can end up miles from where you want to be."

"Regen Valley isn't big enough for that to happen."

Her fingers tightened on her steering wheel. She wanted to get home, slip into a warm bath and forget she'd invited Logan to join her committee.

"It's big enough for us," she murmured.

But obviously not big enough to avoid some-one you don't want to see.

She checked her watch. "I really have to get going now. You should, too. The Hong Kong closes at 9:00 p.m. during the week. Have a good rest of your evening."

"Sure, you, too."

He stepped away and she continued down the street. A glance in the rearview mirror showed he was still standing where she'd left him, but she refused to speculate why.

Back at the house she tried to act as if this had been a normal meeting...instead of one that had ended with a kiss from a man who was utterly impossible. Casual was the key. She didn't want her grandmother to get the idea anything unusual had happened.

"Hey, Grams," she said as she walked inside. "I appreciate you watching Cyndi."

"I love spending time with her. How did the evening go?"

"Fantastic. We've sold over three hundred tickets for the pancake breakfast. With drop-ins, the number could go to over four hun-dred. A Christmas event is also in the works and every store in town has a donation jar by the cash register."

"Was Logan there tonight?"

"Yup, and he might be able to get some clients to be involved with the Flash Fair. If so, Moonlight Ventures will put a notice on their website about it. That way their clients will get some advertising, and so will we. Isn't that great?"

"Marvelous." Grams bit her lip. "Cyndi had an asthma attack while you were gone and had to use her inhaler. She's all right, but I put her to bed early."

Jessica hurried to her daughter's bedroom. The small figure under the blanket seemed so slight. It wasn't right for a kid to have to struggle just to breathe.

Cyndi stirred and yawned. "Hi, Momma. Did you know Teddy Roosevelt had asthma and still did amazing things like exploring rivers and being a cowboy? That's what Grandma says."

"He was also president of the United States."

"And then he went on a safari." Cyndi stuck her tongue out in little-girl fashion. "I want to do that, but I wouldn't shoot any animals, 'cept with a camera. When I grow up I'm gonna have a camera like Logan's, with the big lens thingy, so I can take pictures far away."

"That will be nice. But right now, you'd better get some sleep."

"Okay. G'night, Momma."

Jessica kissed her daughter's cheek and tucked the fluffy blue bedspread around her. "Sleep tight. Don't let bad dreams bite." She'd substituted *bad dreams* for *bedbugs* in the old saying after Cyndi had learned what bedbugs were. "Do you want the light on or off?"

"On, please."

Cyndi usually didn't want her night-light on anymore, unless she'd had an attack. So Jessica turned off the table lamp and switched on the small, glowing orb she'd found for Cyndi's room.

This was reality, and except for her daughter's asthma, a great reality. She didn't need kisses or romantic fantasies to make her life complete.

LOGAN ATE A tasty meal at the Hong Kong. He was surprised to discover such an excellent restaurant in a small town, but that was just his big-city bias showing. He'd have to ask Jessica what other places she could recommend.

Jessica…

His last bite of Mandarin beef seemed to lose its flavor.

He'd frequently thought about kissing her, but had never expected to put that particular thought into action. Though visibly startled, Jessica had handled it well, making light of the moment. Curiosity seemed the best explanation for his behavior, but was it the right one?

Logan pushed his plate away.

The last thing he'd expected when moving to Seattle was to meet someone who unsettled him this way. Jessica was right, his camera *had* become a shield against getting too involved.

The server had delivered his check, along with a fortune cookie, so he broke the cookie open and read the slip of paper inside.

You are energetic and hardworking.

No help there.

Logan paid the bill and left. His dilemma about Jessica wouldn't be resolved by fortune cookies. But he sure wasn't going to ask for advice from Adam and his other friends, either. They'd just suggest he was falling in love.

ON FRIDAY MORNING Penny hummed as she drove to the bakery-café where Kevin had suggested they meet for coffee. They sat in the small patio area that looked into a garden and chatted about world events. Being with him was so comfortable and normal she sometimes didn't remember that everything in their lives had changed.

"Are you really okay if Logan and his partners move the agency?" she asked finally.

Kevin smiled. "Moonlight Ventures is about people, not the location. If this works better for the agency and for Jessica, I'm all for it."

"They may not be willing because of the cost, but I'm so proud of her. She'll do anything to protect other people but rarely stands up for herself. I know she was concerned the idea would upset you."

Penny wondered if it was fair to turn Kevin into a confidant, despite their friendship. Of course, he had a longtime investment in the agency and regarded his old clients and renters as family.

He patted her hand. "I'm thrilled Jess came up with an alternative. Truth be told, I flew home because I was determined to fix everything, but all I can do is sit on the sidelines."

Penny nudged an unopened sugar packet around the table. She was still worried about

Kevin, and hearing him talk about being on the sidelines wasn't reassuring.

"I forgot to tell you that Jessica also recruited Logan for the clinic fund-raiser," she said slowly.

Kevin's eyes widened. "You're kidding."

"I'm serious. He's buying the Satterly House—the one he got the real estate flier for on Saturday—so he must realize how important the project is to the town."

"Interesting."

"Yes, it is. And I've been thinking, why don't you join the committee, too? You don't have to live in Regen Valley to do something for the community."

Kevin shook his head. "I'm too old. They need young, energetic people."

Penny's worry deepened. "Don't be silly. One of Jessica's members is eighty-six and she works her tail off. Don't tell me you can't keep up with an eighty-six-year-old woman."

Another smile tugged at Kevin's mouth. "Maybe Jess doesn't want more help."

"Something this big always needs willing hands. They're having a pancake breakfast tomorrow and a street fair in a couple of weeks, plus half a dozen other projects in the works.

I'm serious, Kevin. You have so much to offer them."

"I'll think about it."

Penny had to be satisfied with that…for the moment. Allison was no longer here to poke and prod, so it was up to her to keep him from giving up on life.

CHAPTER TWELVE

LOGAN DROVE OUT to Regen Valley as the sun was rising, astonished that he'd volunteered to help with the pancake breakfast. They were going to be disappointed. He didn't cook and his social interaction skills were questionable without a camera in hand.

Maybe he could wash dishes.

"Welcome." Perry said and slapped a name tag on Logan's shoulder. "I didn't want to wear one of these at first, but Jessica said we shouldn't assume everyone knows us. Darned if she wasn't right. I was mayor three different times and still meet strangers who don't recognize me."

"Not strangers, Perry," a woman said as she bustled past. "Just friends we don't know yet."

"Yes, dear." Perry grinned, then leaned closer. "My wife. Wonderful woman, just can't resist giving me her opinion."

"I heard that," his wife called over her shoulder.

Perry chuckled.

Logan was grateful for the name tags. Though

he'd met the committee a few days earlier, the names and faces were a blur. He followed Perry toward the kitchen and saw Cyndi in the central room, studiously laying paper place mats on tables. She waved.

"Good morning," Jessica said, coming in while they were donning chef's aprons. "All set?"

Logan doubted she wanted the truth. "Your customers won't all come at once, will they?"

"We're serving until noon, so they should be spread out. Say, I understand you already have the keys to your new house. That was fast work."

He blinked. "How do you know?"

"News gets around. Remember, I mentioned your neighbors would take a friendly interest in your life. You can't claim you weren't warned." She hurried away before he could think of a suitable comeback.

"Logan, your workstation is right over here," Perry said. "I'm assigning you to the pancake griddle."

"Uh…didn't I mention you were getting unskilled labor? I'm not much of a cook."

"You'll be fine," Perry insisted. "Once things get busy we'll have at least three pancake flippers, so you can ask questions if needed. Let me show you what to do."

As it turned out, pouring batter and flipping

pancakes *didn't* require skill. It was repetitive and gave Logan time to consider his plans for the next week and see if there was anything he'd overlooked.

He'd arranged for a local cleaning service to come Monday. According to Carol Foley, the service was popular with people dealing with asthma because they didn't use strong chemicals or scented products. It had been a selling point for Logan, though he didn't want to examine his reasons too closely…after all, Jessica's daughter had asthma.

He pushed the thought away.

The cleaning company had agreed to admit the installer for phone, cable and internet service. And with the majority of his belongings still in storage, he'd arranged for the moving company to deliver everything Tuesday afternoon. His personal belongings in the furnished studio weren't a problem—two trips in the SUV should take care of the lot.

Of course, he still needed to tell the manager that he wasn't renewing his lease. He was tempted to keep the studio in case living in Regen Valley didn't work out, but that didn't make sense. Besides, he could imagine what Jessica might say if she thought he was keeping one foot in the city as a contingency plan.

Jessica again.

Logan abandoned his mental list.

The cheerful, organized chaos in the kitchen was pleasant and he gradually became acquainted with the couple—Shirley and Jim Weston—who were also making pancakes. It helped that there was less time for casual conversation, which was never his strong point.

Perry offered to relieve them with another crew at 10:00, but Logan declined, as did the Westons.

"We want the clinic for our niece," Jim explained when Perry had hurried away. "It'll be convenient for us, but Sandy has childhood diabetes and needs a drop-in facility closer to where she lives."

At the end of the morning, the committee announced they'd raised almost five thousand dollars between ticket sales and extra donations. Cheers sounded, but Logan couldn't tear his gaze away from Jessica.

Her smile lit up the room.

ON MONDAY MORNING Rachel dropped by his office with a broad smile. "Tiffany and Glen Bryant are going to attend that street fair you told me about. They're really excited about it.

Since they're teenagers, I'd suggest a limited autograph period, though. Maybe a couple of hours in the morning."

"That's great news. I'll email Jessica to let her know."

Tiffany and Glen were two of Moonlight Ventures' most successful clients, both as actors and models. They were also Adam's niece and nephew by marriage and he had become their de facto father.

After work Logan drove out to the house and found the cleaning service had done an impressive job. Everything was spotless. He stood for long minutes gazing out the back windows. No buildings were visible, and it would stay that way unless he built something himself—the property extended to the rocky outcropping on the hill.

A doe with two young fawns came into view, nibbling on grass. He automatically reached for his camera, only to remember he'd left it in his SUV. After a while they disappeared into the undergrowth.

Nice.

He went out and began carrying boxes into the house, stowing them in the master bedroom closet. There was more than enough space; it was bigger than some bedrooms.

Though he wouldn't be spending the night, he headed into Regen Valley to buy food and soft drinks to offer the movers when they came the following afternoon. Several customers said hello, including Perry Eastwood, while others just smiled or waved. Thanks to Jessica's insistence on name tags, Logan recognized John Beck, who'd worked on frying the sausage links, and Elinor Boudreau, who had to be at least eighty.

It gave him a warm feeling. As if he belonged.

He left everything at the house before returning to Seattle. At his apartment, he checked his email and found one from his mother.

Dear, Logan,

We were pleased to get your message about buying a home in Regen Valley. I presume that's one of Seattle's bedroom communities. Suburban life could be interesting for you. Let us know a time to visit that would be convenient. Perhaps in the next week or two?

Love, Mom and Dad

A headache began pounding in Logan's temples. He'd sent an email with his new address but hadn't expected his parents to decide on a visit. He would have to consider the right way to put them off. Now that they'd retired, they could come anytime. It didn't have to be this month.

The next morning he hurried into the Crystal Connection for coffee, needing something to jolt his tired brain into action.

"Give me whatever is fastest and has the most caffeine."

Jessica grinned and filled his mug.

"In case I haven't told you," she said, "thanks for recruiting Tiffany and Glen Bryant to attend the Flash Fair, and for sending the info to us so quickly. I forwarded your message to Nora Silvers, who's in charge of publicity."

Logan pressed a finger to his aching temple but couldn't come up with a face to attach to Nora's name.

"The amazing thing is that Tiffany and Glen aren't just local celebrities," Jessica continued. "Their new network television series is a huge hit."

"Rachel is the Bryants' agent. I just passed

the request to her," Logan said, reluctant to take credit.

"You came up with the idea. The students at the high school are frantically promoting their appearance. They've even started a fan club."

"That was fast."

"Never underestimate a teenager."

Logan shook his head, hoping the fog would drift out of his brain. "Glen and Tiff are good kids—fraternal twins who get along. Adam's wife, Cassie, is their aunt and also their guardian."

"Regardless, it's really going to boost our attendance." Jessica cocked her head and studied his face. "You look like something the cat dragged in, as Grams would say. Are you sick?"

"No." He poured sugar and cream into his coffee for added energy and selected a pastry from the display case. "I got an email last night. My parents want to visit in the next couple of weeks—to see me and the new house. I spent most of the night trying to think of a nice way to head them off. Not forever, just a few months."

Jessica's eyes widened.

"You seem surprised," Logan said.

"Oh, well…it's just that I'd love having my mother and father want to visit and wouldn't care if they came when it was inconvenient. Back east, Cyndi and I were only forty miles away, but we only saw them on a handful of holidays. They haven't been out to Washington since we moved."

Logan wasn't sure how to respond. "My folks try to do what's expected of them," he said at length. "Convention says they're supposed to connect, so that's probably why they're making the effort."

Jessica wiped the gleaming coffee bar with a damp towel. "Maybe it's more than that. You're moving into a new house. Unless they plan to help you unpack and get settled, the conventional choice would be to wait. They must sincerely want to be part of your life."

He frowned. Perhaps he was too much in the habit of seeing his parents as gracious diplomats, wholly concerned about appearances. Looking deeper hadn't occurred to him. Admittedly, it wasn't the first time. As much as he'd disliked Jessica's contention that he saw people as surface images instead of looking deeper, she wasn't completely wrong.

"Possibly," he conceded. "But that doesn't change this being a terrible time for a visit."

"It's just that… Never mind."

"Go ahead."

"No. I've said too much already and it's none of my business."

Logan's frown deepened. He wasn't convinced that was true, but it seemed rude to push.

JESSICA WANTED TO dive behind the coffee bar and disappear. Logan's relationship with his parents was none of her business, but she'd given her two cents' worth, anyway.

"Can I get you something else?" she asked.

"I'm fine. About the street fair, I may get more names of clients able to participate by later today, but I'm leaving work early to meet the movers at my house, so I might not be able to let you know until tomorrow."

He strode out the door.

Logan might be groggy from a short night of sleep, but he was the sort of man who moved with confidence. The speed with which he'd purchased the Satterly House seemed in character, as well. Once upon a time she'd been more impulsive and sure of herself, but time and bad choices had made her cautious.

After adding Logan's purchases to his computer bill, she studied the new online catalog her grandmother had prepared. Penny Parrish hadn't actually retired; she'd simply given up certain parts of her work. She had friends all over the world and continued to help them sell their products at decent prices.

Yet the memory of Logan's frustration kept interfering with Jessica's concentration. His parents wanted to see him and he preferred waiting for a more convenient time? Her mother and father loved their children, but it was a detached love. An occasional email or phone call was enough for them.

Abruptly the shop door swung open and Logan marched back inside. He put his mug on the sales counter with a thud.

"Finish the thought you started. 'It's just that *what*?'"

Jessica closed her laptop. "I told you, it's none of my business."

"I still want to know."

Drat him. He had an irritating habit of pushing her to say more than she ought to.

"All right. Did you ever think that having your parents want to visit is a gift? If someone is trying to fix a relationship and you miss the opportunity, there's no guarantee you'll get another chance."

Logan's annoyed expression turned thoughtful. "Fair point. Did you learn that from experience?"

"My problem was more about jumping the gun," she said wryly.

"How's that?"

Jessica shrugged. She'd already told Logan more than he needed to know, but her mistakes weren't a secret.

"Well, I told you about Grams falling for Granddad and chasing after him. I followed her example with my ex-husband, and you've already heard what a mess *that* turned out to be."

Logan scowled. "Is this about you taking too much blame for your divorce?"

His outraged expression was rather sweet.

"Not exactly. I'm just explaining. My parents aren't bad people, but I've never felt very important to them. My twin brothers had each other when we were growing up, but I felt invisible. By the time I went to college, I was practically obsessed with finding someone who would love me the way Granddad loved Grams."

Logan nodded. "I understand, but that still doesn't make it all your fault."

"Aaron would probably disagree. At least I got counseling after he left. I was afraid of messing up Cyndi or asking too much from her, even subconsciously. I still worry about it. Her job is to grow up happy and secure, not fill an empty hole in her mother's life."

"You have nothing to worry about—you're a great mom."

Jessica attempted a grin. "I try, but vigilance is important. Anyhow, what I said about your parents stems from my own hang-ups."

The corners of Logan's eyes crinkled as he smiled. "But you're right. I ought to be grateful Mom and Dad want to visit. It just didn't occur to me with everything going on." He lifted his hand and gently brushed her cheek. "We all have our blind spots. Thanks for the words of wisdom."

"You're welcome…for what they're worth."

"They're worth a lot."

Taking his mug and giving her a casual wave, Logan hurried out again.

Jessica stood with her eyes half-closed, skin tingling from the contact with Logan's fingers. Her body didn't understand that he wasn't coming on to her or intending anything romantic; it had simply reacted.

She had to find a way to deal with the awareness he roused. Even if she moved the shop out of the building, he would still be living in Regen Valley and involved with the work on the clinic project. Avoiding him was impossible.

LOGAN RETURNED TO the agency with his thoughts churning. Jessica had a way of making him see things in a different light.

Though he had little in common with his parents, they loved him and he loved them. However unusual his childhood had been, he'd seen more of the world by the time he left for college than most people saw in a lifetime. And he hadn't seen that world alone. His mother and father had taken him with them when they visited spots like Machu Picchu and the Valley of the Kings in Egypt. True, his dad had lectured like a history professor and his mom had screeched that she didn't want her son breaking his neck climbing the Great Pyramid so he could get a picture at the top, but even that was a fond memory.

Since he'd gone to college, he'd only seen

his parents occasionally. His work had rarely brought him close to where they were posted, and for the same reason, they'd had trouble catching up with him. But now Logan recalled a number of times they'd wanted to get together and he'd put it off, blaming his schedule. Maybe that was why they had simply arrived in Seattle last year unannounced, knowing he'd be there for a few weeks.

He went straight to his computer to send an email.

Mom and Dad, glad you're able to visit. Come whenever is best for you. I'm always busy, but want us to spend time together, regardless. Let me know when you'll be here.
—Logan.

After hitting the send button he wondered if the wording could have been improved, but he'd never pretended to be a great communicator. It was a skill Thomas and Regina Kensington hadn't been able to teach him, no matter how hard they'd tried.

Of course, now he needed to think about sleeping arrangements in case they wanted to stay with him. But before he could decide how to handle that, his mother emailed back saying they'd fly in the following week on Thursday and had reservations at a hotel in downtown Seattle.

He checked the calendar and realized their visit would coincide with the Flash Fair, but he decided it would work out all right. Attending together could smooth over any awkwardness. Besides, his parents were really good with people.

The phone rang on an outside line and he picked it up. "Moonlight Ventures, Logan Kensington speaking."

"Goodness, you sound crisp and professional," said a familiar voice. "It's me, Laurel."

Logan leaned back in his chair with a smile. He'd worked often with Laurel Stevenson since she'd become a model. The camera loved her. "Hey, Laurel, don't tell me you're looking for a new agent. I know one who's available."

She laughed. "Actually, I'm in Washington doing a series of commercials for a cosmetics company. We don't start work until tomorrow, so how about having lunch with me? I'll get something and bring it to the agency."

"Sounds good. But get me real food, not one of those weedy salads you like."

"Will do. I'll be over later."

At noon, Chelsea buzzed to say Laurel had arrived. He went out to the reception area and she rushed forward to hug him.

"Logan, I've missed you. How is your move working out?"

"It's great."

Laurel knew all about Moonlight Ventures. Because she could find it difficult to relax in front of a camera, he usually kept up a running commentary about anything and everything as a distraction. Their last commercial shoot together was just a few months ago, so she'd gotten an earful.

After they'd eaten, he showed her around the agency and then took her into the atrium. "We also have rentals at the other end of the building," he explained.

"I'm impressed, but I saw a sign for coffee at that crystals place. Mind if we get a cup? I flew in last night after a month in Italy, so I'm dragging."

"Sure." Logan knew all about hopping time zones. What surprised him was that she'd called so quickly after arriving. He'd invited his friends in Los Angeles to get in touch if they came to Seattle, but he would have expected her to spend her first day resting. "The Crystal Connection serves a mean cup of coffee. By the way, are you interested in helping a good cause?"

"Of course. What do you need?"

"I'm buying a house in a nearby town called Regen Valley—I actually have to leave before long to meet the movers. Anyway, the town is raising money for a drop-in medical clinic. The next fund-raiser is a street fair, the weekend after next. I volunteered to invite celebrity attendees, so having you show up this way is serendipitous."

"Oh." She flushed. Laurel had never gotten comfortable with her semi-celebrity status. "I guess. We won't be working weekends."

"Terrific. Let's get our coffee."

JESSICA LOOKED UP when the door opened and her welcoming smile wavered. It was Logan with a woman. A very *beautiful* woman.

"Jessica, this is Laurel Stevenson," Logan said. "Laurel is in Washington for a photo shoot, but she's still on Italian time and needs a java pick-me-up. She's also volunteered to be one of the celebrities at the Flash Fair."

"Oh, that's great. What would you like?"

Laurel glanced at the list of coffees offered. "The Southwest Twist sounds interesting."

"I didn't bring my cup, but I'll take an espresso," Logan said.

Jessica gritted her teeth as she headed to the coffee corner. The model was just as striking as Logan's two female partners, but *they* were comfortably married. Laurel's present marital status was unknown, but a few months ago her name had hit the headlines with speculation that she was being romanced by a European prince.

"Is something wrong?" Logan asked. He'd followed her, leaving his companion, who was looking at a collection of quartz crystals.

"Not at all. Why?"

"You seem tense. Thanks for what you said earlier about my folks visiting. I emailed an invite and they're flying in next week on Thursday. I'll bring them to the Flash Fair."

"That's nice," Jessica murmured.

She was not, repeat, *not* jealous. On the contrary, Laurel's appearance in the store was a healthy reminder of how silly it was to engage in romantic wistfulness. Besides, the hollow expression in the model's eyes suggested something was bothering her. Nobody's world was perfect.

"Is everything okay with your friend?" Jessica asked in a low voice. "She looks unhappy."

"Probably just tired. Those long flights are killers."

Jessica wasn't so sure, but she put both cups on the coffee bar and smiled at Laurel when she came over. "Here you go."

"I'd like to buy this," the model said, holding out a sterling silver necklace. The pendant was a quartz cabochon, shot through with gold needles. "Your informational material says this kind of stone may help with decision-making. I can use all the help available."

Jessica didn't dare look at Logan for fear of laughing. Poor guy, he was surrounded by people willing to consider something beyond what they could see in front of them.

"That's right." She rang up the purchase and put the necklace in a nice box. "Have a good day."

She breathed more freely when they were gone. It wasn't easy running a store frequented by women renowned for their beauty, but she rarely felt a twinge of insecurity around them.

The only explanation for her reaction to Laurel was that she'd seen her with Logan.

Jessica had almost regained her equilibrium when the model returned a short while later, but at least she was alone this time.

"I know Logan mentioned me coming to your street fair, but he forgot to say you were one of the people in charge. Is it okay with you?"

The vulnerability in her eyes made Jessica sigh. Beneath the skin, they were both dealing with insecurity. "We'd love having you, Laurel."

"Thanks. Logan has all my contact information. I need to get going. My agent called and they want a preproduction meeting. Anyhow, Logan had to leave before we could really talk. Something about the movers. I... I've been needing a friend and he's always been someone I can confide in."

Jessica tried not to reveal her amazement. Maybe Logan was better at relationships than he seemed to think, or maybe it was different when a gorgeous woman commanded his attention. "You'll probably have time if you're staying until after the Flash Fair."

"True. Oh, and see?" Laurel gestured to

the rutilated quartz pendant at her throat. "I couldn't wait to wear it."

"Great. I'll see you a week from Saturday."

As the model left, Jessica told herself it was wonderful to get so much help on the fundraiser. She emailed Nora the news about Laurel Stevenson, then sat on the stool behind the counter, wishing she wasn't in the usual afternoon lull between customers. It gave her too much time to speculate whether Logan and Laurel were *more* than friends.

They weren't, were they? None of the signs had been there...the secret, unspoken communication, the casual touching, the little smiles meant only for each other.

Jealousy reared its head again and flutters of panic hit Jessica. She couldn't fall for Logan. It would only lead to heartbreak.

CHAPTER THIRTEEN

THE FOLLOWING THURSDAY Logan waited at the airport for his parents' plane to arrive. Smiles wreathed their faces when they spotted him, though they'd insisted it wasn't necessary to be met because they were renting a car.

"It's so good to see you," his mother declared with her usual hug.

His father hugged him, as well, which *wasn't* usual. He'd been prepared for a firm handshake.

"I'm glad you're here," Logan said, meaning every word. At first he'd decided to make the best of things on their visit. Then he'd remembered the bleak resignation on Jessica's face when talking about her own parents and had decided he should do better than "make the best of it."

He conducted them first to claim their baggage and then led them to the car rental area. He made sure they had the agency address to put into the GPS and went to collect his own car. Since they wanted to check into their hotel before coming to Moonlight Ventures, he stopped to see how a new client's first job was going. The model was all smiles and the photographer was pleased, saying she was refreshingly easy to work with.

Logan drove into the agency lot and parked as Jessica was locking her car. "Aren't you late getting here?" he asked.

"It was my turn to bring snacks to Cyndi's classroom, so Grams opened the store. You look pleased with life."

"I am. I just visited a job site for one of my new clients. She's off to a good start. It's nice to think I played a role in that happening." He paused. "Is that similar to how a parent feels when their kid does well?"

"A little, but parenting is a marathon, with endless ups and downs."

"I suppose parents have to be careful not to get too invested in their child's successes," he said, thinking of the struggles his friend Adam had experienced with his mother and father on the same issue.

Jessica nodded. "Isn't that what stage moms and dads do? I've seen a version of it at soccer and Little League games."

"I guess." Logan shuddered. "I've met stage parents who could curl your toes. Just to reassure you, Cassie Wilding isn't like that. She's keeping Tiffany and Glen grounded and Adam is helping."

"Everything I've heard about the Bryant twins is positive. We're going to have autograph stations in the park for our celebrities, but nobody is being asked to do more than a two-hour stint. The assigned times are shown in publicity releases, along with signs to be posted around the fair."

Just then his mother and father arrived. They got out of their rental and looked at Jessica curiously.

"Hi. I didn't expect you so soon," Logan said.

"Our hotel room wasn't ready, so we came straight over." His mother smiled at Jessica. "I hope we aren't interrupting."

Logan saw speculation churning in her eyes and groaned silently.

JESSICA INSTANTLY KNEW the couple was Logan's parents.

He closely resembled his father, a distinguished man whose hair was lightly peppered with gray. And his mother was so perfectly dressed and coiffed she could have stepped off the cover of a fashion magazine. How did they look so polished after a plane ride, especially a red-eye?

"Mom, Dad, this is Jessica Parrish," Logan said. "She rents one of the spaces in our building. Jessica, these are my parents, Thomas and Regina Kensington."

Jessica smiled. "It's lovely to meet you, Mr. and Mrs. Kensington."

"Please call us Tom and Regina," his mother said quickly.

"Logan told me you were coming to visit and see his new home. You'll be impressed—it's a beautiful place."

"You've been there?"

"I live in the same town and had a chance to tour the house before it sold," Jessica explained. "Mostly out of curiosity. My daughter and I live on the other side of my grandmother's duplex."

"She must appreciate you being so close."

"I'm the lucky one, and Cyndi loves having her great-grandmother next door. She thinks I don't know how much Grams spoils her."

Regina's smile widened. "What an amazing

coincidence, son. Jessica rents a space in your building, and now you're buying a house in the town where she lives. How lovely."

Oooh.

Jessica choked down a laugh. Logan had mentioned his parents were longing for grand-children. Did his mother hope the "amazing coincidence" was founded in romance?

"Not so amazing," Logan said. "I saw the house when I went to do a photography presentation for Cyndi's girl rangers troop. Cyndi is Jessica's daughter."

"I see." Thomas nodded in a solemn, grave manner. "It's important to encourage children in their interests."

"Jessica, how old is your daughter?" Regina inquired.

"Seven, almost eight."

"That's a wonderful age. When Logan was seven we were in…" She cocked an eyebrow at her husband. "Was it Tokyo, or were we living in Rome by then?"

"Rome," Logan interjected. "We visited the Colosseum on my eighth birthday."

"That's right. You were fascinated when the embassy aide said the early Romans filled it with water and fought mock sea battles." She let out a light laugh. "And then the aide made a joke about Lucrezia Borgia poisoning people, and *you* informed him that Lucrezia was a victim of unfounded rumor and he should know better than to keep blackening her name. It lacked tact, but I loved your sense of fair play."

Logan grinned as if he hadn't expected his mother to remember that level of detail.

Jessica made a show of checking her watch. "Tom, Regina, it was great to meet you, but I should get to work."

Pleasant goodbyes sounded and she went inside to where her grandmother was tidying shelves.

"Hey, Grams. Thanks for the help."

"My pleasure. I had a huge sale...that tall amethyst geode, the one over four feet high? A company in Kirkland bought it for their lobby."

"Fabulous."

Large pieces, with equally large price tags, were slow sellers. But Jessica had spent hours cleaning the geode a few days earlier. She was pleased her work had paid off.

"Who are those people outside?" Grams asked.

"Logan's parents. We may see them at the Flash Fair."

Tom and Regina were very cosmopolitan

and sophisticated, but from the little she'd seen, Jessica thought the family might be able to have a closer relationship.

Was it Tokyo, or were we living in Rome by then?

Imagine not being able to recall which fabulous city you'd been living in at a given moment. And Regina's designer suit must have been purchased in a very exclusive boutique. Just another reminder, as if Jessica needed one, that Logan came from a very different world. She couldn't fit into that world, even if she wanted to. But life was all about choices, and despite the mistakes with her ex-husband, she was satisfied with her life.

Her satisfaction was harder to remember when Laurel came into the shop a while later.

She gave the model a determined smile. "Hi. Let me introduce my grandmother, Penny Parrish. Grams, this is Laurel Stevenson, though she's so famous she might not need an introduction. Laurel is one of Logan's friends."

"Not famous," Laurel protested.

She might be uncomfortable with her supermodel status, but a lot of people knew who she was.

"Coffee?" Jessica asked.

"Actually, my mother's birthday is coming up. I'm looking for a gift."

"Let me know if I can help."

Laurel bobbed her head and began perusing a display case of necklaces, rings and earrings. Though the Crystal Connection wasn't a fine-jewelry store, Jessica had brought in a selection of unique, hand-crafted pieces as an experiment. Sales had been brisk, and despite the uncertainty of her rental situation, she'd ordered more.

Logan arrived several minutes later. "Hey, Laurel, I thought I'd find you here. My parents just left for their hotel. Sorry I was tied up for a while."

"That's okay. It gave me a chance to shop. I'll be done in a minute."

She quickly chose a pair of opal earrings and Jessica put the purchase in a gold gift bag. Logan waved as they left and she ground her teeth. He hadn't said a word to her, which should suit her fine but didn't.

"Is everything all right?" Grams asked a few minutes later.

"Of course. Why do you ask?"

"You look annoyed. Did you have a fight with Logan?"

"I'm fine," Jessica assured her, but was glad when her grandmother decided to stay and help for the remainder of the morning. It was comforting to have her warm, loving support.

While Jessica served coffee and checked her inventory, Grams answered the portable phone and rang up purchases. On the latest call, she put her hand over the mouthpiece and gestured to Jessica.

"It's Logan. He wants to talk to you."

Jessica took the receiver, wondering if there had been a decision on the rental. "Hello?"

"Hey, I was calling to see if you'd be free after the store closed, but since Penny is there, can I steal some of your time right now? It's personal. Not for me, for Laurel. She has a decision you might be able to help her with. Do you mind?"

"It's fine. I'll come right over."

Jessica hoped the model didn't want to discuss being in love with Logan. Surely not. After all, why would he think someone else could help with that one?

Next door, Chelsea sent her to the Moonlight Ventures break room, where both Logan and Laurel were waiting.

"This is so nice of you, Jessica," Laurel said. "I hate taking up your time."

"No worries."

Once they were seated around the small table, Laurel drew a deep breath. "I've told Logan about my problem and he thought you'd understand because of the situation with your daughter and ex-husband. You see, my...my biological father contacted me a few weeks ago. I've never met him. He says he's sorry that he hasn't been there for me and wants us to get acquainted. I'm torn about what to do. Logan mentioned your daughter might face the same decision one day."

"That's right."

Jessica had often wondered what she'd do if Aaron asked to see Cyndi. As Logan had pointed out, she and Cyndi wouldn't be difficult to locate. And what if Aaron waited until after Cyndi was eighteen? Cyndi might come to her mother for advice, but the decision would rest on her shoulders. Jessica shivered, sensing the years rushing away.

"Um, are you angry at your biological father?" she asked.

"In a way, though I don't know the whole story. From what I understand he and my mom had an affair and it was over quickly. Mom may have insisted he stay out of our lives."

Logan leaned forward. "Jessica, do you think Cyndi will be angry about her father eventually?"

She shrugged. "It's hard to know. Right now she's a little curious because so many of her friends have daddies and she doesn't. But someday she'll start asking hard questions. I won't bad-mouth Aaron, but I also won't pretend he's helped support her or asked to be a part of her life."

"I'm also afraid Mom will be upset about this, so I've wondered if I should tell her," Laurel explained. "How would you react if Cyndi was my age and decided to meet your ex-husband?"

Jessica thought for a moment and realized she *would* be upset. Not with Cyndi, but with Aaron. She didn't blame him for walking out on her, but he'd also walked out on his child and never acknowledged her.

Her gaze caught Logan's and she had the oddest feeling he understood what she was thinking.

"I'd have mixed feelings," she finally admitted. "But our circumstances might be different from your situation. Did your biological father know about you from the beginning?"

"I don't know. My mom has never wanted to talk about it."

"But you're curious," Jessica guessed. "How could you not be?"

"Yeah. What do you think?"

"I'd want Cyndi to meet her father, if that's what *she* really wanted. At the same time, I'd be livid if it didn't go well and she got hurt. I can't speak for your mother, but if you don't say anything, it becomes a secret, and secrets can turn into walls between people."

Laurel looked forlorn. "You're right."

They talked for another few minutes until the alarm on Laurel's phone chimed. "I have to get back to the set," she exclaimed. "I'll see you on Saturday. 'Bye."

"I hope that wasn't too hard for you," Logan said when they were alone. "She needed to talk to someone who understands and is good with people."

"It's fine, and it gave me a taste of what could be in the future for Cyndi."

"I'm sure you'll handle it well. And from what I've seen, Cyndi will, too."

"Thanks." Although nobody could predict

what the future would bring, a surge of confidence went through her. Motherhood had its ups and downs, but if she could offer something of value to someone like Laurel Stevenson, she must be doing okay.

PENNY FURIOUSLY CHOPPED the pecans on her cutting board.

"What do you have against those nuts?" Kevin asked. He'd come over to help make candy to sell at the Flash Fair.

Penny stirred the mangled pecans and sighed. "I'm just working out my frustrations. I spent the morning at the Crystal Connection. Logan came in looking for Laurel Stevenson, who was there, shopping for a birthday gift."

"That's the supermodel doing a series of commercials up in Bellevue. The newspaper interviewed her and she did a fine job of promoting the street fair. Attendance could triple with folks coming to get her autograph. It's a great development."

Penny whacked the pecans again. "Yeah, *great*. Logan is very friendly with her."

Kevin reached over and took the knife. "He must know a thousand models."

She swept the pecans into a bowl. So far

she'd made several double batches of fudge and two trays of peanut brittle. Now she was starting on English toffee. Divinity was her personal favorite, but nobody seemed to eat it these days. Tomorrow morning she'd make soda cracker candy.

"Never mind me," she said briskly. "We thought we were doing the right thing by giving Jessica the Crystal Connection, but now it could all fall apart."

Kevin frowned. "I thought Logan and the others were seriously considering her idea."

"They are, but all we can do is wait, and I'm terrible at waiting. I go after what I want. I don't just sit around."

He laughed. "Eric once said you were a human tornado and people were wise to get out of the way, but good things generally followed."

Pleasure stirred inside of Penny. She and her husband had been opposites. She'd rushed around to make things happen while he'd quietly done his work, taking life as it came. They'd balanced each other beautifully.

"It could be an adventure to just watch and see how everything unfolds," Kevin suggested.

"Except adventures don't always have happy endings."

It didn't feel like an adventure when she couldn't do anything to fix a problem. That was how she'd felt when she saw Laurel Stevenson's closeness with Logan. Jessica had pretended not to notice, but Penny knew her granddaughter too well.

If Jessica honestly didn't care, that was one thing; but if Logan was too blind to fall head over heels with such a wonderful woman, he was a fool and didn't deserve her anyhow.

"Penny, give it time," Kevin cautioned. "You did your best by giving Jessica the Crystal Connection, but you can't manage her life. She has to find her own way."

It pinched, but he was right. Everyone had to make their own decisions.

LOGAN MET HIS parents for dinner that evening, apologizing that he hadn't been free to spend the day with them.

"Nonsense," his mother said. "You have a new career to establish."

The maître d' showed them to a table and gave them menus.

"Are you certain you don't mind going to the street fair on Saturday?" Logan asked.

He'd told them earlier about joining the Flash Committee and the work being done to raise funds. They'd gotten a positive first impression of Jessica, but their approval had skyrocketed upon learning about the clinic she wanted to get built.

"Not at all. It sounds entertaining," said his mother. "And the medical facility is an excellent cause. When we get home, I'll speak with some of the people we know and ask for contributions. I just hope Jessica won't think we're stepping on her toes."

"I'm sure she'll appreciate anything you do. Tomorrow afternoon I'm going to help with setup, but I can meet you for a late dinner."

"We'll help, too," his mother volunteered.

Logan considered refusing, not knowing what two people more accustomed to state dinners than street fairs could do, but Jessica might say the same of him.

"Okay. I'll take you to see my new house after the fair is over. But be prepared, almost everything is still in boxes. I've only spent a few nights there."

Regina waved her hand. "Quite understandable. Tell us more about Jessica. It will help when I'm soliciting donations for the clinic."

Logan narrowed his eyes, but his mother had phrased the inquiry in a way that made it impossible to refuse.

"She's quite talented and has been able to motivate the Flash Committee to an extraordinary degree. She's also secured a private grant that will match a maximum level of funds raised over the next two years."

"Excellent. Donors love that. They feel as if they're giving twice as much. Is she married?"

Prickles of warning crawled up Logan's spine. "Divorced."

Thomas frowned. "It's hard to raise a child alone. What is her little girl like?"

"Cyndi?" Logan relaxed as he thought about the exuberant seven-year-old. "She leaps into something with both feet. After seeing the advance copy of my calendar, she became enamored with photography. That's why she asked me to give a talk to her girl ranger troop."

"You seem to know them both well," Regina said.

"I've been working with Ms. Parrish on rental issues. She owns the Crystal Connection, so her daughter is often around."

The conversation was going more smoothly than Logan had expected, though it was a topic that put him on edge. Still, with his parents' support behind the clinic, Jessica's fund-raising worries could soon be over, along with his membership on the Flash Committee.

"Jessica is a fine young woman," Regina murmured. "Don't you agree, Tom?"

He nodded. "Are you finally thinking of settling down, son? An instant family has its challenges, but so does any marriage. Cyndi sounds like a nice child and I assume we all agree that Jessica is special."

Logan suppressed a groan. If his parents had their way, he'd be married by July.

"There's nothing like that between us," he insisted, uneasily remembering one of the sweetest kisses he'd ever experienced. "Jessica Parrish is a business associate who asked me to join her committee for the clinic. Don't get your hopes up, because the last thing I'm thinking about is settling down."

"You're buying a house," Regina argued. "You've always rented condos or apartments before."

"It isn't a family home. More of a retreat in the country."

They looked disappointed. Until now he'd assumed that they were interested in grandchildren mostly because their friends expected it. But Jessica had made him wonder if he was wrong. Maybe they truly wanted a closer relationship that included a daughter-in-law and grandkids.

So, how could he explain that he didn't feel equipped to be the kind of husband a woman would want?

No matter how many attractive qualities he saw in Jessica, it wouldn't be fair to her, especially after what she'd told him about her childhood and marriage. She deserved the kind of love that wouldn't leave her feeling as if she came second to a camera.

CHAPTER FOURTEEN

THE NEXT DAY Jessica closed the Crystal Connection at 3:00 p.m. Her grandmother was picking Cyndi up from school, so she went straight to the town square and got a job assignment from Carl Sheffield, the general manager of the Flash Fair. Carl had been a colonel in the US Marines and was an expert at marshaling forces.

Logan was already there, dressed casually in a worn black shirt and black jeans. At the moment he was helping construct the booth that would feature barbecued hamburgers.

"Hello." A voice broke into her thoughts. "Jessica, right?"

It was Regina Kensington.

She turned and smiled as naturally as possible. "Yes, Jessica Parrish."

"Tom and I admire your efforts to build a drop-in clinic. We'd like to get donations from a few of our friends to help hurry things along.

We hope that will be all right with you and your committee?"

Jessica was stunned by the generous offer. "Wow. No, I mean, yes, we'd so appreciate that. Thank you." She grinned.

"Now, in the meantime, is there something we can do right now to help out?"

Still flustered, Jessica tried to think of jobs that might suit the sophisticated couple but then pointed toward Carl.

"See the guy with the red ball cap? That's Carl Sheffield. He's in charge. I'm sure he can find a project for you."

Regina nodded and collected her husband. They immediately went to talk with Carl.

Jessica didn't have time to watch what happened. She went to help set up tables and chairs near the food booths. Luckily, most of the booths for food, games and merchandise were being run by assorted Regen Valley organizations and businesses. The committee was having a contest to see which group could raise the largest contribution—the winner would have their name added to a donor plaque at the clinic. The response had been overwhelming.

"If this goes as hoped, we should have a

Flash Fair every year," Carl said as they crossed paths an hour later.

"Sounds good, but don't suggest it until our feet have stopped hurting."

He chuckled. "On another note, it was a great idea to get Logan Kensington involved with the project. Public figures like Laurel Stevenson and the Bryant kids will attract people of all ages."

"Inviting Logan to join the committee was an impulse when I heard he was buying the Satterly House. He's something of a celebrity himself."

"Good impulse."

Good for the committee, Jessica thought, *not so great for my peace of mind*.

She threw back her shoulders and continued working.

KEVIN CARRIED BOX after box of Penny's homemade candy into the empty building being used as a drop-off area for goods at the street fair. On his next trip to his truck, he was astonished to see Logan hammering nails into a booth on the city square.

Everywhere Kevin looked, people were putting up posters, setting up booths or hauling in supplies. At least the police had set out signs saying that except for authorized vehicles, no through traffic or parking was allowed until Sunday morning.

"This is incredible," he said to Penny. "I've never actually *seen* organized chaos before."

She laughed and he marveled at what a remarkable person she was. Penny would always be beautiful, but the passing years had added character and a depth of experience to her face that made her even more attractive. He didn't say so, because she would just make a joke about being old with wrinkles and creaky knees.

Not old, just well seasoned, Jessica liked to tease her.

Kevin agreed.

Despite telling Penny that people had to find their own way, he was struggling with letting go himself. Maybe he shouldn't have sold Moonlight Ventures, but he'd started the agency with Allison and running it alone had depressed him. He just hadn't realized what it would be like to see the agency marching on, leaving him unable to fix problems for his friends. Knowing Jessica's shop was at risk was especially painful.

The only compensation was having more time to spend with his family. And friends like Penny.

TO HIS SURPRISE, Logan was enjoying the preparations for the street fair. The labor wasn't difficult and there was a cheerful camaraderie amongst the volunteers.

Early that morning he'd called his mother and father at their hotel and suggested they all go for a drive to Mount St. Helens. They had protested he needed to work, but it hadn't taken much convincing for them to agree to a short sightseeing trip. Now they were in Regen Valley to help. Their eagerness to be involved in a small-town event seemed unusual, but Logan was beginning to see he'd made a number of wrong assumptions through the years.

He ran into Jessica as the evening's work was concluding. "Where are Cyndi and Penny?" he asked.

"I tried sending them home an hour ago, but they wouldn't go. They're across the street with your parents."

Logan glanced at his mother and father, who were adjusting the red, white and blue bunting on a booth. Their faces were so happy that it astonished him. He looked back at Jessica.

"In case I haven't told you clearly enough, I appreciate what you said about Mom and Dad wanting to visit. We've had our share of rocky moments, but I think we're going to be okay. I hope you'll have the same opportunity with your own folks."

Her smile had a wry quality. "That would be nice, but I have to be careful about expressing hopes in that direction. I don't want Cyndi to start believing something is wrong with her just because Aaron and my parents aren't part of her life. It isn't her fault."

"It isn't yours, either. How can you help Cyndi believe that, if you don't?"

A myriad of emotions flickered across Jessica's face. "It's easier to understand something in your head than believe it in your heart. But I'm trying."

At least she wasn't instantly declaring she was wholly to blame for her divorce. He admired how hard she'd worked to defeat her personal demons, not only for herself but for Cyndi, as well. A lot of people just kept making the same mistakes over and over without understanding why or trying to correct the problem.

Logan cleared his throat. "I, uh, thought a pictorial history of the Flash Fair might be useful, so I took photos tonight and I'll get more tomorrow."

Jessica looked ready to say something, but his parents were approaching and she closed her mouth.

"Carl says we're finished for the evening," Thomas explained. "Jessica, we've been getting acquainted with your grandmother. Her stories about living abroad are much more interesting than ours. We'd love to hear more of them, so please let us take you all out to dinner. Penny told us she's free, but that she couldn't speak for you and Cyndi."

"We hear there's a good Chinese restaurant in town," his mother added, "but would your daughter prefer pizza?"

"Uh…sure," Jessica agreed, "the Hong Kong would be fine."

Thomas clasped his hands together. "Excellent. Shall we meet there in twenty minutes?"

"Sounds good. I'll go talk to Grams."

Logan's mother gave him an apologetic look

when they were alone. "We're sorry. We should have asked you ahead of time."

"It's fine," he assured her. "We all need to eat."

"Good. You know, Penny Parrish is a remarkable woman. Her stories make us wish we'd gotten away more often from cities in the countries where we lived. Diplomatic circles can be stifling."

Thomas nodded and Logan's brain reeled. He felt as if the entire world as he'd known it was being spun on its axis.

THE LAST THING Jessica wanted was to eat dinner with Logan and his parents. But it would have been rude to wriggle out of the invitation.

Her grandmother and daughter were sitting on a bench.

"Hungry?" she asked. "We're going to the Hong Kong with the Kensingtons."

"Whoopppee." Cyndi jumped with enthusiasm.

"It was thoughtful of them to invite us," Penny said. "They wanted to include Kevin, but he had to get home for a video visit with his daughter and son-in-law."

"Uncle Kevin mentioned they were talking

online a lot. Why don't you take Cyndi to the restaurant, and I'll meet you after I do a final check with Carl?"

She half hoped that Carl had something urgently needing resolution—that way she could phone Grams with an apology to the Kensingtons. But he shook his head.

"We're good," he said, tossing a sleeping bag over his shoulder. He and a group of high school students from his shop class were spending the night in the park to keep an eye on everything. The kids were excited about camping in the middle of town.

Jessica drove to the Hong Kong, where the Kensingtons had gotten a large round table. Thomas seated her next to Logan, while he and his wife sat opposite.

"Why does this feel like a job interview?" she murmured to Logan.

"Because that's what it is," he replied in an equally low tone. "You're being vetted as a prospective daughter-in-law."

"*Jeez.*"

"Exactly. I expected more subtlety with their background in diplomacy. But chin up, you only have to survive one dinner."

His amused exasperation took the edge off

the situation, so Jessica focused on her menu. She didn't honestly think the Kensingtons saw her as a prospective daughter-in-law. They were probably just wondering how their world-traveled son had gotten tangled up with a local town project like the Flash Fair.

Rather than perusing the menu himself, Logan lifted the camera around his neck and began taking pictures until she nudged him with her elbow.

"Visit more, take pictures less," she whispered.

He put the camera down.

Grams took Cyndi to the restroom to wash her hands, and when they returned, Regina looked around the table. "How about eating family style? We can each choose a dish we like, and then add a few more, and share."

There was a chorus of agreement. Ordering went quickly and won ton soup was soon delivered to the table. As they ate, Regina and Tom exchanged memories with Grams about life abroad. Cyndi listened with bright-eyed fascination.

"I'm amazed by her concentration," Logan murmured. "She does well in a group of adults."

"She can get the wiggles the same as any

child, but she usually stays quiet for Grams's stories."

"I'm still amazed. Before I forget," Logan said, "this morning Chelsea mentioned a concern about limited parking at the wedding next Saturday. I understand Kevin is driving Penny with some other friends, so why don't we ride-share, as well? I'm taking my SUV, so I'll have plenty of room for you and Cyndi, even with all my photography equipment."

"Are you attending as a friend, or as their photographer?" Jessica asked.

"Chelsea and Barton have a photographer—somebody his parents know—but I want to take pictures as a backup. I've seen horrendous wedding photos over the years."

If it was anyone other than Logan, Jessica might accept that as a reason, but his discomfort with marriage made her think he preferred watching the festivities from behind his camera. Not that it was her place to object. He'd offered them a ride, he hadn't asked her to be his date.

"I'm okay with ridesharing," she agreed. "Let me know when you want to leave. We can meet at your house or in town, if you aren't moved in by then."

"Nah, I'll pick you up. I've started sleeping at the house instead of the apartment, though not this evening since I need to run my parents back to their hotel and pick them up in the morning. They have a rental car, but I'd prefer us all coming together."

Cyndi was yawning by the time the fortune cookies arrived, so Jessica stood and smiled at the elder Kensingtons. "I should get my daughter to bed—we have a big day tomorrow. But thank you for dinner."

"The pleasure was ours," Tom said. "We'll see you in the morning."

Jessica urged Cyndi from her chair and led her to the car.

She wondered how Logan felt about the evening, jokes about daughter-in-law interviews aside. Still, he could probably handle a cozy family meal, provided long-term commitments weren't involved.

BACK AT HIS APARTMENT, Logan copied the photos he'd taken to his laptop and studied them. They weren't unique, just shots of people working and laughing together. But using his telephoto lens, he'd also gotten several of Jessica. Her vitality leaped off the screen. It was mesmerizing, the way she seemed to inspire people to action.

Or maybe she was just plain mesmerizing.

He frowned. Both Penny and her granddaughter were beautiful, dynamic women, and Cyndi was a bright, eager child who took after them. He just wished he could call Jessica's parents and ask if they had a clue what they were missing.

Churning inside, Logan dropped into bed. The city traffic outside his window seemed unusually loud, and then he realized it was just in contrast to the quiet of Regen Valley.

Unbelievable.

He punched his pillow. He'd slept in every imaginable place—some noisy, some quiet and some miserably uncomfortable. Most of the time, he dropped off like a rock.

Logan closed his eyes again, only to see Jessica's face, and it wasn't through a camera lens.

It was bad enough that after the movers had left on Tuesday last week, he'd started imagining a woman's purse hanging on the hook by the door. A child drawing pictures. The scent from a pot of chili wafting from the kitchen. And the sound of a baby crying in a room that didn't even exist. Was it possible that his longing for a home betrayed a deeper desire to belong? Perhaps he wasn't as detached as he had always thought.

Logan turned over again.

It was going to be a long night.

LOGAN DRAGGED HIMSELF into the shower the next morning, hoping a cold dousing would make him more alert. On the way to his parents' hotel, he stopped at a coffee kiosk and ordered a cup with an extra shot of espresso. He nearly gagged on his first gulp—Jessica's coffee was infinitely better.

Though they were early, the traffic into Regen Valley was heavier than he'd ever seen it. The street fair wasn't officially open for another half hour, but they still had to park six blocks from the sectioned-off downtown area.

"Attendance should be good," Thomas said with satisfaction. "Jessica will be pleased."

Logan didn't doubt it. "I just got involved a few weeks ago, but the committee has put a huge amount of time and effort into the event."

"You've contributed, too," his mother said stoutly. "Penny says you're donating photography sessions for the auction and that you've gotten several celebrities to attend the fair. It was sweet of you to do that for Jessica."

He wanted to protest that he hadn't done it *for* Jessica. After all, it was a good cause. But he wasn't convinced himself, so how could he convince anyone else?

Perhaps it was his guilty conscience about the stress he and his partners were putting her through. Ultimately they couldn't force the Crystal Connection to move in the near future, but she had to be wondering what would happen if she refused. It was to the point he'd be willing to personally pay for the entire remodel of the back area, but that wasn't feasible. He had some savings, but not the kind of finances for what would be involved. So he was devoting a huge amount of time to get the information needed for a decision. In fact, he'd just gotten in touch with a fourth contractor for ideas and costs.

"I wonder where Jessica might be?" mused his mother.

As if in answer, Jessica came around the corner with Carl Sheffield, both in red T-shirts. They were laughing and Logan found himself taking pictures again. She wasn't wearing makeup and her soft hair was already sliding free of her French braid, but he couldn't imagine a better subject for a photo.

"Hi," she called, coming over. "We officially open at nine, but with so many people here, most of the booths have opened early."

"We can't wait to explore," Regina told her. "It's remarkable how everything has come together."

Jessica grinned. "I feel the same. Logan, the Bryant twins are scheduled to begin signing autographs at 10:00 a.m., and Laurel Stevenson at eleven. Cara Williams will start at noon, followed by Alyssa Jeffries and Martin Carter at one o'clock. We thought it might be best to stagger the start times. Remember, the autograph stations are in the park if you want to be there."

"I remember."

"Then go enjoy yourselves."

His parents wanted them to stay together as a group, so after they wandered around for while, they all headed for the park. Long lines had already formed in front of the Bryants' autograph stations. Adam and his wife arrived shortly afterward, along with Tiffany and Glen.

The day before, Adam had announced that

Cassie was pregnant and he still looked exhilarated.

"Are you ready for this?" Logan had asked.

"More than ready," Adam had declared with unquestioned confidence. He was even looking forward to diapers and 2:00 a.m. feedings. He'd told Logan that with Cassie's niece and nephew they'd jumped into parenting in the middle; now they'd find out what it was like to start at the beginning.

Logan was happy for his friend. Fatherhood no longer seemed like such an odd choice for Adam, though he hadn't changed his mind about becoming a father himself.

Nevertheless…he looked at Jessica, who had just arrived. As she chatted with Adam and Cassie, she stroked her daughter's hair, and for the first time in his life, Logan seriously wondered what it would be like to have that kind of connection. *To be a husband and father.*

His time wouldn't be his own, and he couldn't just disappear for the weekend to take pictures. He'd often been told that children required routine and he'd always hated the idea of following the same schedule, day after day.

But still…

CHAPTER FIFTEEN

JESSICA KNEW ADAM WILDING but had met his wife only once.

They were a nice couple, busy raising Cassie's niece and nephew. Today they were positively glowing. The reason seemed clear when Jessica spotted the large round button on Tiffany's T-shirt that announced *I'm Going to Be a Big Sister.*

"I'm just guessing, but are congratulations in order?" she asked.

"That's right." Adam grinned from ear to ear. "Cassie is six weeks along."

Since pregnancy had prompted a far different reaction from Jessica's ex-husband, she appreciated his excitement. He was a proud, ecstatic papa-to-be.

"That's wonderful. Any cravings yet, Cassie?"

"None so far, but the food I can smell from the booths is driving me crazy. We try to eat healthy, so I'm going to blame my indulgences on the baby."

"Sounds good to me."

Adam put a hand on Glen's shoulder and leaned forward to say something to both kids. They nodded and headed for their respective autograph stations. The people waiting in the two lines—predominantly other teens and preteens—cheered.

Jessica held up a pair of gift bags. "These are for Tiffany and Glen to thank them for coming."

"That's so thoughtful," Cassie said, accepting the bags. "Though totally unnecessary. The twins were thrilled to be asked. Tiff practically did handstands."

"Well, I hope you enjoy yourselves. If you need anything, ask somebody wearing a T-shirt like mine." Jessica gestured to her bright red shirt with *Flash Committee* printed on it.

"Thanks."

Jessica's cell phone beeped. It was a text, reminding her that the fire department's skit on fire safety would soon be starting.

"I hope I see you later," she said to Tom and Regina before leaving. "Thanks again for dinner last night."

"It was our pleasure."

Jessica headed for the fire station with Cyndi. She didn't need to return to the autograph stations in the park; Carl was delivering Laurel's gift bag, and other members of the Flash Committee would greet the remaining three celebrities. Right now she was just on call, though later she was taking her turn on the dunk tank.

A crowd had already gathered outside the main doors of the firehouse. The department had been performing the same skit for twenty-five years, but they enjoyed doing it so much that everyone else had fun watching. Jessica's favorite part was when the fire chief started singing and his crew doused him with a hose.

"Thank you," said Chief Delgado at the end. He bowed, still dripping with water. "We'll be back in an hour."

"I took bunches of pictures," Cyndi said, coming over to join Jessica. She'd been at the front of the crowd, watching with the other kids.

"It's okay just to watch, too," Jessica reminded her gently. She didn't want to make a big deal about it, but she also wanted her daughter to learn balance.

"I know, but I gotta practice."

An hour later they crossed paths once more with Regina Kensington, who still looked spotless in her cream linen slacks and white silk blouse. Jessica wouldn't have dared to wear clothes like that at a street fair; they'd be ruined in five minutes.

Regina looked at Cyndi. "Are you having a good time, little one?"

"Uh-huh." Cyndi lifted her camera and took a picture of her. "See? I want to be just like Logan. Momma, can I go take pictures of Grandma selling candy? And to help her," she added quickly.

Jessica hesitated and then nodded. "That's fine. Stay until I come for you." The candy booth was just a short distance away, but she watched until her daughter was safely inside before turning back to Logan's mother. "When do you fly home?"

"Monday morning. We love being here, but we don't want to take too much of Logan's time. How long have you known him?"

"A little over a month."

"I would have guessed longer. You know, Regen Valley is such a peaceful little town that it hardly seems possible we're so close to metropolitan Seattle."

Jessica understood how she felt. "Several communities in the Pacific Northwest have the same hidden-away feeling, probably because of all the hills and waterways. Naturally I think Regen Valley is the best, but I'm biased. I spent summers here with my grandparents as a kid. It's always felt like home."

Regina's face turned wistful. "Logan doesn't have a place like that. Our assignments were usually a few months…a year or two at most. It's difficult to form ties."

"He's mentioned living in a number of different countries. He must have enjoyed the travel, since he continued doing it in his career."

"Perhaps, but I know we shouldn't have remained in the diplomatic service for so long. Tom tried to resign when Logan was five and they begged him to stay. He has special skills that always seemed to be needed somewhere, and each new country required learning different protocols and customs. We were constantly walking a political tightrope, which meant our son had to walk it right along with us."

The intimate conversation was surprising, but maybe Regina needed reassurance.

"Logan is a good person," Jessica said firmly. "He said it's been hard to spend much time together over the past few years, but I know he wants you to be part of his life."

Regina's smile quivered. "That's kind of you. It's a comfort knowing you're his friend. But I mustn't be selfish and keep you from your responsibilities. The boys will be back soon. I bought some patchwork quilts and pillow covers, so they took everything to the car."

Friend? Jessica blinked. Her relationship with Logan was more frenemy than friend given the agency's request to relocate the store, but the other woman wouldn't appreciate hearing it.

"I'll volunteer to help in the candy booth," Regina added. "It would be good for the boys to have time together without me."

The way she called her husband and son "the boys" was endearing, but Jessica didn't have time to really consider it—her phone beeped for the ninth time that morning with a text message. She pulled it out and looked at the screen.

"Is something wrong?" Regina asked.

"I'm needed at the health station. We have a lost child looking for his parents. See you later."

"I DON'T KNOW how she expects to get this home on the plane," Thomas Kensington grumbled as they stowed his wife's purchases in the back of Logan's SUV. There were seven patchwork quilts and other assorted handiwork that she'd explained were gifts for potential donors to the clinic.

"I know Mom. She usually has some room in her luggage. The rest can be shipped."

Tom snorted. "Room? She brought three times the number of clothes she needed. Maybe she was nervous about the trip, because it simply isn't like her."

Logan agreed. He'd learned his minimalist travel style from his mother, not his father. Regina Kensington believed in bringing exactly what she needed and no more. It helped that his parents usually stayed in the kind of establishment that provided laundry and dry-cleaning services.

They headed back to the street fair and he saw his mother waving at them from inside the candy booth.

"I'm volunteering for a while," she explained. "Maybe you can find the health station and help Jessica. They have a child looking for his parents."

Obviously Jessica and his mother had spoken, which led Logan to wondering what they'd spoken about.

"Happy to help. Can't have a lost child," Thomas said.

But when they reached the health station they were told the family had been reunited.

Jessica was talking to a paramedic and Logan began snapping pictures. He'd put four extra memory cards in his pocket early that morning, just in case, and it was starting to look as if he'd need them.

Through the viewfinder he saw her glance his direction and wrinkle her nose. She finished her conversation and came over.

"Don't take so many pictures that you forget to enjoy the fair," she urged. Her light tone didn't fool Logan. She'd called his camera a barrier between him and the rest of the world.

"Sure. What food do you recommend?"

She shook her head. "I can't recommend one vendor over another. The competition between them is too fierce and I might be accused of favoritism."

"Perhaps we should get a sample from each of them."

"Then you'll need an unusually hearty appetite and patience for long lines."

Logan eyed the crowds of cheerful people queuing up at the different booths. The lines were moving quickly, but he probably wouldn't have the patience to wait in one, much less all of them. Ironic. He was willing to wait hours for a single great photograph of a bear. But not for food.

He wasn't even hungry because of the hearty breakfast burrito he'd gotten earlier when things were quieter.

A family went by, carrying heaping plates of barbecued ribs and potato salad. Logan's mouth watered. Maybe he could handle *one* line today; the question was which one.

"Uh, I'll talk to my folks and see what they want to do."

"Good decision."

Jessica walked away, hips swaying gently while the sun sparked fiery glints off her hair. For once Logan didn't lift his camera—this was one image he couldn't store electronically. He needed to capture it in his brain.

PENNY WAS PLEASED with the brisk candy sales. Even though cooks from all over Regen Valley had contributed their homemade confections, they were already running low on supplies.

"My great-grandma made that one," Cyndi told a customer, pointing to a container of cappuccino fudge. "It's the best and it's almost gone."

"All the fudge is good," Penny scolded in a light tone.

"But yours *is* best, Grandma."

The customer, a woman wearing a Seattle Seahawks T-shirt, just laughed and followed Cyndi's recommendation.

Regina Kensington had been helping with the sales, but now she took money from her purse and bought the last container of cappuccino fudge. "I don't want to miss getting some," she explained, tucking her purchase into a new tote, decorated with a patchwork square.

A short time later Jessica brought them cups of coffee. "Grams, someone is replacing you at one o'clock, right? Though it doesn't look as if they'll have much to sell by then."

"Yes, at one. Carl has someone getting more candy from a warehouse store. Anyway, it should be quiet for a while. Over the noon hour people are more interested in hamburgers than sweets."

"That's true. Call if you need anything."

She smiled at Regina and left with Cyndi.

"Goodness, your granddaughter is a bundle of energy," Regina said when they were alone.

"She knows how to get things done." Penny surveyed their remaining stock of candy with exasperation. "I wish we had more fudge and English toffee. Store-bought candy won't be as popular and the profit margin will be smaller. Still, every bit counts."

"You sure sound like a savvy businesswoman."

"I should be after so many years in business. My husband and I started the Crystal Connection. It's Jessica's now because we wanted her to have it after he was gone. But I still manage the trade network we set up with our friends in other countries."

Regina traced the lettering on the cash box.

"If you don't mind me asking, how long have you been alone?"

"A lifetime in emotions, nine months now by the calendar."

Regina shivered. "Tom had a health scare in February. It turned out all right, but we were both reminded that time shouldn't be wasted."

"Then his problem was a blessing in disguise."

"I suppose. I—" Regina stopped, her attention caught by something down the street. Following her gaze, Penny saw Logan, and looking in the direction his camera was pointed, she saw Jessica and Cyndi.

"Do you think there's anything between them?" Regina asked wistfully.

"I've wondered, but don't get your hopes up. Jessica's marriage ended badly and I suspect your son isn't too keen on permanent relationships."

"Logan likes his freedom. But what about you? Do you think you would ever consider remarrying? I'm only asking because Kevin McClaskey seems to be such a close friend."

"I'm not ready for anything like that," Penny said, though she'd been thinking a lot about Kevin. Lately their relationship had been changing—it was even beginning to feel as if it was more than friendship.

But romance? She still thought the idea was ridiculous for a woman her age.

Wasn't it?

Her mind was buzzing as a customer came up to buy a package of soda cracker candy.

She didn't want to upset her relationship with Kevin, but it would be best to get things out in the open and discuss their expectations honestly. After all, she was too mature and they'd known each other too long for silly games and girlish embarrassment.

LOGAN CAUGHT UP with Jessica again at the silent auction booth. An impressive collection of items were displayed—restaurant gift certificates, small appliances, antiques, pieces of art and everything in between. Ten items were being auctioned off each hour and people were engaging in friendly rivalry.

"Your calendars are doing well," Jessica told him. In addition to four professional photo shoots, he'd donated several copies of the calendars for the auction. Jessica had insisted he sign them, though it felt pretentious, especially since his name was already on the front.

"That's nice. Just to keep you in the loop, I'm moving as fast as I can to get the figures and information together for my partners."

A shadow crossed her face and Logan kicked himself. Today of all days, Jessica didn't need to be reminded of the rental issue.

"Thanks. I knew it would take a while."

Carl strode up to them. "Jessica, a television crew is here to interview you."

Her eyes widened and she tensed. "You're the head of the event. You should talk to them."

"But you're the committee chair. Besides, your pretty face is much more appealing than mine." Carl gestured and a man hurried over, a cameraman following.

"Are you Ms. Parrish?"

"Yes."

"Mr. Sheffield tells us you're responsible for getting the Flash Committee together. Can you tell us about it?"

Logan watched as Jessica explained the need for a clinic with the same clear, passionate voice that must have gotten the project started in the first place.

"We've had phenomenal people working on this," she concluded. "Carl Sheffield has worked tirelessly as the guy in charge of the

Flash Fair. I can't thank our volunteers enough, or the members of the community who are raising money in the different booths."

The reporter thanked her and asked the cameraman to get general footage of the booths and games.

"Great job, kid, you're amazing." Carl kissed her cheek and then checked his phone. "And you didn't even miss your turn on the dunk tank. You have just enough time to change."

"Come on, Momma," Cyndi urged, pulling on her mother's hand.

Logan's father approached, and Logan had a feeling he'd been waiting until Jessica was gone.

"That's an incredible young woman," Thomas said. "I've known ambassadors who couldn't handle an interview so well."

It was the highest praise his father knew how to give.

"Right," Logan agreed. "Are you enjoying the fair?"

"I haven't gone to anything like this since I was a boy. The family warmth here is so… Let's just say that it's become increasingly important to me lately."

Logan was caught by the sheen in his father's eyes. He'd never seen Thomas Kensington so emotional before. "Is something wrong, Dad?"

"No, no, not now. But Regina made me promise to tell you that I needed surgery a few months ago. The tests were negative and I'm fine, but she thought you should know."

Adrenaline sent Logan's heart racing. "*Of course I should know.* I should have known when it was happening. Why didn't you tell me?"

"You were busy, in Japan, I think. We didn't want to worry you unnecessarily."

Logan tried to calm down, juggling both alarm and relief. And on its heels came another question—did his parents keep him in the dark because they hadn't believed he'd be there for them, anyway?

"I'm glad it turned out all right," he finally said. "But don't ever do that again. If something is wrong, call me. Please."

"You do the same. Now, let's see what's going on with this silent auction."

They examined the items currently being auctioned. Logan wrote down a bid on a good watercolor landscape by a local artist, but his father promptly outbid him by a generous amount.

"I hope I win. It would be a fine souvenir of our visit," Thomas said with a grin.

Together they strolled through the bustling crowd. Before long they came to the dunk booth, where Jessica was perched over a deep tank of water.

"You have to do better if you're going to turn me into a mermaid," she called to the man throwing balls at the release mechanism. She was laughing and her hair was wet, so she must have been dunked at least once. The red Flash Committee T-shirt was plastered to her slim body, but she'd changed from her jeans into a pair of nylon shorts.

"Remarkable," Thomas marveled. "I've never known anyone quite like her."

Logan had to agree.

WHEN JESSICA FINISHED her turn at the dunk tank she dashed into the changing tent clutching a towel. She shivered. Spring in the Pacific Northwest was unpredictable, but they'd gotten lucky for the street fair—it was sunny, if not that warm.

Yikes. She dropped her wet clothes into a

plastic bag and shimmied back into her jeans and a dry T-shirt.

"Hi, Momma," Cyndi squealed when she came out of the tent. "Is it okay that I threw balls to dunk you? Grandma and Regina said you wouldn't mind. They bought me tickets."

"You bet it's okay." Jessica hugged her daughter and smiled at the two women who seemed to be forming a friendship.

Logan walked up between Grams and his mother and put an arm around each of their shoulders. "Dad is holding a table. I got pit barbecue plates for everyone from the Flash Committee's booth. Jessica, since the booth isn't in the competition, you won't be showing favoritism to eat with us. Come on, you must be starving after getting dunked."

She couldn't refuse, not with Grams nodding agreement and Cyndi jumping up and down with her usual excitement.

Initially the elder Kensingtons regarded their plates with caution, but that didn't last.

"Delicious," Regina declared after taking a tentative bite. "I've never had pit barbecue before."

"Ed Schindler is famous for it in Regen Valley," Jessica said. "He not only offered to take charge, he found his own volunteers and got a packing company to donate the meat."

"I admire the strong community spirit everyone seems to have." Tom seemed to be enjoying the food as much as his wife. "Metropolitan areas have community pride, but this is special. We thought Regen Valley was an interesting choice for Logan, but we're starting to understand."

"I already like it here," Logan said.

Jessica smiled faintly as their gazes met. She remained skeptical about his long-term residency but wouldn't say so in front of his parents. Part of her still wished he'd decide Regen Valley wasn't the place for him, but he was an undeniable asset to the community. News about the celebrities he'd invited had gone viral and he'd worked hard in every other way.

It would be petty to deny Logan's good qualities.

And she shouldn't keep prodding him about staying behind his camera. But he'd rejected love without having any idea of what he was missing…though considering how badly it had worked out for her, maybe he was the smart one.

CHAPTER SIXTEEN

A WEEK LATER, Jessica glanced at the mirror as the doorbell rang, hoping she wasn't over- or underdressed. Chelsea's wedding invitation had said to be comfortable, so she'd chosen outfits for Cyndi and herself that she hoped would be nice enough to honor the occasion without looking too casual.

Cyndi opened the door. "Hi, Logan. We're all ready. Momma says it isn't polite to keep people waiting."

"That's very considerate, but before we leave, I want to give you something." He carried a box to one of the Morris chairs and set it down.

Cyndi looked inside and jumped up and down with excitement. "Momma, look!"

Jessica came over. In the box were a large number of matted photographs. She flipped through them and saw portraits of the kids from her daughter's girl rangers troop. But they weren't the kind you got from a photography studio—they were natural, unaffected, charming pictures.

She looked questioningly at Logan. "How?"

"With digital cameras you can take more photos than anyone realizes. Remember at one point I had the troop pose for a group picture? I used it to be sure I could get a portrait of each of them from the candid shots."

Cyndi hugged him. "Thank you bunches and bunches."

"You're very welcome. I thought you could hand them out at your next troop meeting."

"I'm going to get extra points!"

His grin made Jessica's stomach flip.

"That took a lot of time and effort," she said. If they'd been dating, she might have thought he was trying to impress her through her daughter, but they weren't. Besides, a man like Logan Kensington didn't need to impress women; they probably flung themselves at his feet.

He shrugged. "It wasn't that much. I finished them after Mom and Dad flew home. Shall we go?"

"Sure." Jessica collected her daughter's booster seat by the door, along with her purse and the sun hat she'd gotten for the occasion.

"Cyndi is still small enough to require a child's safety seat in the car," she explained.

His nonplussed expression almost made her laugh. He truly didn't have a clue about parenting. "Uh, can I help?"

"No need." She positioned the booster in the back of the SUV and buckled Cyndi into it.

"Has everyone recovered from the Flash Fair?" he said when they were on the road.

"They seem to be. We hope to announce the final figures at the meeting next week. Preliminary counts are unbelievably good. Carl is our high school shop teacher and his students have made a ten-foot-tall 'thermometer' to put in the city square so the community can track our progress."

"Good idea."

Silence followed until Jessica couldn't take it any longer. "I seem to remember that Chelsea is related to Nicole."

"They're sisters-in-law. Chelsea is her husband's younger sister. We hired her before Nicole and Jordan got serious, but Nicole knew both of them as kids."

"They were childhood sweethearts?"

"Not exactly." His dry tone suggested there was a story behind the story.

"Amy Gonzales says she already knows who she wants to marry," Cyndi said. "That's silly. The only boys we know are yucko."

Logan coughed. "You, uh, might change your mind someday."

"No way. Timmy Stines eats crawfish. And Johnny Richards likes spiders. Not to eat, he just likes them. The other boys are worse. Totally yucko."

"I can see why you'd have a problem with marrying one of them," Logan choked out.

Jessica rubbed her mouth to keep from laughing. "Sweetheart, why don't you tell Logan about your new kitten?"

Cyndi didn't need more encouragement. The doctor had ruled out an allergy to cats, always a concern with asthma, so a few days ago they'd adopted a twelve-week-old brown tuxedo tabby from the Regen Valley Shelter. Buster and Cyndi had quickly become inseparable. He slept on her bed and lay on her lap when she was reading, purring so loud it made her giggle. She was still talking about him when they reached their destination, where her attention was quickly diverted.

"Look, Momma, more kids!"

She immediately ran to join the group of children.

Logan grinned. "Barton and Chelsea just met last year. It's a good thing, or I'd spend the whole ceremony wondering how many times she'd called him yucko growing up."

"Did you have a yuck factor as a kid?"

"Do you think I'd admit it?"

"Probably not."

Tall and handsome, his eyes crinkling with humor, Logan wasn't yucko anymore, if he'd ever been. Any woman in her right mind would be thrilled to have him as her escort to a wedding. But he wasn't escorting her, Jessica reminded herself. He had merely offered them a ride. It was important to keep her feet firmly planted on the ground.

KEVIN WAS UNCOMFORTABLE on one of the little white chairs that people rented for weddings, but he was happy to be sitting next to Penny. They were quite early, so they'd gotten seats in the back and were enjoying the fresh country air.

"What a beautiful place for a wedding," Penny murmured. "It's nice that Chelsea's in-laws-to-be have such a large garden."

"Yeah, it's great."

She turned toward him. "Listen, there's something I've been wanting to discuss. We... well, we've been friends a long time, and I hope we can be honest with each other."

Fear clutched Kevin's stomach. Was Penny sick? "Of course. What is it?"

"Lately it seems as if our friendship is changing."

"I think so, too," he said, his anxiety easing. He hadn't consciously thought about what those changes meant, but Penny was becoming important to him in a way that extended beyond friendship.

She put her hand on his arm. "But we need to consider whether there's a real bond growing between us, or is it mostly loneliness and wanting to be with someone comfortable?"

A laugh rumbled from his belly and Penny frowned.

"This isn't a joke, Kevin."

"I realize that. It's just funny how you've always challenged me to go deeper. You challenged all of us. Eric might have been the anthropologist, but you understand people."

"Okay, then what do you think?"

He gazed at Penny, evaluating what she'd

said. She was so much like Allison, and yet so different. Yes, he was lonely. His wife had shared everything with him—they'd been companions, best friends and lovers, the finest foundation he could imagine for a marriage. But he didn't believe loneliness explained his growing feelings for Penny.

"It's more than loneliness," he said finally.

She inclined her head. "Okay. But you should also know that I'm not ready."

"That's all right, I'm not going anywhere. Time will tell whether we stay friends or become something else."

He curled his fingers around hers.

PENNY SMILED.

It was nice to just sit and hold hands with someone. Kevin would be an easy man to love. He was honest and dependable, caring and thoughtful. And he had a sense of humor, an essential quality in her opinion.

But it was too soon for her. It wasn't because Eric would have objected. She knew he'd tell her to get on with life, the same way she knew he was patiently waiting for the time they'd be together again.

As Kevin had said, time would tell.

Across the yard she saw Jessica with Logan. Her granddaughter had stressed it wasn't a date—they were only driving together to save parking. But date or not, he seemed to be hovering nearby. From a distance it was hard to read his expression, but a stranger would assume they were a couple.

"You're wondering about Jessica and Logan, aren't you?" Kevin guessed.

She turned around. "How did you know?"

"Because I keep wondering the same thing. There's an energy that happens when they're together. Logan seems more aware and Jessica seems more yearning."

"It would break my heart if she got hurt again."

"We can't protect her, no matter how much we both want to. I'm afraid we have to just wait and be patient."

Penny squeezed Kevin's hand, thinking it would be polite to get up and meet some of the other guests.

But maybe she'd wait another few minutes.

LOGAN HAD EXPECTED to circulate and take pictures, not stay at Jessica's side, but he knew she wasn't acquainted with many of the guests.

It was mostly an excuse; he didn't know that many of them, either. Now, seeing her against the background of flowers and wedding decor, he wondered if she'd had a real wedding. She would make a beautiful bride.

"Weddings are nice," she said.

"Was yours?" Logan winced. "Sorry, I shouldn't have asked."

Her smile was shaded with sadness. "I'm not sensitive about it. Essentially we eloped, so there weren't any picture albums or wedding garters to throw away after the divorce."

"You didn't want a more formal event?"

"I didn't care. I thought getting married would make everything okay and we'd be magically healed of anything that had ever hurt us. It was almost laughable. I wanted to play house and Aaron wanted to be beer pong champion of his college fraternity. We were two immature kids who didn't understand anything about marriage or how to make it work. My neediness scared him."

"Shouldn't a husband and wife be able to rely on each other? Marriage isn't just about raising kids and having someone to eat dinner with every day."

Jessica focused on the group of children

where Cyndi was playing. "I agree. A couple should learn and grow and be better people because they're together. But in a healthy way, with both of them working on it."

Since Logan had never seriously contemplated the wedded state, talking about it seemed bizarre. But Jessica's regrets were forcing him to think. "Maybe part of the answer is loving someone else as much as you love yourself."

"You're right. No one should always be giving, and the other always taking. Over the long haul it should balance."

Logan chuckled. "For two people determined to stay single, we're waxing philosophical about marriage."

"It's in the standard wedding handbook—rule 263. 'Guests are to consider the significance of two people making vows.'"

"You're making that up."

"You think?" Her laugh made the day seem even brighter.

"Logan, Jessica, come sign the book," Nicole called to them. "We're asking everyone to write a short message to the bride and groom."

"Where does this go?" Jessica held up a gift bag.

"There's a table by the pink rhododendron."

Jessica wrote on a page and went to deposit her gift.

Logan read her inscription.

To Chelsea and Barton,
Your love and commitment will give you
joy in the good days and help you through
the hard ones. Wishing you the very best.
—Jessica Parrish.

"Can't figure out what to write?" Nicole asked as he hesitated.

"Are we supposed to give advice? Anything I say would be a contender for one of those lists. You know, the 'Ten Worst Things Ever Said to a Bride and Groom.'"

"Advice isn't necessary. Anyhow, it's difficult to come up with something on the spur of the moment, though I must say, I like what Jessica wrote."

Logan liked it, too. Still dubious, he lifted the pen.

Chelsea and Barton, I hope you find
something to be glad about, even on the
worst days. You deserve it. Logan.

Nicole read the brief message and looked at him. "That's unexpected."

"Just building on what Jessica wrote."

A worried crease appeared in Nicole's forehead. "That reminds me—when do you think you'll have the information together on the potential remodel?"

"Sometime next week."

"Good. It's admirable that Jessica didn't simply dismiss our request for her to move, though I've been feeling more and more guilty about it. According to the lease she has the right to stay put, at least for the time being, but she's giving it serious thought and even suggested an alternative for consideration."

"I know."

Cassie and Jessica were talking by the gift table and as Logan caught up with them, he felt like a moth attracted to a flame. Jessica was wearing a rose-colored gown with short sleeves and a full skirt that fell in long, graceful folds. Its simplicity gave it an air of elegance…or was that the woman inside the dress?

"Hey, Logan," Cassie said. "We were just saying that Barton's parents could rent this place out as a wedding venue."

"Or for fashion shoots," he agreed.

He put his gift with the other wedding presents. He'd considered asking Jessica's advice about what would be appropriate, only to dismiss the idea and choose something from the wedding registry. The agency's official gift was a set of Waterford Crystal goblets and three weeks of paid vacation for Chelsea to use for her honeymoon.

"Are you all right, Cassie?" he heard Jessica ask urgently. "You suddenly went pale."

He wheeled in time to see Cassie wrinkle her nose. "It's just morning sickness. I was fine until a second ago, then whoosh. But I'm so happy about the baby I can't complain."

"Should I get Adam?" Logan asked.

"Don't you dare. He worries too much."

"How about peppermint candy?" Jessica asked, taking a bag from her purse. "It might help."

"I'll try anything. This is Chelsea's special day and I don't want to spend it in her in-laws' bathroom."

Cassie unwrapped a piece and stuck it in her mouth while Logan fetched a chair. He felt like a fish out of water. Everything in the air was about pregnancy, love and romance.

She sank down and a few minutes later the color crept back into her face. "Thanks, I think the peppermint helped."

"Keep them," Jessica said as Cassie tried to return the bag. "I have more. When you have a chance, consider getting ginger lozenges, too. Both helped when I was pregnant."

"Good idea. I'll share the info with Rachel. She's in her first trimester, just like me."

An older man approached them. "Is everything all right?"

"Absolutely." Cassie smiled up at him. "I'm Cassie Wilding, and this is Jessica Parrish and Logan Kensington."

"Don Smith. I'm the grateful father of the happy groom. We're delighted to have Chelsea joining our family, though she's already so much a part of us the wedding is just a formality."

"That's how it should be," Jessica said. "Oh, and thanks for including my daughter in the invitation."

"Ah, which one is yours?"

Jessica pointed. "Cyndi is in the lavender dress."

"She seems to be having a good time. Just so you know, we don't have assigned seating for the meal. There's a children's table, but Cyndi is welcome to sit with you if preferred. Also, anyone without a camera or phone for pictures is being invited to use one of the disposable kinds for candid shots. There's a whole basket of them."

As the conversation continued with Don and Cassie, Logan just watched, absorbing Jessica's warmth and beauty. The contrast between her easy grace with people and his own stumbling efforts seemed to mock him.

To regain his equilibrium, he began roaming back and forth, taking photos as he went.

JESSICA HATED SEEING Logan withdraw behind his camera. At the Flash Fair he'd finally seemed to loosen up and enjoy himself. Now he was back to snapping pictures as if his life depended upon it.

To be fair, weddings weren't his milieu. A man who'd rejected love and marriage wouldn't be comfortable surrounded by white lace and roses. She didn't blame him; her own feelings about it were mixed.

She'd often questioned whether she'd genuinely loved Aaron. It had felt real at the time, but now she'd met a man who was so compelling he made her college romance look like child's play. If she hadn't learned from her old mistakes, she might pursue Logan, believing love was worth the risk. In theory she still believed that, but whenever she thought of taking the chance, cold reality brought her up short.

Despite the counseling and years of dealing with her issues, she still could repeat her mistakes. If Logan ever got married, which seemed unlikely, he'd want someone independent, who wasn't emotionally hungry. Besides, he erected walls and lived behind them. Life would be complicated with such a man.

Trying to subdue her inner turmoil, Jessica went to speak with Cyndi, who was having a wonderful time taking pictures and playing games with the other children.

"Look, Momma," she said, holding up a disposable camera. "These have film, but they aren't as much fun 'cuz you can't see the picture right away. They have to be developed, like Logan told us about at my girl ranger meeting."

"The disposable cameras are to make sure Chelsea and Barton get lots of different pictures. You don't need one—we'll give Chelsea a copy of all the pictures you take on your own camera."

"I just want to give her the good ones," Cyndi said gravely. "Wanna see?"

"Of course, I do." Jessica sat down on the grass and pulled her daughter onto her lap.

For a moment, she almost forgot everything else. At this moment in her life, Cyndi was all she needed.

LOGAN STOOD PARTLY concealed by bushes and took picture after picture of the milling guests. It was akin to capturing photos of wildlife. Models were accustomed to cameras, but outside the industry, people could be uncomfortable having a lens pointed at them. By stepping back, he could get shots that were truly candid.

Would Jessica call it intruding on their privacy? He didn't know, but he couldn't resist focusing on her again and again as she sat on the ground with Cyndi.

He held the shutter release button down, taking bursts of pictures. A long time ago he'd tried to set up a similar shot at a fashion shoot, only to have the designer balk at the risk of grass stains. "Do you want to sell your product or worry about a dry-cleaning bill?" he'd snapped impatiently.

But he doubted Jessica was worried about stains. She enjoyed Cyndi's questions and youthful prattle. He did, too, come to think of it.

Someone blocked his view and he looked up. "Hey, Jordan."

"Hey, yourself. I know you offered to be my sister's wedding photographer. But when she refused and said guests should just enjoy themselves…she meant it."

"I realize that. But what would I do without a camera in my hands?"

Jordan glanced at Jessica and Cyndi. "Spend time with a beautiful woman and her daughter, instead of taking pictures of them. That's Jessica Parrish, isn't it?"

"Yes, but Jessica and I talk all the time."

"Well, talk to her some more. I have to go. The wedding starts in ten minutes and I'm a groomsman."

Logan hesitated before going over to help Jessica to her feet. "We should probably find seats," he told her.

Several minutes later strains of music filled the air and the bridesmaids walked down the aisle, followed by the bride. The ceremony was short, but long enough to prompt damp eyes at the obvious devotion between bride and groom.

As for Jessica? Her face revealed a mix of emotions—true happiness for the couple, but also a trace of sorrow and fear.

Logan understood the sorrow, but not the fear.

CHAPTER SEVENTEEN

To HIS SURPRISE, Logan enjoyed the reception, though it was usually the time at weddings when he started coming up with excuses to leave. He smiled at Cyndi when she trotted up with a curious expression.

"Can I look through your camera?" she asked.

"Sure."

He crouched and held his heavy camera up to her face. She didn't wiggle and take a fast look before dashing away. Instead, she stared intently through the viewfinder.

He put her hand on the lens and showed her how to focus it on distant objects, a process quite different from the autofocus on her small camera.

"It makes things so close." Then she giggled. "Momma is coming and I can see her big toe, just like my nose is right in front of it, except I need to keep changing the focus thingy."

A few moments later, Jessica stood looking

down at them. "Cyndi, they're serving home-made ice cream. Both vanilla and chocolate."

"Yum." Cyndi ducked out of Logan's arms and then turned to kiss his cheek. "Thank you. It's just like magic."

He straightened as Jessica smiled.

"I understand some of the science behind your fancy lenses, but I prefer Cyndi's explanation. We can all use a little magic."

Though he was more of a pragmatist than dreamer, Logan nodded. "I guess taking the wonder out of things would be a loss, especially at Cyndi's age."

Her head tilted in a questioning attitude. "But is it possible to experience wonder through a camera lens? I remember seeing that award-winning wedding photo you took in Venice—the one at sunset, by the water. It was hauntingly beautiful. But did you personally feel the enchantment and romance of the moment?"

"Photography is an art form," Logan said. "I wasn't part of the wedding. I was taking pictures."

Yet it wasn't entirely true. The groom had been a friend and Logan had taken the photographs as a gift. When he recalled the wedding in Venice, it was mostly as a series of images he'd carefully constructed…which probably proved Jessica's point.

"That's fair," she said, mercifully oblivious to his inner thoughts. "I just think there shouldn't be too much emphasis on recording the moment instead of living it. I know we've already discussed shades of this and I'm not trying to goad you," she added hastily. "But about Cyndi, she's fascinated with photography, which is fine, except I want to encourage her to have a rounded life."

Logan was certain that he didn't want Cyndi to live the way he did. He wasn't even sure it was possible; she was too vibrant, the same as her mother. And the thought of Cyndi growing up and being alone… He released a harsh breath. Why was it okay for him and not for her? Or was his kind of alone the same as being lonely?

Music started, providing a welcome distraction. "How about living in the moment and dancing with me?" he asked.

"I… Sure."

After setting his camera on a table, Logan drew Jessica onto the small dance floor brought in for the wedding. After a few minutes, he realized two things.

One was that she danced extremely well.

The other was that she was a perfect fit in his arms.

IT HAD BEEN a long time since Jessica had danced, but after a minute she loosened up. Part of it was Logan confidently swinging her around with perfect timing, sometimes slow, sometimes fast. One musical number flowed into the next and then another.

Eventually, the musicians took a break.

"Momma." Cyndi ran over with another girl following. "I didn't know you could dance. Can you teach me?"

"Sure."

"Not now," the second girl scolded. "We're s'posed to play a game with Lena and Mike."

"You'd better go play," Jessica advised her daughter. "I can teach you to dance at home."

"Okay."

"Maybe she'll switch her interests from photography to something else," Logan said as the girls ran off together.

"Perhaps, but she's particularly drawn to art and there's something intense about her fascination with cameras. Cyndi is curious about everything. Her extramural classes have included things like weaving and gymnastics. She also wants to learn about fixing computers, astronomy, cheese-making, woodworking and car repair. Most of it will have to wait until she's older."

"You didn't mention crystals and geology."

Jessica grinned, feeling mischievous. "She likes crystals, just as much as you like them."

Logan's eyes narrowed. "Excuse me?"

"I'm pointing out that you actually *do* like crystals. Have you forgotten what LCD stands for? Liquid crystal displays are heavily used in technology, including your beloved cameras. And what about quartz crystal timing mechanisms? Why is it so far-fetched that crystals might have a healing resonance if they can keep our clocks on time and help display pictures on a screen?"

He held up his hands in a show of surrender. "I apologize for every narrow-minded thing I've said or thought about your customers. They could be on the leading edge of innovations we'll take for granted in fifty years."

"That would be nice," Jessica said, deciding to trust the sincerity she saw in his face.

"By the way, I'm sorry for what I've said about you just recording experiences. If you were a complete emotional hermit, you wouldn't have such good friends."

"That's nice of you to say." He chuckled.

A waiter came by with a tray of goblets. She chose sparkling cider and saw Logan did the same. The table where he'd left his camera was free, so they sat down. Every couple of minutes she looked to where Cyndi was playing, to be sure everything was all right. It was instinctive. She couldn't predict an asthma attack, but to be safe, she had an inhaler in her purse and Cyndi had one in her pocket.

After their break, the musicians returned and the drummer spoke into the microphone.

"Ladies and gentlemen, let's keep the dance floor free for Chelsea and Barton's first dance as husband and wife."

Applause rose for the young couple. Chelsea looked shy. Her dress was charmingly old-fashioned with a fitted lace bodice. Her dark hair fell from the top of her head in a cascade of curls intertwined with rosebuds and tiny, sparkling crystals. In a dark suit, Barton looked uneasy but proud, and his face glowed with love for his bride.

"They make a nice couple," Jessica said as the music ended.

"Yeah. I've always liked Barton, though Nicole and Jordan know him best since he's their neighbor. That's how Chelsea met him. She needed a place to stay when she started working at the agency and Nicole offered the use of her guesthouse."

They watched as the bride's dance with her father was announced.

"I never thought about it before, but it seems as if weddings are a chance to strengthen bonds between friends and family," Logan said. "Kind of a neutral ground where everyone can put their differences aside to support the bride and groom. It probably doesn't always happen, but it should."

Jessica glanced at Logan. He understood more about people than he believed.

It had been too easy to see herself in Chelsea's shoes during the ceremony, looking into Logan's eyes as they exchanged vows. The thought terrified her.

Even if she changed her mind about marriage, Logan was the wrong guy...except for all the reasons he was right. His physical attractiveness aside, he was intelligent, decent, cared about people and had a sense of humor. He was also good with Cyndi, though it was partly because they'd bonded over photography.

Jessica reminded herself that Logan Kensington was also far too sophisticated for someone who didn't wear designer clothes or eat in fancy places. He'd traveled all over the world and had hobnobbed with the rich and glamorous. As for his parents? They were pleasant, but she must seem pretty simple and limited to them. From Regina's stories, it sounded as if they'd lived in most of the major cities across the planet.

They were retired diplomats, for heaven's sake.

Besides, Logan wasn't interested in being a husband and father, or at least that was what he'd always claimed. And she hadn't seen any evidence that he'd changed his mind.

FOLLOWING THE BRIDE'S dance with her father, the dance floor began filling again. Logan immediately spotted a man heading toward their table with a determined stride, his gaze fixed on Jessica.

Not a chance, buddy.

Logan stood and held out his hand. "Shall we, Jessica?"

Her smile seemed strained, but she nodded. The approaching man seemed to recognize that his prospective partner was taken, because he stopped short of the table and disappointment filled his face.

Logan couldn't blame the guy for wanting to dance with Jessica—she was a sweet armful. What he didn't understand was his green-eyed urge to keep him away.

He pushed the thought aside for the rest of the festivities.

In the early evening, he and Jessica buckled a chocolate-smeared, grass-stained and smiling little girl into her booster seat and he drove back to Regen Valley. It was still light and the sun cast long, golden rays across the town.

"Thanks for ridesharing with us," Jessica said as he pulled up in front of her house. She got out quickly.

"My pleasure." Logan opened the back door, where Cyndi drooped, sound asleep. He unbuckled the belt, trying not to wake her. It had been a big day for a little girl, full of new places to run, people to play with and treats to eat.

Jessica held out her arms, but he shook his head. "Why don't you bring the booster seat? I'll carry her inside. Where do you want her?"

"The couch is fine."

In the house he laid Cyndi on the sofa cushions, warmth flooding through him at the way she curled into a tighter ball. From the corner of his eye he saw Jessica smiling at her daughter.

Logan turned. Wisps of hair had escaped the clips and formed a shining frame around Jessica's face. He'd never seen a more beautiful sight.

He leaned toward her slowly, so that if she didn't want him to kiss her again, she could make a move to stop it. There were conflicted emotions in her eyes, but she leaned into him.

Her lips were soft and sweet and it felt utterly right to hold her in his arms. But after an interlude of deep, mind-spinning kisses, she pulled away.

Logan suddenly remembered Cyndi. He snatched a look at the couch, but she still seemed to be asleep.

"Sorry," Logan murmured as Jessica half pushed him to the door. "I forgot she might see us."

"That's okay. No harm done. Chalk it up to spending the day at a wedding. Inhibitions get lowered by all the romance and music."

Her reasoning was entirely plausible…and completely wrong. His feelings for her couldn't be explained away. He just didn't know if she saw him in the same way.

"Have a good rest of the evening," he said. "I'm, uh, I'm not sure Cyndi's dress will ever be the same."

"It isn't important—she enjoyed herself. In any case, kids outgrow their clothes with light-ning speed and that one won't fit her much longer."

Since Jessica stood waiting to lock up, Logan couldn't prolong the moment to explore the sensations flooding him. Strongest of all was the urge to ask if he could stay, have a cup of coffee, watch television, play cards…or even wash her car. Anything that didn't entail him driving away.

As he turned toward his SUV, he heard the door close and the dead bolt slide into place.

Back at his house, Logan realized some-thing—for the first time in his life, he knew he was lonely. Yeah, he was bad with people. But instead of trying to improve, he'd used his cameras to cover it up. He'd gathered his solitude around himself like a suit of armor.

What if he'd given his problems a fraction of the effort Jessica had made to become a better mother and person after her failed marriage? Maybe his father wouldn't have faced an alarming biopsy without his son at his side. Perhaps his mother would feel she could call when she was worried or just wanted to talk. He might even feel remotely qualified to be the kind of husband Jessica deserved and the father Cyndi ought to have.

Logan went out the back door and headed for the rocky outcropping up on the hill. A rabbit, startled from its hiding place, shot across the overgrown path. Farther away, a raccoon paused to look at him and blinked, as if insulted that a human was intruding into his space. A Steller's jay hopped lower on an evergreen and began scolding.

Higher on the hill Logan could see bits of Regen Valley through the trees. It was easier to think in the open air and he inhaled deeply.

Jessica deserved the best a man had to offer. So did Cyndi. A part-time husband and father wouldn't cut it. It was possible that his disdain for domestic routine and following a schedule came partly because he'd never found someone worth upending his life for.

Maybe he just had to make a sincere commitment, not only to Jessica and Cyndi, but to being genuinely connected. He could take pleasure in his career, while putting home and family first. That was what his friends were doing. They enjoyed their work and were passionate about helping clients get good career opportunities, but the balance in their lives had shifted. And he couldn't deny they had a new-found joy unlike anything he'd ever known before.

Logan's breathing quickened at the thought he could feel the same way.

Life was about choices. He could *choose* to put Jessica and Cyndi first. It might have to be a choice he made every single day to be sure he didn't fail them, but he could do it.

Still, Jessica also had to choose…and there was no certainty that she would choose him.

CHAPTER EIGHTEEN

JESSICA GOT TO the shop early on Monday, determined to be optimistic.

So Logan had kissed her again.

So what?

Soon the scent of coffee brewing wafted through the air and she filled the small display case with pastries from the Regen Valley Bakery. A few people had suggested she offer breakfast sandwiches, but she was keeping things simple. The Crystal Connection wasn't a café.

A deliveryman arrived with the new pieces of jewelry she'd ordered and she unpacked the box. Sales were going well. She'd even started getting orders through the new website.

At opening time she unlocked the door and found Logan waiting on the other side. She glued a determined smile on her face. Why did he have to be the first test of her optimism?

"Good morning, Mr. Magellan Einstein

Stanley. Hey, it just occurred to me that we could use the initials of your nickname instead of the whole mouthful."

She waited to see if he'd take the bait.

"Magellan Einstein Stanley?" he repeated. "Wouldn't that be MES?"

"But with only one S. If you like, I can do some research and find another explorer whose name also starts with S."

"I'm not sure it would do your business good to have a frequent customer with the name of Mr. Mess. Besides, Einstein was a scientist. He doesn't fit with Magellan and Stanley."

"Spoilsport. Besides, he explored mathematical concepts. So, what's your coffee preference today?"

"Surprise me. Anything you pick will be great."

She wasn't sure about that, but she'd been experimenting with her own combination of coffee beans, so she filled his mug with the new brew.

"This is great," he said after taking a sip. "What is it?"

"My latest stab at creating a special Crystal Connection blend."

"It's a winner." His smile seemed different

than usual, but she was probably just misinterpreting it.

"Good to know. Can I get you anything else?"

"Nope, though I wanted to tell you that I finally have all the contractor estimates and other information. As soon as I can get my partners together, we'll talk about it. I know they want to make a timely decision, so I hope to have news by the end of the week."

"Thanks for letting me know," she said, hoping it didn't sound too much as if she was rushing him out, even though she wanted him to leave. "Have a good day."

A few hours later Nicole came in for her second cup of coffee. "Latte, with a second shot of espresso," she moaned. "With Chelsea on her honeymoon, we're all pushed. She trained an assistant, but Sara doesn't have Chelsea's experience."

Jessica made the latte and poured it into Nicole's cup. "I'm glad I can run the Crystal Connection by myself."

"There are pluses and minuses. Having four of us helps because we can rotate special tasks. It's my turn, which is why I'm extra busy with Sara."

Jessica watched as Nicole rushed out. The

agency's custom of rotating responsibilities was what had thrown Logan so thoroughly into her life. She'd be sleeping much better at night if it had been one of the other partners who'd asked her to consider moving.

LOGAN JUGGLED HIS morning between working for clients and finalizing his presentation on the remodeling proposal. But in the back of his mind, he kept thinking about Jessica.

He'd spent Sunday in the mountains shooting pictures, yet all he'd thought about was being with Jessica and Cyndi, or having them with him. With every passing hour he was more and more certain that he wanted them squarely in the center of his life.

Complications abounded.

They hadn't resolved anything about the Crystal Connection. It was important, though not a central issue. What concerned him most was Jessica's wariness about him. She had every right to question his ability to commit, but it was more than that. What had she said about marriage—the risk of repeating her mistakes was too great? She'd worked so hard at getting herself into a good place she couldn't see how well she had achieved her goals. Marrying him wouldn't mean a loss of independence or strength.

He also wasn't worried about Jessica becoming too needy; in fact he was more concerned that she didn't need him at all.

By noon Logan was practically climbing the walls. It would be impossible to discuss a future with Jessica while the store was open for business, but he still wanted to see her.

Grabbing his mug, he headed next door. The shop had several customers and he hung back, listening as they asked questions about different rocks. Interesting stuff. He didn't know if crystals had healing properties, but she'd made some good points at Chelsea's wedding. The possibility wasn't as far-fetched as he'd thought.

He came over when there was a lull and she was free.

"Coffee?" she asked.

"Oh, yeah. The same as before." Logan handed her the mug and followed her to the coffee bar. "Would you have a chance to talk after the shop is closed?"

Her expression turned puzzled. "I suppose. Is something wrong?"

"No. Though I have a gift for you." He

fished an envelope out of his pocket and gave it to her. "It's a flash drive with pictures from the wedding. There are some good ones of you and Cyndi."

"That's nice."

"My pleasure. Has Cyndi recovered from the festivities?"

"She seemed okay yesterday, but she had an asthma attack last night that left her a little tired this morning."

"Did you have to go to the emergency room?" he asked, a stab of retroactive worry making his pulse jump.

"No, we managed to get it under control."

"That's a relief. I'll see you later."

Shaken, he turned and went back to the agency. They *had* to get the clinic built as soon as possible. Not that it would be open at night. Maybe he could convince Jessica to move somewhere closer to around-the-clock medical care.

He groaned as he sank into his desk chair. Jessica loved Regen Valley and she wouldn't have moved there if it posed a serious risk to Cyndi's safety. But he couldn't help worrying about the little girl who was entwined in his heart along with her mother. He'd have to map out the best routes to hospitals.

The afternoon crept by slowly.

JESSICA COULDN'T IMAGINE what Logan wanted to discuss. He'd said it would probably be another few days before his partners made a decision.

During the slow part of the afternoon she stuck his flash drive into the computer and was awed by what she saw. Photo after photo of both her and Cyndi. Some were close-ups of her, others were Cyndi's face, her expressions ranging from disgusted to happy to ecstatic. They looked like something out of a magazine. No wonder he'd been in such high demand as a fashion photographer.

But why had he taken so many?

Jessica's heart skipped a beat as she wondered if it meant something special, but it was an absurd speculation. He'd probably taken just as many of the other guests. And she'd seen what he could do, selecting an individual out of a larger photo to create a portrait. It didn't mean anything.

Logan returned, just as she was flipping the Open sign to Closed.

"Hi." Jessica kept her voice bright. "I had a chance to look at the flash drive. The photos are wonderful. Thanks for taking the time to sort them out for us. Digital technology is amazing. You must have thousands from the wedding."

"Not even close. I took a fair number to add to Chelsea's wedding collection, but I mostly concentrated on you and Cyndi."

She pulled in a quick breath. "Why would you do that?"

"To be honest, I wasn't sure at the time, except that you're both so photogenic. It wasn't until I got home that the truth dawned on me—I was taking pictures of the two people I want most in my life."

Her brain tried to spin but she refused to let it loose. She must have misunderstood. "Oh?"

"Jessica, I'm tired of just being the guy behind the camera. I love you with all my heart and I want to be with you and Cyndi, every single day."

Now her brain froze.

"Uh…"

His eyes were warm, full of energy, and seemed utterly sincere. "I'm impressed. For once I've stunned you into speechlessness."

Jessica straightened her back. "I'm not sure that you… That is, you've been quite clear about avoiding commitment."

"I've said a lot of dumb things. Now I know I was waiting for you."

Trying to think clearly, Jessica glanced around the shop. As a child it had been a place of safety and love. She still felt the love, echoing through the years, but it no longer seemed quite as safe. Finally she focused on Logan again.

"I can't discuss this. Not today."

"That's understandable. It probably feels as if this has come out of the blue, but it hasn't, at least not for me. I just want you to know how I feel, and that I'm sticking around. We can take this slowly. What about dinner some night? We haven't had any traditional dates." He grinned. "I might be able to find an ice-cream parlor. How about an old-fashioned chocolate soda?"

"Maybe. I don't know. I'll think about it."

Logan's hand reached up to caress her cheek and the sensation shivered through her body. He could do as much with his hand and his eyes as he'd done with his kisses.

"Jessica, I know we have all sorts of things

to figure out, but I also know it can be done. We can make a relationship work."

Though she'd said she didn't want to talk, Jessica couldn't stop herself. "Following a schedule would be too dull for you. Don't forget that I'm the mother of a young child with a health problem. Cyndi needs to rely on certain things happening at certain times. You'd be bored silly. Your life has always been glamorous and exciting."

"Glamorous? Try sitting under a damp bush for eighteen hours to get a picture of a pair of foxes," Logan retorted. "And fashion photography isn't nearly as exciting as people think. Frankly, it was a treadmill. Sometimes I had a hard time telling which fashion shoot I was doing since they all blended together."

"You also know supermodels like Laurel Stevenson." Jessica hated the jealousy that had prompted her comment. It wasn't that she disliked Laurel, who seemed kind, not to mention vulnerable and uncomfortable with her fame. But how many other drop-dead gorgeous women might show up, wanting a shoulder to cry on?

"Laurel is a star," Logan acknowledged, "but Nicole and Adam were even bigger stars, and you know them, too. They'd all tell you the same thing about our work. It can be rewarding, but it has less enjoyable aspects that can be downright tedious. You compromise and accept the parts you don't like."

He gazed intently into her eyes.

"I've had positive experiences, but my life wasn't *full* until I met you and Cyndi. That's when I realized what I was missing."

Logan was making good points, but Jessica was still struggling with disbelief and shock.

"If you don't love me, that's one thing," he continued. "Just don't reject me for reasons that shouldn't have anything to do with two people who belong together. I admire how hard you've fought to be strong and independent. But you won't lose yourself if you share responsibilities with someone who cares."

Logan glanced out the window where people were heading to their cars in the parking lot, then turned back to her. "I'd kiss you, but this is the wrong place. And I don't want you to talk yourself into a corner."

The warm focus of his eyes was almost like a kiss and they brimmed with emotion a woman could convince herself was love. He took a step forward, his hand outstretched as though he might still pull her into an embrace. Then he seemed to regain control and walked out.

Jessica locked the door and hurried into the stockroom, where she could fight her emotions without risk of being seen by anyone passing outside. Before long she realized her cheeks were damp.

She felt as if she'd glimpsed paradise and didn't know whether it was a gift...or a mistake.

PENNY WAS PLEASED that Cyndi had made it through the school day, despite her late-night asthma attack. Keeping her later than usual wasn't a problem, but she wondered why Logan had wanted to speak with Jessica.

When Jessica got there to pick up Cyndi, her face wore the same tense mask Penny recognized from years past.

"Any news?" she asked.

"Not really. Logan won't have anything to report until he talks with his partners."

That was disappointing but not unexpected. "Would you like to stay for dinner? Kevin is coming over."

Jessica gave her a hug. "Thanks, but last night I cut up vegetables for stir-fry. Say hi to

Uncle Kevin for me." She called to Cyndi and they left.

Penny fretted until Kevin arrived and she could explain what had happened. "Do you think something is wrong?" she asked. "Her face… I haven't seen her look that way in years."

He'd been holding her hand and gave it a squeeze. "We both know there are a number of possibilities. She may not be ready to discuss it, especially where Cyndi might overhear."

"You're right."

"We're so much alike. Given the chance, we'd rush in and fix everything for everyone, but people mostly need to sort out their own lives." He heaved a sigh. "Lately I've been wondering if I was too overprotective as an agent. It might have been better for my clients if I'd encouraged their independence, the way Logan and the others are doing."

He sounded melancholy, so Penny nudged him with her elbow.

"That's the problem with hindsight—you can torture yourself over what you could have done better or differently. But your clients loved you and you helped them in the way that worked for you. Besides, Logan and the others wouldn't have bought Moonlight Ventures if they hadn't respected you and the work you'd done. It meant they got an agency with a reputation for honesty and integrity."

Kevin smiled. "You're good for me."

"And don't you forget it, either." She left him in the living room while she got a pitcher of iced tea from the refrigerator. Their discussion at the wedding had relieved the strain she'd felt. Everything was out in the open and they had time to make sure they were both ready to move on and wanted the same thing.

Kevin settled on the couch with his tea. "I told my daughter about your idea of doing volunteer work. She suggested looking for a grandparent program, where they match you with a kid who needs extra attention. What do you think? I like the idea of doing something that helps children."

"That's the spirit. You wouldn't have any trouble passing a background check. But you can do more than that. Docents are needed at museums or historical sites, and I already plan to take you to the animal refuge center where I volunteer. They can always use a helping hand. There are lots of ways to make a difference in the world."

"Hmm. I may be busier in retirement than when I was a talent agent. Sounds great."

His delighted expression made her feel warm all over.

ON FRIDAY LOGAN presented the information he'd assembled to his partners. He didn't want to make his feelings for Jessica part of the equation, so he laid out the proposal in simple financial terms.

The discussion went on for over an hour and Logan's partners looked puzzled when he didn't want to express his opinion.

"I'm too close to the situation to be unbiased," he excused himself. "I'd rather hear what you think."

"It's expensive," Nicole said finally, "but we'd be getting a huge amount for our money."

"I agree." Adam tapped the chart showing the increased space they'd have at the back of the building. "We can have everything we want there. Besides, we could reduce the initial outlay by simply renovating the space needed for ourselves and two or three new agents, and do the rest when it's required. Though I have to admit a genuine meeting room would be helpful right away, not to mention a place to do training."

Rachel nodded. "The Crystal Connection location would only give us enough space for two more offices and a smallish meeting room. Future expansion would require us to move eventually, or displace more tenants. On top of that, the projected rental income for our current space would eventually pay for the remodeling cost since the units at the back are usually empty."

Adam looked around the room. "All right, let's vote. Who is in favor?"

All hands went up, Logan's lagging a second behind the others'.

"Then we're in agreement," Nicole said. "But, Logan, why wouldn't you tell us what you thought until we voted?"

"It's exactly what I said—I'm biased. I can't be objective and I didn't want to unduly influence the decision."

Adam seemed to choke down a laugh. "Ah, so the mighty have fallen. I knew you'd succumb sooner or later, but I didn't realize it would be *this* soon."

Logan should have realized they would guess; they'd been friends for too long.

"What happened to 'I'm leaving romance to the rest of you?'" Nicole's eyes danced as she quoted him.

He held up his hand. "It's okay if you tease, but please don't say anything to Jessica."

"You haven't told her how you feel?" Rachel asked.

"No, I mean yes, but nothing is settled."

"Not a word," Adam promised, and the others nodded. "But we reserve the right to continue giving you a hard time about love and marriage in private."

Logan didn't mind. He'd been outspoken about his intentions to avoid commitments, so his friends were entitled to their fun. The only thing that worried him was convincing Jessica that he was worth the risk. Giving her time to think had been hard, but it was the right thing to do, so while he'd continued going for coffee, he hadn't pushed for an answer.

The question was, when should he properly propose? Was it best to tell her first about the decision on the building? He didn't want relief or gratitude to be part of her choice. And he didn't want her decision colored by knowing he had power over her future as a landlord.

In his office he stewed about it before shoving the question aside. Jessica was a mature, intelligent woman. He'd simply have to trust her.

CHAPTER NINETEEN

AFTER CLOSING THE Crystal Connection on Friday, Jessica hurried to her car, not wanting to give Logan another opportunity to seek her out. He had been attentive all week, reminding her in a hundred different ways that he loved her.

It was confusing. She wasn't used to being pursued. For that matter, she wasn't used to romance, either.

Recovering from her failed marriage had been painful, but it had helped her realize that she was responsible for her own mistakes. She'd decided to do her best to be Cyndi's mother and forget the happily-ever-after stuff.

But now Logan was offering her a forever kind of love. He wasn't the kind of man who to declare something he didn't feel and she knew if it didn't work out, the hurt would last forever, as well.

At least Logan's declaration had put everything with the Crystal Connection into perspective.

When she got home, she sat down with Grams for a cup of tea. Cyndi was in the back-yard playing, and they watched her through the sliding glass door.

"I still don't know what will happen with the store," Jessica said finally. "I don't have to move right away, even if they say no, but it's tricky. I'm not worried about supporting us. Internet sales are starting to pick up, and I can always get a new job. But the Crystal Connection is especially important because of you and Granddad."

Penny sipped her tea. "It upset me when I found out what Moonlight Ventures wanted, but even if the shop closes eventually, the memories will remain. Your grandfather believed in focusing on the present and the future, and that's what we need to do." Grams stared into her cup as if she was trying to find answers in the contents.

"I've been meaning to tell you something," Jessica said.

"What's that, dear?"

"It's just that if you find someone else who makes you happy, I'll be happy, too."

"Is it that obvious?" Penny murmured.

"No, but I've known you and Uncle Kevin all my life."

"I'm still exploring how I feel about him and I'm not ready for such a big change. This isn't the same as with Eric—it's gentler, and I'm figuring it out, a little at a time."

"Of course it isn't the same. Uncle Kevin is a different person and should be loved in his own right. Besides, didn't Granddad always say that one good love deserves another?"

Penny chuckled. "He certainly did. Well, nothing is decided and we're biding our time." She looked up. "What about you? I keep getting the feeling you and Logan have become more than just business associates."

DISMAY HIT PENNY as her granddaughter's eyes brimmed with tears.

"I'm sorry, honey, I shouldn't have said anything."

"No, it's fine." Jessica's voice was choked. "He says he loves me and I believe him, but it's a big step and it affects Cyndi."

"Logan is a good man."

"No question, but even good men can get tired of routine when they've spent their lives avoiding it."

Penny didn't want to push Jessica one way or the other. "Do you love him?" she asked gently.

"Yes. But we come from completely different worlds."

"That makes a relationship a challenge, but no one said marriage was supposed to be easy."

Jessica pushed her cup aside. "He hasn't asked me to marry him. Not exactly."

"A man like Logan? He wouldn't say he loves a woman without intending to make it permanent."

"Maybe."

Penny reached over and patted her granddaughter's hand. "You'll figure it out. Now, why don't I order a pizza and we spend the evening playing a game with Cyndi?"

"That's a good plan. I'd rather think about something else tonight. Anything else."

It seemed unlikely to Penny that Jessica's plan would work. A woman's brain chewed on love no matter how hard she tried. Perhaps a man's brain did the same, but she only knew about women.

She'd have to ask Kevin his opinion.

LOGAN HAD BEEN disappointed to find that Jessica had already closed the shop and left. He'd wanted to tell her that his partners had voted for Moonlight Ventures to move. With that issue out of the way, he could work on the most important one—their relationship.

After calling her home number several times without getting an answer, he sat back and considered his next move. He'd never gotten Jessica's cell number and didn't want to leave a message on the home voice mail and risk Cyndi overhearing it. Email wasn't the best solution, but he finally sent a message asking Jessica if she was free for dinner the next evening for a private discussion.

Several hours later he got a reply saying she could do dinner, but if it was more convenient, they could talk on Monday over coffee.

Logan frowned at his computer screen. She made it sound as if he just wanted to talk business. Granted, he needed to let her know about his partners' decision, but he'd made his other intentions clear during the past week.

He walked to the back of the house and looked out on the moonlit scene. It was different viewing nature through a window instead of lying covertly under bushes or on a rocky ledge to get a photo. A movement at the edge of the garden made him peer intently, but despite the full moon, he couldn't tell what animal it might be.

He hadn't asked Jessica if she returned his feelings, though she'd expressed doubts about him being able to handle domesticity and routine. It was a valid concern and he needed to show her how committed he was.

True, as a photographer his jobs had been varied, but no matter where he was or what he was doing, there had been moments when he'd wondered how often he could keep doing the same thing before getting redundant. But all jobs and lives had routines, and that included marriage and family. He'd just never recognized the upside of domestic life.

An image filled Logan's mind—of Jessica at the wedding, looking at Cyndi's bright, excited face as the little girl showed her mother the pictures she'd taken.

Nothing negative about that.

He'd take routine with Jessica any day. There would always be the challenge of getting to know each other better, watching their children develop and grow, and building memories they could share over a lifetime. Those memories would ideally include travel, sometimes just the two of them, sometimes with their children. He could easily see himself teaching Cyndi how to get a panoramic picture of the Grand Canyon.

Logan typed back a message saying he'd pick her up at 6:00 and they would go to the same restaurant where he'd taken her a few weeks ago. But as soon as he hit Send, he reconsidered the location. That night they'd talked extensively about the Crystal Connection moving. And he had a feeling she really didn't like the place.

He needed to come up with a better plan.

THE NEXT EVENING Jessica came to the door wearing a basic black dress. Logan's experience on fashion shoots told him it was the kind of outfit a woman wore when she wasn't sure what garb was appropriate.

"You're beautiful," he said. She'd look great in anything, but he was no longer a dispassionate judge.

Emotion flickered in her eyes, but he wasn't sure if she was flattered or doubtful. "Thank you."

He helped her into the SUV, but when he turned left instead of right on the main road, she frowned. "This isn't the right direction."

"I thought of a better place." He drove to a quiet spot he'd found that overlooked Regen Valley. The evening sunlight shone across the trees and rooftops and hills beyond; it seemed an appropriate location for a discussion about the future.

"Alfresco?" Jessica asked, a smile growing on her face.

"Dining alfresco has its advantages. The service may be a little lacking here, but the privacy and view can't be beaten."

Logan set up the table and chairs he'd brought. It would have been a nice touch to cook for Jessica, but he didn't want her getting a bout of indigestion.

Before unpacking the food, he sat forward. "Let's get business out of the way. My partners and I have carefully gone over everything. It's unanimous. We love your idea of Moonlight Ventures moving and apologize for the stress we've caused you and Penny."

He expected to see relief and happiness instead of the concern that crowded Jessica's eyes. "Are you sure the financial risk is acceptable? I can guess how much the agency means to all of you—a new beginning and proving yourselves in a second career. Not to mention your initial investment. Uncle Kevin is a sweetheart, but he wouldn't have sold it to you for a pittance."

That was Jessica, a woman who cared about people, instead of blithely expecting them to make way for her.

"It's fine," Logan said firmly. "Mostly we wish that we'd thought of doing it from the beginning. But we've weighed the options and think this will serve us best in the long run."

JESSICA WAS GLAD she wouldn't have to make a decision about the Crystal Connection moving, yet the glint in Logan's eyes told her that the discussion was only beginning.

"I wasn't sure when to tell you about our decision because I know how important the shop is to you and Penny and Cyndi. It's more than just a business to you. It even seems like more than just a store to many of your customers."

She nodded. "I've been torn between the needs of three generations. But Grams and I have talked about it and she's made peace with whatever happens. As for Cyndi and myself? I've always supported us, and could find another job if necessary."

"Fortunately, you won't have to do that. I've

been torn, as well. For that reason, I didn't tell my partners what I wanted us to do until the final vote."

"Why not?"

"Because while Nicole and Adam and Rachel are my closest friends, you're the woman I love."

Jessica's heart thudded. Though he'd already told her that he loved her, it was breathtaking to hear him say it again.

"Anyway," he continued, looking at her intently, "I didn't want conflicting emotions to interfere with us talking about the future. Then I decided you're much better at understanding yourself than I am, and if you need more time or breathing space, you'll simply say so."

There was something dynamic about the way he was opening up to her. It was the way people should relate to each other.

Could they really make things work?

"I'm glad you're being open about it," she managed to say.

"We need to discuss things like that." His eyes were serious and intent. "I may not have your gift of understanding people, but—"

"You're better at it than you think," Jessica

broke in. "If you weren't, then Laurel would never have sought you out."

A broad, embarrassed smile suddenly split his face. "Thanks for saying that."

"It's the truth."

"Anyhow, I know some of your concerns are whether I'll get restless with the routine of family life and work. But don't you ever feel that way?"

Jessica shifted uncomfortably. Of course she did. She loved her life, but it was human nature to think about paths not taken.

"Yes," she admitted. "But mostly I've been leery of being too spontaneous, considering my mistakes."

"That's understandable. Who we are today is partly built on what happened in the past. I can't deny there will be times that I'm restless and want to travel or have some sort of adventure. But that won't mean I'm unhappy being married. I'll just want to have those adventures with you and Cyndi, along with any other kids we might add to the family. Isn't it good for children to have new experiences?"

The doubt began easing in Jessica. Logan wasn't just throwing out offhand comments;

he'd spent a great deal of time seriously reflecting what it meant to be a family man.

"THEN YOU'RE INTERESTED in having more children?" Jessica asked. The expression on her face was encouraging to Logan. She seemed open, instead of erecting her usual defenses.

"Yes," he said, "but that's a mutual decision. You'd need to want it, as well."

"More, um, sounds good."

Electric shocks seemed to travel down his spine. "In the interests of complete honesty," he said carefully, "I have to confess that the idea of being a parent is both wonderful and terrifying."

Jessica broke into one of her merry laughs. "That just means you're sensible."

"You and Cyndi can train me properly," he said, smiling. "Like all fathers, I'll make mistakes and we'll have to do a lot of talking and sharing, but that's one of the good parts of marriage. Of course, I'm still waiting to hear how you feel about me."

Faint pink stained her cheeks and she lifted her lovely eyes to meet his gaze. "I don't know when I started loving you, but I do."

For a moment Logan's muscles turned into mush and his lungs gasped for air.

"So, Jessica…will you marry me?"

Instead of an enthusiastic yes, Jessica traced an outline of the infinity symbol on the small table he'd brought to the overlook. "The thing is, you and I come from such different worlds. Regina and Tom are nice, but they're ultra-sophisticated. They've traveled everywhere. And you've probably gone even more places and done more things than they have."

Logan thought about the longing he'd seen on his parents' faces during their visit, the regret of not being closer to him.

He shook his head.

"Jessica, deep down, Penny and my mom and dad are very much alike. We talked most of the night before they flew home. They're *glad* I didn't join their world of diplomacy and power connections. I think they loved the Flash Fair so much because it celebrated the kind of values and community ties they long to rediscover."

"But that's about them, not you."

"Actually, I'm just getting to the same realization sooner. I want community and love, parenthood and marriage. But even if they didn't feel the same way, it doesn't mean anything. After all, you chose a different set of values than your mother and father. Is it impossible to believe that someone else could do the same?"

Humor rippled across Jessica's face. "That's an excellent point."

"Maybe love can conquer all," Logan said, "because real love includes the commitment to work on it."

"I have a feeling you're right." Her voice was husky and he saw happy tears in her eyes.

JESSICA BLINKED RAPIDLY as Logan came around the table to draw her into a kiss.

"I love you so much," he said. "I didn't know the heart could hold this much love. But I have a feeling the more someone loves, the more space their heart has to love."

"Love can do that for you."

"Isn't it grand?"

His arms held her tightly and he could feel his pulse matching hers, beat for beat.

"We can do anything," he said against her lips, "so long as we do it together."

EPILOGUE

Seventeen months later...

LOGAN STARED IN wonder at the tiny bundle he held.

"She's so small," he breathed.

"Bigger than Cyndi was," Jessica told him. She smiled, though her face was tired and flushed after the hours of labor.

"Really?"

"A whole pound."

Taking parenting classes and reading a dozen books hadn't prepared him for this moment.

"I'll go out and get everyone," he said, carefully putting little Anne Regina back into her mother's arms.

In the waiting room, Cyndi flew into his arms. "Is Momma okay?"

"Absolutely," he said, hugging her tight.

He looked around the room. Penny was sitting hand in hand with Kevin. That Christmas they'd officially declared themselves a couple and everyone expected them to get married soon. Logan's mom and dad were there, as well; they had flown to Seattle as soon as they'd learned Jessica had gone into labor. He had never seen them look happier.

Sadly, while Jessica's folks had sent a flower arrangement to the hospital, they'd declared that the demands of work wouldn't allow them to come right away. At least they'd made it to the wedding fifteen months ago, along with Jessica's brothers. Logan liked the elder Parrishes, despite himself. Someday he hoped they'd slow down and be a bigger part of their children's lives. After all, the renovations they'd done to the Satterly House included a private guest suite where their respective parents could stay during visits.

Rachel and Simon were also waiting with their kids, along with Nicole and Jordan and their little one. It was too bad about Jessica's mother and father, but baby Anne and Cyndi had lots of people who were choosing to be family.

"Is everything okay?" Adam asked, holding

his baby daughter in his arms, while Cassie held their twin son.

"Great." Logan lifted Cyndi, thinking she was growing so fast he might not be able to do it for much longer. "As expected, a beautiful baby girl. Eight pounds, two ounces, twenty-one inches long."

A chorus of congratulations sounded, while Cyndi hugged his neck. It was hard to remember that he'd adopted her—she was so much a part of his heart.

"I have my camera," she whispered in his ear. "Did you already take the first picture?"

"Pictures weren't as important as just being there with your momma," he said softly. "In a little bit, you and I can take the first one together."

Then they led the whole family toward Jessica's room to introduce them to the newest member of the clan.

* * * * *

For more great romances from author Callie Endicott, visit www.Harlequin.com!

Get 4 FREE REWARDS!

We'll send you 2 FREE Books <u>plus</u> 2 FREE Mystery Gifts.

Love Inspired® books feature contemporary inspirational romances with Christian characters facing the challenges of life and love.

FREE Value Over $20

YES! Please send me 2 FREE Love Inspired® Romance novels and my 2 FREE mystery gifts (gifts are worth about $10 retail). After receiving them, if I don't wish to receive any more books, I can return the shipping statement marked "cancel." If I don't cancel, I will receive 6 brand-new novels every month and be billed just $5.24 for the regular-print edition or $5.74 for the larger-print edition in the U.S., or $5.74 each for the regular-print edition or $6.24 each for the larger-print edition in Canada. That's a savings of at least 13% off the cover price. It's quite a bargain! Shipping and handling is just 50¢ per book in the U.S. and 75¢ per book in Canada.* I understand that accepting the 2 free books and gifts places me under no obligation to buy anything. I can always return a shipment and cancel at any time. The free books and gifts are mine to keep no matter what I decide.

Choose one: ☐ **Love Inspired® Romance Regular-Print** (105/305 IDN GMY4)   ☐ **Love Inspired® Romance Larger-Print** (122/322 IDN GMY4)

Name (please print)

Address   Apt. #

City   State/Province   Zip/Postal Code

Mail to the Reader Service:
IN U.S.A.: P.O. Box 1341, Buffalo, NY 14240-8531
IN CANADA: P.O. Box 603, Fort Erie, Ontario L2A 5X3

Want to try 2 free books from another series? Call 1-800-873-8635 or visit www.ReaderService.com.

THE FORTUNES OF TEXAS COLLECTION!

18 FREE BOOKS in all!

Treat yourself to the rich legacy of the Fortune and Mendoza clans in this remarkable 50-book collection. This collection is packed with cowboys, tycoons and Texas-sized romances!

YES! Please send me **The Fortunes of Texas Collection** in Larger Print. This collection begins with 3 FREE books and 2 FREE gifts in the first shipment. Along with my 3 free books, I'll also get the next 4 books from The Fortunes of Texas Collection, in LARGER PRINT, which I may either return and owe nothing, or keep for the low price of $5.24 U.S./$5.89 CDN each plus $2.99 for shipping and handling per shipment*. If I decide to continue, about once a month for 8 months I will get 6 or 7 more books but will only need to pay for 4. That means 2 or 3 books in every shipment will be FREE! If I decide to keep the entire collection, I'll have paid for only 32 books because 18 books are FREE! I understand that accepting the 3 free books and gifts places me under no obligation to buy anything. I can always return a shipment and cancel at any time. My free books and gifts are mine to keep no matter what I decide.

☐ 269 HCN 4622   ☐ 469 HCN 4622

Name (please print)

Address   Apt. #

City   State/Province   Zip/Postal Code

Mail to the **Reader Service:**
IN U.S.A.: P.O. Box 1341, Buffalo, N.Y. 14240-8531
IN CANADA: P.O. Box 603, Fort Erie, Ontario L2A 5X3

50BFT19R

Get 4 FREE REWARDS!

We'll send you 2 FREE Books <u>plus</u> 2 FREE Mystery Gifts.

FREE
Value Over
$20

Both the **Romance** and **Suspense** collections feature compelling novels written by many of today's best-selling authors.

STRS19R